AMERICAN BLUES

AMERICAN BLUES

Evan Guilford-Blake

HH
Holland House

www.hhousebooks.com

Hardback ISBN 978-1-909374-93-5
Paperback ISBN 978-1-909374-24-9
Epub ISBN 978-1-909374-25-6

Cover by Eric Gaskell

Typesetting by handebooks.co.uk

Published in the USA and UK

Holland House Books
Holland House
47 Greenham Road
Newbury
Berkshire
RG14 7HY
United Kingdom

www.hhousebooks.com

In memory of Sonny Criss

For Roxanna

Acknowledgements

The author would like to thank the many people whose time, patience, faith and insights contributed to the writing, and the betterment, of this book. Foremost among them are my wife, Roxanna, and my publisher, Robert Peett. There are many others to whom I'm deeply grateful, but the actors and directors who helped develop the plays on which "Nighthawks," "Tio's Blues" and "The Easy-Lovin' Blues" are based were particularly invaluable to their creation. Special thanks, then, are due to Steve Gillam, Derrell Capes, Karen Skinner and the original cast of *Nighthawks*: Joy Ovington, Dean Kharasch, Eliot Wimbush and Randy Hoel; and Neil Ellis Orts whose support of the play was largely responsible for taking on the task of adapting it, and the others, to prose.

CONTENTS

SONNY'S BLUES

November 12

Sonny's tired. He blew till 3:00 on maybe four hours sleep, the adrenalin provided by the rest of the quartet, the between-sets bourbon, the music itself. Then he sat—had one more drink—with Harper for almost an hour after that, till he'd come down from the high. Now and then it came from the audience though, sure, most of the time, didn't matter that they were there: The music was for him, not them, and he couldn't hear 'em, or see 'em: His eyes were closed, focused on the rolling, fluid blue in his head, and all he heard was Harp's piano, was Cole's bass, was Alan's drums; his own alto, blowing hard and clear, the blue behind his eyes made audible to anyone who knew to hear. And all he felt was the vibration. Even the pain picked itself up and floated away on a river of blues. Didn't need no drugs to do that, just the reed and the saxophone's smooth keys.

He's worn out, too, maybe more worn out than he oughta be at fifty. Too much bourbon, too much smoke, too much sweat and too little food. Still wasn't really hungry, hadn't been, again, all day, but he ate a bologna sandwich when he got home, four slices of meat on white bread smothered with mayo. When he ate (his appetite had kinda deserted him the past few weeks) he ate heavy during the day—fried chicken and barbequed pork (not as good as his Mama made, but still pretty good) and smoked ham, and fried potatoes and fried rice ("Man, you eat *all* that shit and you look skinny as hell. 'Cept for your belly," Harper laughed and shook his head)—but he forgot when he was playin': forgot everything except the music, Norma'd said. And that was true. The breaks, well, they were just long enough to get a drink, dry his face and piss, chew a coupla antacids and have a smoke. Maybe change his shirt. Norma hated the stains his sweatin' left. *Hard to get out, Sonny. And they* stink *somethin' fierce!* Well, Norma didn't wash his shirts no more, he did, and he had plenty. They were all white, all cotton-and-somethin', all wash-and-wear. He could throw 'em in the machine in the basement and leave 'em hangin' on the shower curtain bar before he left, by the time he got back they'd be dry.

Too much coffee. He lifts the white mug and swallows from it. Still hot. On the stove, the pot's still steaming. Three more cups in it. He'll drink them too, before he goes to bed. Probably make his gut hurt worse—these days, everything seems to—but right now the hot feels good inside. Sometimes, he passed blood. Not much, but the Doc said it "concerned" him and Sonny oughta be concerned, too, but he's not. Hell, wasn't much a horn man could do about it. Man's got a problem, man's got A Problem if the man don't got the money to take care of it, and horn men? they don't got it. Yeah, he gets paid pretty good for club gigs, but there ain't so many of those anymore, clubs are bookin' comics instead of jazzmen, folks are goin' to discos where the music all sounds the same and is all recorded, they wanna dance 'stead of listen, and the record companies got plenty of sax players to play that background shit: tenormen— that was what the public wanted to hear, those softly rounded notes, watery like undercooked grits, instead of the tight-squeezed reed-chewed alto ones like Sonny's which were smooth as breast milk, Maryjane said. Sweet as it, too; he'd as soon suck the notes out of the horn as her titties. He gets sessions, too— Harper always tries to get him called in on his—but there ain't a lot, 'specially in Chicago where there ain't but a few record companies left, and they don't pay much when your name's nowhere on the album cover. When he's "at liberty" he'll sit in somewhere, make a few dollars or maybe just his bar tab, but that, he knows, ain't ever gonna be enough to take care of A Problem.

He sighs, thinks *maybe I oughta go back to L.A.* and swallows more coffee, his third cup since he got home. The kitchen is dimly lit, a bare bulb glares from the ceiling and casts shadows into the corners, highlighting the used-to-be-white walls that have needed another coat of paint since the day he moved in, five years ago. He can see the living room with its raggedy-ass olive sofa, matching lounge chair, two plastic-that-looks-like-wood side tables, a radiator that clinks in the winter and, as far from it as possible, his record player, with albums stacked, straight up and spines facing out, in a wood case beneath it. The Hawk, Ben, Pres, Bird. Clifford and Monk and Mingus and Bill Evans; Milt and Max and Harp's buddy Chet Baker. A couple of him and Harper that they'd produced themselves; the one he'd made in Paris as leader. He took good care of them, like he did his horn, and they took good care of him in return. He could put one on, close his eyes and everything that wasn't the music—life and all *its* blues—went away. Just like when he played.

They were his, the phonograph and the albums; everything else came with the place. Same with the bedroom: Single bed, big enough to hold him and a woman if it needed to, so long as neither of them tossed too much. Closet and a dresser and drapes which didn't block out the light during the day when he slept, so he bought shades. Another radiator, this one noisy as hell but he's got used to it in five years of livin' here.

Now, his gut hurts somethin' awful. Always does after four, five, six hours playin' but tonight it's worse than it's been in weeks. He's had indigestion and heartburn before, but not this bad. Not this long, either. He even went to a doctor this afternoon, first time in years. Doc looked Sonny over, ran a whole bunch of tests, took x-rays, scraped skin from a couple places, and drew blood. Doc'd said that since it had been goin' on so long, might be an ulcer. He told Sonny to drink skim milk and cut out all the fat and alcohol and at least cut back on the cigarettes. Sonny laughed to himself: Fat and alcohol and cigarettes—hell, 'cept for the tunes and the women, wasn't much else made life worth livin'.

"Can I get somethin'; for the pain?" Sonny asked. Doc looked at him long and careful, and shook his head. Nothin', not till he knew what the problem was. "And when you gonna know that?" Sonny asked. In a few days, he said, when all the results were back. In the meantime, drink milk, take pain relievers that weren't aspirin. Sonny sighed and said "Okay," made an appointment with the sweet-faced receptionist for Thursday afternoon, paid her the fifty bucks for the Doc's time.

"We'll bill you for the tests," she said.

Phone rings. He sighs—who in *hell* is callin' at four-thirty in the goddam mornin'? Harp's asleep now, or with some girl— and pushes his body up from the table. A knife stabs his belly as he rises and he leans on the table and waits till the pain eases, then goes to the living room. He stares as the phone continues to ring, then finally answers it on the ninth.

"Yeah," he mutters, his voice soft and raw, "What you want?"

"Hi, baby, what you doin'?" Maryjane's soft voice melts into his ear. "I know I ain't wakin' you up."

"MJ" he says, rubbing his throbbing stomach.

"Sure is."

"Hang on."

"Only got a minute 'fore I got to go back on."

"Be right back." He lays the phone down and gets his bottle of Jack from the side table, takes a swallow. It burns going down but it feels smooth lyin' inside him. He swigs again.

Sonny sees the gun on the arm of the sofa. He took it out to clean before he left, and forgot it there. He bought it years ago and carries it in his sax case. He lives in an old part of town that's between a high-crime ghetto and a middle-class neighborhood that's working hard at gentrifying itself, but the places he plays, and the hours he comes home, aren't usually the safest. He's never fired it except at the practice range, where he goes a couple times a year: He knows how to use it, and he keeps it nearby and ready.

The gun scared Norma. Maryjane? Hell, she grew up in a house where everybody includin' the girls knew how to use one. Had to know. Maryjane, her little-girl life hadn't been real pleasant, but she grew up and was makin' it better.

When he goes back to the phone his stomach feels a little better. He clears his throat. "I'm back."

"That's good," coos MJ.

"So, what you want?" he says more affably.

"I get off in half an hour; less," she says. "Like a little company? Been a week and I'm, y' know…?"

He pulls his cigarettes from his pocket and lights one, squinting in the flame from the lighter. "I'm pretty tired," he says.

"You too tired for *me*?"

"I'm like to fall asleep."

"I bet I can wake you up."

He laughs; it turns into a cough.

"You all right, Sonny?" Maryjane says, her voice changing from coy to concerned.

"Yeah, jus' tired."

"Tough night?"

He coughs again. "Like I been rode hard and put away wet."

"Sure know *that* feelin'."

"Yeah." He takes another hit of Jack. "Tell you what. You come over, you can rub my back."

Now Maryjane laughs. "You got a nice back, Sonny," she says, "but it ain't my favorite part to rub." She sighs. "But yeah. I guess I'm tired too. Maybe we both just sleep. How's your belly?"

He shrugs. "It's okay," he lies. "Saw a doc; he run some tests."

"Mm."

"You gonna want some coffee? I'll save you a cup."

"Nah," says Maryjane. "I've had plenty. 'Less you gonna give me some jelly roll to go with it."

Sonny laughs again. "My jelly roll, it gone all stale, Sugar. But I get a few hours sleep? Why, I think it's gonna be just like fresh out the oven."

MJ laughs. "I'm countin' on it. I got to go back on. See you in a while."

"Right," he says, but she's already hung up. He takes one more—small—swig from the bottle, puts the gun into his sax case, turns out the light in the kitchen and returns to the living room, where he carefully puts The Hawk on the turntable. He sits in the dark and closes his eyes as "Body and Soul" fills the room.

The record has ended and he's asleep when she buzzes, dreaming about something he can't quite remember, about bein' a boy, eight or nine, before he had the sax anyway, in Los Angeles, his Mama cookin' supper for him and his sister and Harper. He wipes the sleep out of his eyes and presses the buzzer, stands by the door till she knocks softly, then opens it. Maryjane steps through. She's a small woman with silver and blonde highlights in her hair and a scar that runs down her jaw from her right ear almost to her chin. She's had the scar since she was twelve. She was twelve when she learned how to shoot a gun, and thirteen when she killed the man who scarred her. Shot him in the chest, then shot him in the balls, "so if he *got* better, he couldn't do to no other girl what he done to me." Pushed the body into a pile of garbage that was home to a million rats. No one ever found it. She had the abortion the day after she killed him.

She'd come to hear him play, three nights in a row, and after the third she came up to him and asked, could he play *her* the way he played *it*? and pointed to his sax. There wasn't nothin' long-term there, they both knew it, but the sex was good and she had a way of purrin' that helped him fall asleep. It'd been five, six months now; for her, he knew, he was just someone to tide her over till she got restless, and that was okay. Was a time in his life *he* got restless too, right after Norma'd got the divorce and he was alone in Paris, still young and without a belly, and with lots of energy built up after playin' most every night for hours.

"Hey, Sonny," Maryjane says.

"Hey."

She wraps her arms around his neck, pulls him to her and kisses him. He returns it carefully. Truth is, her pressin' on him so hard hurts.

"You *are* tired," she says, and he nods and yawns. "You wanna just go to sleep? It's okay."

"Yeah, honey. I do."

Maryjane nods. "Lemme jus' take a shower first. Wash off some a that stink of all them hands." Maryjane dances, topless. She covers her scar in silver, adds a matching one on her left cheek and calls herself Silver Streaks. She's twenty-six or -seven and makes good money, and nobody touches her—no*body*, no*where*, 'cept Sonny—except to stuff ones and fives, the occasional ten or twenty, into the waistband of her short silver pants or the tops of her thigh-high silver boots.

When she comes out of the shower he's lying in bed with the lights out, listening to Dex and Bud Powell play "Willow Weep for Me" on the radio. She steps into the bedroom wrapped in a towel; he can see her outlined in the faint light spilling from the bathroom.

"You want a drink?" he says.

"Nah," she says and shakes her head. "I'm gonna turn on the little light. That okay?"

"Yeah." He covers his eyes as she turns on the small lamp next to what's her side of the bed when she stays. It's only twenty-five watts, and there's a shade, but it jars Sonny. "Ow," he says, "that's bright."

MJ laughs and peels away the towel. Her damp, perfect body glows in the light. She looks good and she knows it, wants Sonny to know it. "You just turn that way" she says teasingly, and points to the wall, "so you don't got to see it."

He takes one long look at her, mumbles "Umm," and does.

She snorts a laugh. "You *surely* are tired," she says, and sits on the bed beside him, picks up the bottle of isopropyl, pours some on his back and rubs it in. "Feel good?" she asks.

"Yeah," he murmurs.

She kisses his ear. "You just rest up, Sonny Curtis," she whispers. "You don't got to worry 'bout nothin'. MJ is here." She rubs some more, his stomach relaxes and he falls asleep.

His sleep is hard, like his waking. His belly awakens him repeatedly and he sits up chewing antacids one after another. The pain eases up for a while, and between the bouts, he falls asleep. Maryjane, still as the dead oak in his Mama's back yard, sleeps peacefully beside him, but he dreams of Norma. Norma just got wore out, like he's wearing out; only difference is, she walked away while she still had somethin' left to wear. "Sonny," she said, "I love you but you ain't got nothin' and you ain't never gonna have nothin', long as music means more to you than breathin' does." They never had no kids, him and Norma; sometimes he wonders why: Was it him, was it her, was it just luck—bad or good? She's been gone nine, ten years now. Sonny was in Paris when he got the letter. He'd been expecting it but that didn't make it no easier. He called her, all the way from France, and she kept sayin' over and over "It just ain't workin', Sonny. I can't be a wife to a man I don't get to see but once or twice a year, for *three years* now." It was true, and he knew it, but there wasn't no work in L.A. no more, not much in New York or Chicago, neither. He hated traipsing around the country, a week here, a weekend there, just for enough to buy food and pay the rent on the apartment he was always leavin' her alone in. Norma went with him sometimes, but she hated it too. "I want a *home*," she told him. Well, so did he, but the jazz scene in America? Hell, there wasn't one, not like there'd been when they got married, ten, twelve years before he went to France; that was why he left. There was a lot of work in Paris, where they still loved American jazz, and blues, and all the players who played it. Money wasn't great but it was steady. He could even put a little aside. But Norma, she'd come there once and didn't want to live in France. "Ain't a thing for *me* to do," she said. "You got that horn. Me, all I got is cleanin' floors. They got plenty a girls in Paris already who can do that."

November 17

He gets to the doctor's office a few minutes before three, and he feels good. He slept well, woke up late and refreshed and, for the first time in maybe a month, really hungry ("You losin' some major pounds, man!" Harper said last night. "You gettin' *awful* thin."), made a couple over-easy eggs and some toast and his stomach was happy to receive them. It feels, well, okay now—least, there's nothin' but the feeling he gets sometimes after eating, like he's all filled up with water. But he hasn't passed blood today, didn't yesterday, neither. *And* he's "got prospects," as Harp likes to say: He doesn't have to play tonight, but Harper called him about a session tomorrow morning.

He gives the receptionist his name, she smiles and asks him to have a seat, the doctor will be with him in a few minutes.

"Thank you," he says, and finds a cushioned blue vinyl chair, drops into it and leafs through the magazines on the table beside it. There's nothing he wants to read—Sonny's never been much of a reader, one of the reasons he didn't do so good in school (the other: He discovered the sax when he was ten, by fourteen he was playing in dance bands and by fifteen, in dark, smoky clubs where nobody cared about his age, only how well he blew, and where he got his nickname. *You play pretty good, Sonny boy,* a trumpeter told him one night, and turned to the others and said, *Don't Sonny here play good*? Even Harper called him nothin' besides Sonny after that. He'd turned eighteen a month after VJ Day—didn't have to worry 'bout school no more so he'd been playin' instead of readin' ever since). But there's a *National Geographic* and he looks at the pictures: places he'd like to go, like New Zealand, and Thailand (now that that war's over; he's been through most of Europe but nowhere exotic like Japan or Rio or Africa), lots of birds and animals that're pretty. Brightly colored. He likes bright colors. He don't wear 'em, nothin' but black slacks and white shirts, but he likes them. MJ wears a lot of red 'cause he likes it. Norma wore yellow.

He's looking at a picture of a large toucan, its yellow-orange bill holding a fish, the one visible blue-ringed eye seemingly focused on the camera, when a girl in a white uniform comes out and says "Mr. Curtis?" He says "Uh-huh" and she smiles and asks him to come with her, the doctor is ready for him. Silently, she leads Sonny to a different office than he was in last week, this one with a big, dark-wood desk and books and certificates, no examining table. The desktop is clean, neat. *He could lie down on that*, he thinks, *with that girl* without *her white uniform*. Behind the desk there's a large mahogany leather chair, a bigger, castered version of the side chair to which the girl points him. The girl says "He'll be in in a minute," smiles at him and leaves—the door clicks behind her—and he waits, looks out the wide third-floor window that's behind the wheeled chair. It's a clear day, unusually warm for a Chicago November. Maybe he'll walk home 'stead of takin' the bus. Maybe he'll call MJ: if she don't got to work tonight, see if she wants to have a picnic in the park, they can pick up some cold cuts, maybe some ribs, and some bread, and slaw, pickles, olives, whatever, a six pack and a pint, laze out on a blanket and watch the sun go down, go back to his place when it gets cool, *get warm*. MJ, she ain't gonna have on any uniform.

His daydreaming is broken by another click as the door

opens and the doctor enters. He's a slight man who squints, maybe thirty-five but already balding, with a mustache that'd make him look dashing if he had a head of hair to go with it—and a chin. He smells of disinfectant and his face looks freshly shaved, even if it is three o'clock in the afternoon. Sonny stands up to greet him. The doctor smiles, says "Mr. Curtis" and they shake hands briefly. "Please," he says, "have a seat. How 're you feeling?"

Sonny chuckles. "Pretty good today," he says. "Pret-ty, *good.*"

"That's good to hear," says the doctor; he picks up the phone, presses a button and says easily "Rae, hold my calls, okay? Thanks" and hangs up. "Now," he says, and takes a folder from the center drawer of the desk, reviews its contents quickly, and sits, hands folded on top of it. He looks at Sonny. "Mr. Curtis" he says, and stops.

Sonny waits. The doctor continues to look at him, like he expects Sonny to say something. When he doesn't, the doctor clears his throat. "Mr. Curtis," he says again, and Sonny is aware the doctor is forcing himself to continue to look at him. "Your tests came back, I mean, the results of your tests came back this morning." He takes a quick breath. "This is the hard part of being a doctor, Mr. Curtis," he says, and lifts up the folder, then sets it down again. Sonny watches with a mix of curiosity and detachment and foreboding. *This man*, he thinks, *he wants t' tell me somethin' he* don't *want to tell me.*

The doctor squints into Sonny's eyes. "You have cancer of the stomach, Mr. Curtis," he says, clearly, simply, so there will be no misunderstanding the words.

Still, it takes a Sonny a long heartbeat to understand. He watches a distant plane appear at one corner of the window and fly from one side of the doctor's head, behind it and past, and disappear beyond the other side of the glass, going someplace Sonny can't imagine. "Cancer," he says.

The doctor nods. "Of the stomach." He takes a breath and lets it out carefully. Sonny thinks of a dragon trying not to breathe fire, that the doctor's stream of air will cause an explosion in the room if he releases it too quickly. "I - wish we'd found it earlier," the doctor says, "we might have been able to ..."

Sonny watches the doctor work not to say the words. "You tellin' me I'm gonna die, ain't you?" he says.

The doctor nods. "Yes," he says quietly, with dignity.

The world whirls. Sonny is dizzy. He grips the arms of the chair and closes his eyes. It takes him several moments to regain his balance, during which the doctor gets up quickly and says "Are you—I mean, can I get you something? Water? Mr. Curtis?"

Sonny opens his eyes. He's very tired. "Cancer" he says. "In my stomach."

The doctor sits again. "Yes." Sonny takes a deep, deep breath, filling his lungs, his head, his gut with air, like balloons. *There's no pain.* He does it again. *Still:* **no pain**. He touches his shirt, white, and like all his other shirts growing loose against his neck, his wrists, his skin.

"So," he says softly.

"I also need to tell you: It's pretty far advanced. The x-rays show it's metastasizing."

"What that mean?"

The doctor continues to force himself to look into Sonny's eyes. "It's spreading, Mr. Curtis, to other parts of your body. It's beyond the point where we can treat it—cure it—or remove it surgically." He folds his hands on the desktop and takes a breath. "You have a few more months, perhaps," he says kindly. "We can - make you comfortable, in a hospital, help control the discomfort."

Sonny nods and reaches for his cigarettes. Quietly the doctor says "You can't smoke in here." He tries to soften the words with a smile. "It's not safe; all the"—he waves vaguely—"around."

"Mm," Sonny murmurs. "Well."

They are silent.

Finally, the doctor sits straight up. "I'm going to give you a prescription, Mr. Curtis, to help with the pain you've been having. It's pretty strong, so be careful with it. *Only* take it as directed. And," he begins to write on a pad, "you shouldn't use alcohol while you're taking this, and you shouldn't drive." He looks up. "You understand?"

Sonny nods.

"Good." He finishes writing the prescription, tears it off and hands it to Sonny. "I'm sorry, Mr. Curtis," he says. "I know this is a shock. If you like, I can ask a counselor to talk with you, someone who can help you with the... issues."

Sonny shakes his head. "I got no issues, doc."

"Well." The doctor gets up. "Can we call someone to come get you? Or would you like to just sit here for a while?"

"No. Thanks." Sonny gets up. He's a little unsteady on his feet but, damnedest thing, there's *no* pain, not even the filled-up feeling. He takes the doctor's hand, shakes it and starts to leave.

"Mr. Curtis?" The doctor stops him.

"Yeah?"

"I can make arrangements for you. At the hospital. If you'd - like me ..."

"I don't know. Got to think. Think it over. Y' know?"

The doctor nods. "You'll think about it? We *can* make you more comfortable."

"Yeah. I will. Think about it."

The doctor nods again. "If you decide *not* to go into the hospital, right away I mean, we'll need to monitor your condition. You can come in whenever you need to, but I'd like to see you once a week, just to see how - whether the drugs are working, give you a refill or something else if you need it."

"Okay," Sonny says.

"I'll walk you to the reception area. The nurse will give you some information about... that you can read that may answer some questions you'll have."

Sonny nods. The doctor opens the door and, as if Sonny

had changed to glass in the last ten minutes, guides him slowly, gingerly to the lobby.

At home he drinks a glass of water, goes into the living room, calls Mama. Mama is seventy-eight now, frail but with her faculties very much intact—more than his own, Sonny thinks sometimes. Like now. He sits on the frayed sofa, another glass of ice water on the side table, and dials the 'phone.

Vernita, his sister, two years older, answers and calls "Mama, it's Sonny." They don't talk much now, never did, really. 'Nita spent her whole post-girlhood life with Mama in Phoenix, moved out when she finally got married in '65, but she visits nearly every week, practically lives there instead of Tucson with her husband, while Sonny hasn't been to see Mama in two, three years. Partly it's the money, partly it's the trip—flying has always upset his equilibrium, train ride's too damn long and he doesn't have a car—and, partly, he always feels like he's let her down, done nothin' with his life, least, not as much as she always told him he *could* do when he was a boy. All he's ever done is play the sax; that never meant much to anyone, except him.

"Vernon, that you?" Mama says into the 'phone. She's the only one ever uses his given name anymore. "How you doin'?"

He doesn't know what he can tell her, or how. *I'm gonna die, Mama, in a couple months, and I'm hurtin' bad a lot of the time*, he wants to say. But he can't. For one thing, he's not sure he believes it yet and, for another, how can he say something like that to her over a telephone, how can she *hear* something like that on a 'phone? He says instead, "I guess I'm doin' okay. Keepin' busy. How you?" He says it, and he wants to cry.

"I'm good, son. Workin' in the garden a lot. Sold fourteen cactus plants this week. Can't believe folks in Arizona wanna *buy* cactus." She chuckles.

"Four*teen*!" says Sonny.

"Uh-huh. That's so far. And it only Thursday. Last week I didn't sell but eleven the whole week." She sniffs. "Still hopin' you gonna give me a grandbaby 'fore I pass." She raises her voice. "Your *sis*ter ain't never gonna have none."

He hears 'Nita's voice in the background. "That's for damn sure" she says.

Sonny smiles, then winces. He got the prescription filled and his stomach is beginning to hurt; he has the clear plastic bottle there on the table—"take as needed, no more than one every four hours" it says—and wonders if he should take one now. He decides to wait. Pain ain't *that* bad yet.

"So how come you callin' me out a nowhere, middle of the day?" Mama asks.

"Mama," he begins, and falters.

Her voice changes. The lightness that's almost always there, that reflects the tenderness, disappears and is replaced by the darkness of concern: her love. "What is it, Vernon," she asks. "Tell Mama."

"I ... I got the cancer, Mama. In my stomach." He hears Mama suck in her breath. "It's... bad."

Mama smacks her lips, what she always does when she's thinking. Then she says: "You wanna come home, son, I take care of you. You my boy. You *always* gonna be my boy."

"I know, Mama" he says weakly. He wipes his eyes.

"You gettin' treated?"

"Yeah. Best 's they can."

"What that mean?"

Sonny shrugs, aware she can't see it and glad of it, glad she can't see him right now. "It just means they doin' what they can do."

"You in the hospital?"

"Nah. No need for that. 'Sides, wouldn't do no good, I mean, there's nothin' they can do for me in the hospital they can't do for me out."

"Well..." Mama sighs.

"I'm doin' all right, Mama. I got some med'cine. And the doctor, he's gonna check me every week. I got appointments."

"You gonna tell Norma?"

Now Sonny sighs. "Mama, I don't even know where Norma is no more. You know that."

"She's in Los Angeles. *You* know *that*. Prob'ly get her number from 'Information.'"

He shakes his head. "I don't know."

"Well," Mama says again. Then there is silence.

"I got to go, Mama," says Sonny finally. "Got to get ready."

"You playin' tonight?"

"Uh-huh, I—" he grunts as the pain suddenly jabs him. "Shit" he mutters through clenched teeth.

"Vernon, what's happenin'? You—"

"I'm, I jus'—spilled something, is all" he says. "Glass of water. All over me."

"Didn't *sound* like you spilled no water."

He hates lying to her, but he needs to get off the 'phone. The pain suddenly erupts like a gush of oil from a just-drilled well, glorious and black and uncontrollable. He clenches his teeth and his gut. "Jus' water," he tells her. "Look, I got to go. I'll call you over the weekend."

"Saturday. I'll be at church almost all Sunday. They holdin' a yard sale and a barbeque. Asked if I'd make the ribs."

"Well," says Sonny, "you save some for me then."

"You come out here and get 'em, I'll make ribs for you, every night."

"Sounds good, Mama."

"And you can play that song for me, that one by what's his name, the Little Tramp?"

"Charlie Chaplin, Mama." He is straining hard to hold back the pain. He can feel the strain in his throat as he speaks. "Tune's called 'Smile.'" First time he heard it was in a movie Mama took him to: 1932 or '33. He was five, six. She spent the dime 'cause he wanted to be with her.

"Yeah. That the one. I like *that* song."

"I know."

"You play it real good. Prettiest thing I think I ever heard. Your record."

"Thanks, Mama. I'll play it for you."

Mama sighs. "Well."

"You get your rest now, Mama. Say 'Hi' to 'Nita for me."

"Nita," Mama calls, "Vernon says 'Hi.'"

"Hi, Vernon," 'Nita calls back.

"'Bye now, Mama" he says.

"'Bye, son." He starts to hang up, but, in the low, concerned voice, she adds: "Sonny, you take care. I love you."

"I know. I love you, too."

"'Bye," she says.

"'Bye," he whispers, and waits for her click before he hangs up.

When she does, he sits back and looks at the pill bottle. He opens it and taps out one of the small orange tablets. He looks at his watch: 5:45. "You better work," he says to the tablet. He swallows it with a swig of water, sits back and waits. The pain grows worse, then, in fifteen or twenty minutes, begins to ebb. He closes his eyes and hopes it will stay away.

November 18

When Harper calls it's past midnight and Sonny doesn't want to talk. Talking will make the pain worse. He tells Harp he's tired and he'll see him at the gig.

He sits in the living room, the lights out, smoking and listening to Ben Webster play ballads. The long, breathy notes of his tenor are as blue as Sonny's, and they mingle with the smoke and the spilled light from the sign across the street that flashes

"OP N ALL NIG T" in bright white neon. He wants a drink, but he's got a pill in him and he won't do somethin' stupid like that.

He's known Harper forever: since they were kids in L.A. Harp was the one turned him on to the sax. He thought they looked cool so he stole one for Sonny from a pawn shop, reeds, case and all, and Sonny just picked it up on his own, listenin' to records and sneakin' into clubs with him. Told their Mamas Harp'd bought it with money he made playin'. Which coulda been true. He was the wild child who played the piano like he was born at one, even played in the church both their Mamas went to when he wasn't but seven. Harp's Mama's passed now. He never knew his Daddy. Sonny hadn't known his, either, but that was because he'd died when Sonny was four. Harper's Daddy never knew he had a son.

They lived only a few doors apart, walked to school together in the morning and got into trouble together when school let out. Till they started playin' music together. Then they didn't have no time for trouble. Harp is his friend, the big brother Sonny always wished he had. Sonny is two months older but Harper was the protector, the one who made the rules that Sonny followed and took the chances Sonny reveled in.

Last few years, though, Harper's been gettin' into trouble again. Usin'. Did that, just a little, experimenting, when he was a kid, seventeen, eighteen, playin'—and livin'—like crazy with guys who had habits. Sonny knew about it then, didn't want to know any more about *that* and Harper never offered to teach him. He got over it, though; least, Sonny thought he did. Spent six months in jail while Sonny was off touring. He wrote to Harp, picture postcards mostly, and Harper wrote back.

He don't talk to Sonny 'bout it now, either, but Sonny can tell. There's that look in his eye he knows, *because* he's known Harp forever, because he's been playin' with men like Harp forever and he's seen their eyes, a little too bright, a little too wide, filled with a gaze that's a little too at the world inside them and not at all at the world most of the rest of the world is seeing. That pains Sonny too: They been friends so long. Used to see each other two, three times a week, even when they weren't doin' a gig. Go out, have a drink, maybe with MJ and whoever Harper was seeing at the time—his girls changed often as the colors of the sky at sunset. Now, Harper calls him, late, wantin' to talk, wantin' to say the somethin' he can't say, or won't, or just 'cause it's late and he's high. Sometimes, they talk for a couple hours; *Harp* talks, mostly, and Sonny listens. Last couple months though, since his gut's been botherin' him, Sonny finds it hard to listen, to concentrate on what he's sayin'. That don't bother Harper. He needs to talk and Sonny hates tellin' him *no* like he did tonight, but the pill's mostly wore off and the pain keeps gettin' worse and he needs to take another one, and *he* don't want to tell *Harper* that: Fool'd start worryin' himself into usin' more a whatever it is he's swallowin', or sniffin', or shootin' into his arm. Sonny's never tried it, not even when Norma quit and he stopped carin' about anything—*even* the music—for a while. He don't even like takin' these orange things. *Man's got pain, he's got to deal with it.* Unless the pain fucks up the man's mind even worse than the drugs do.

He avoids taking another pill till after one, then falls asleep quickly under its influence. He sleeps and doesn't dream.

The alarm is set for 7:00 but he wakes up at 5:30 and knows he's awake for good, so he gets out of bed and takes a shower. He sits on the toilet. When he gets up he looks and sees the water's a dark reddish brown, a little brighter than the color of watery shit. He's not hungry and he doesn't eat or drink anything except two, three glasses of water, no pill—pain isn't too bad— and when he gets to the session he looks like he feels, drawn and worn. He blew a little before he left, just to make sure he could.

They start at 10:00, layin' down background for some girl

singer who's got a nice voice but he's heard a thousand like her. The music's Muzak and boring as hell, it doesn't require much effort. And they're only laying three tracks today, conductor's gotta be somewhere, the rest'll be Monday. Sonny's glad. He's supposed to play the club tonight, startin' at 9:00. He can get some rest, take a pill: By the time they wrap the second track, he knows he's gonna need it.

They break at 3:00, and Harper suggests they get something to eat. Sonny's still not hungry and his stomach is hurtin', but he oughta eat somethin' before the gig and he knows if he don't do it now he won't do it at all. So he walks with Harp into a diner where Harper orders a Greek salad and a gyro and a bowl of bean soup and Sonny asks for scrambled eggs and dry toast. Harper looks at him with too-bright eyes. "That all you eatin'?" he says. "Or did you have a big breakfast for a change."

"Nah," says Sonny. "Jus' ain't hungry."

Harp cracks a short laugh. "You lose any more a that belly, you gonna be concave. Girl's head just gonna sink, she tries to lie it on your chest."

Sonny smiles. He knows he's got to tell him, too, but not here. Not at the club, either. After he tells Harp, ain't neither of them gonna be able to play worth a damn. "Look, man," he says, "I'm kinda wore out. Didn't get much sleep? And it's *hard* playin' shit like that"—he waves in the direction of the studio—"all that time."

"Know what you mean, brother. *Know* what you *mean*." Harp looks at his fingers and cracks the knuckles. "That crap? It make my hands sorer in a hour than they get in four at the club. Got to play too *sloooow*."

They talk for a few minutes, nothin' in particular. The waitress brings coffee and Sonny sips his, then the food. Sonny takes a bite of toast, moves the eggs around, drinks more coffee and takes another bite of toast while Harper wolfs it down.

"Man," he says, "I was hungry like a bear."

"Yeah," says Sonny with a grin, "I noticed."

Harper laughs. "Look like you hungry as a bird," he says.

"I just ain't got much appetite. Prob'ly 'cause I didn't sleep much."

"Somethin' on your conscience?" Harp smiles. "Or is somethin' *else* botherin' you." He says it lightly, but Sonny knows what he's askin'.

Sonny shakes his head, says "Unh-uh," drops a five on the table and gets up. "I just got to get me some rest, Harp. I'll see you tonight."

Harper grabs his wrist. "Sonny?" he says, "Somethin's goin' on. You look like shit, man. You sound like shit."

"Jus' tired, is all."

Harp stares right into him. "You seen the doc yesterday."

"Yeah."

"What'd he say? About your *stom*ach, boy."

Sonny shrugs. "Didn't say nothin' 'bout it. Why you think he said somethin' 'bout my stomach?"

"'Cause *you* ain't said nothin' about it. Not last night on the phone, not before the gig, not durin' breaks, not since we been sittin' here. Only time you don't talk about somethin' is when somethin's wrong, *bad* wrong." Harper pulls him down into the booth and leans across the table, speaks quietly. "I've known you forty-some years, Sonny. You got no way to lie to me." He sits up straight and stares into Sonny's eyes. "*No* fuckin' way."

Sonny looks down at his hands and breathes carefully. "I - can't talk about it, Harp. Not now." He stands up; Harper eyes his every move. "I *do* got to rest. I, we'll talk, maybe tomorrow."

"Why not tonight? After?"

"If I ain't too tired."

"Okay." Harper gets up from the booth as the waitress approaches with their check, steps around her, and does something he's only done one other time in their lives, the day Sonny married Norma, right before she came down the aisle. He puts his arms around Sonny and holds him, hugs him to his bulky chest, squeezing Sonny like he was the last man on earth and there was no way he was gonna let him get away. Sonny is surprised, and the pressure makes his gut ache, but he doesn't move. He just lifts his arms and he hugs Harper back, not so hard, but hard enough.

"'Scuse me," says the waitress. "You boys want anything else?"

"Nah," mumbles Sonny, still in the embrace.

"Okay," she says, and drops the check and leaves.

Harper lets go. Sonny steps back: Harp is crying. Sonny's embarrassed. "Hey, man," he says, puts his hand on Harp's shoulder and tries to smile.

Harper clasps the hand with own massive, lissome fingers. "You my brother, Sonny."

"I know. You're mine."

"You all I got."

Sonny nods and squeezes Harp's shoulder.

"Shit," Harper says. He wipes his face. "Look - at - this - *shit*!" He laughs, and Sonny joins in. "Hey: You go get that rest now. I'll see you tonight."

"Yeah, man," says Sonny. "Tonight."

He lies in bed, the radio on, unable to sleep. The pain won't back off. He took a pill, finally, but it's not helping: His gut's on fire and he's passin' blood again. He called the doctor who again suggested he come into the hospital; they could give him something IV that would help. And he would sleep. "I got to play tonight," Sonny rasped, "and tomorrow night. How'm I gonna pay for anything if I don't? 'Sides," he went on, "how'm I gonna think straight with that shit goin' through my brain?" "It's up to you," the doctor said, "but I strongly recommend it, Mr. Curtis." He cleared his throat. "It's not going to get better, only worse."

In the end he agreed to see Sonny Monday morning, first

thing, and Sonny agreed, if it kept getting worse, he'd maybe go in then. He hung up, turned on the radio, set the alarm for 8:00 and lay down.

He tries to breathe slowly and shallowly, so his belly won't blow up, and wonders where he's gonna get the breath to play tonight. Well, he's got to. He needs the money, he needs to get away from the pain. The music, it can do that, move him along like a cloud in a summer sky. Even a stormy summer sky.

He finally does fall asleep, he's not sure when, but the alarm startles him. He rubs his eyes and shuts it off, lies there trying to figure out how his stomach is. He takes a small breath, then a slightly larger one, then a deep one. That hurts, but it's not as bad as before he went to sleep. Pill is still workin'. And he can take another one at, what, 8:30?

He gets to the club just before 9:00. It's busy, lots of people and noise. Harper's at the bar, with Cole; Harp waves to Sonny who waves back but keeps going, into the dressing room. There's a pitcher of ice water there and he pours himself a glass, takes out a pill and swallows it. His stomach is still hurtin' but it's nothin' like this afternoon, and he waited so this one'd last as long as possible. He's not supposed to take another one till 1:00, but he figures if he needs it he can take it sooner. Just so's he can get through the night. Then he can go home, sleep some more, maybe he'll feel better when he wakes up tomorrow.

When he comes out Harp, Alan and Cole are on the stand, jokin' and laughin', loose and eager. He steps onto it, one hand on the sax hangin' from the strap. He smiles and waves at all of them.

"How you doin'?" Harp says, his eyes clear this time, sharp and focused.

"Okay" says Sonny. He blows a couple notes and does a sound check, takes the song list from his pocket and looks it over while Harp says into his mike:

"Ladies and gentlemen, welcome to Club Riff, one of the—few—places around where you can still hear *jazz* the way it's meant to be heard, intimately, played the way it's meant to be played, right before your very ears." The audience applauds, a little more enthusiastically than usual; most of the time it's just polite, least till they get warmed up, lost in the music like the players do. "Thank you" Harp says and arpeggios.

"My name is Harper Howell, and tonight we got Mr. Alan Towson on the drums"—Alan riffs; the applause is polite—"Mr. Cole Amber on acoustic bass"—Cole plunks a couple bars; more polite applause—"and, on the alto saxophone, Mister, Sonny, *Curtis*" he says with a flourish. Sonny blows up and down a scale, nods as the applause rises. He thinks about his stomach. So far, so good.

"We're gonna be here till three o'clock, so you just sit back, drink up so the owner'll think you love us and he'll pay us better"—there's a small laugh; Harp smiles his widest smile—"and *listen* up, 'cause you gonna hear some great music tonight.

"We're gonna start with a tune that features Sonny Curtis, written by another Sonny—Sonny Rollins. It's called: 'Sonnymoon for Two.'" He moves the mike away, says "Two, three, *four*" and they're off. Sonny wets the reed again, slips it between his teeth and lips, closes his eyes and blows.

And there it is: a great skein of notes woven into a crazy quilt of such otherwise-inexpressible beauty that it can only exist because *he* weaves it. It wraps him and he feels warm within it. Like Norma's hands when she loved him, like his Mama's when he was a little boy. Like Harp's when he put the bear-hug on this afternoon. Yeah, there's some pain—in his gut, in his memory—but it don't matter. He thinks of something somebody read him once, that he never forgot: The dying dream of ecstasy like the living dream of love.

Well, he's dying. He's entitled to dream of anything he wants.

By the end of the second set he knows he's gonna need another pill. Breathin' deep, like he needs to, is hard. At the break he asks Harp to change the song list, pick pieces that have fewer solos for him, and shorter ones. Harp looks at him and says sure, Sonny, and you keep it to eight bars no matter what; and offers to buy him a drink. Sonny shakes his head.

"You turnin' down a *drink*?" Harp asks. He looks worried.

"I'm takin' some med'cine," Sonny says. "Doc says I ain't supposed to drink while I'm takin' it."

"Mmm," murmurs Harper. "It for...?" and he taps Sonny's gut, not hard, just a little tap, but Sonny jumps back. "Sonny?" says Harper, "hey, what—."

"Yeah," Sonny concedes. "It's for my stomach. Look, I'm gonna go sit a while, you come get me when break's over. Okay?"

"Yeah," says Harp, and Sonny heads for the dressing room.

It's only a quarter after eleven, he can't take another pill yet. He pours a glass of water, drinks it, closes his eyes, tries to breathe slow, even. Behind his eyes he can see patterns, shapes shifting, like paisley, all shades of blue and purple, floating around images: his sax, the bedroom he slept in as a boy, 'Nita's body the time he glimpsed her comin' out the shower with the bathroom door open, when he was twelve; Paris, first time he saw it, huge cathedrals, narrow streets, lights flashing like Vegas' did now. Man, he was happy there, at first anyway. Music everywhere. Everything a man could want.

He hears footsteps and a hand touches his shoulder. "You 'bout ready?" Harp says softly. Sonny nods and opens his eyes. "Yeah," he says. "Let me piss and I'll be out."

"Sonny, you *sure* you can play?"

Sonny laughs; it hurts. "Now, Harper," he says, "when'd you ever know me *not* be able to play?"

"Okay," says Harp, with raised eyebrows.

"Two minutes," Sonny says and goes into the bathroom. He fills a paper cup with water, takes a breath and swallows it with a pill. He looks at his watch: 11:31.

By the last break the pain is blinding and he's gasping between notes. Harper tries to convince him to go home, they'll play the last set as a trio, and even Cole, who, like Sonny, usually sees nothing but the music, has noticed and commented. But Sonny's determined: He can finish out the night. He'll go home and rest, that'll make him okay.

Harper shakes his head. "You one stubborn son of a bitch, Sonny Curtis," he says. "*And*, sick or not, you one hell of a horn man."

"Thanks," Sonny mutters. He heads for the bathroom and takes another pill. *I got to last one more hour*, he whispers to the mirror; *not even a hour, just three-quarters a one*. He drinks more water. *I can do that* he thinks. *I can do that.*

When they finish the last set Sonny sits on stage, eyes closed, breathing in and out slowly and shallowly. In his whole life he has never hurt this bad. Harp comes up to him, asks if he can do anything and Sonny, unable to speak, shakes his head. He sits that way five, maybe ten minutes, he doesn't know how long. Harp sits beside him, pretending conversation so that when Mr. Orrin, Club Riff's owner, comes up and asks if everything's okay, Harp can say, "Yeah, we just talking while Sonny catches his breath. He's just tired." He grins. "Late night with his girl, know what I mean?"

Mr. Orrin is sympathetic and goes away. Harp gently lays a hand on Sonny's shoulder. "C'mon, man," he says, "let's get you home." Sonny nods.

Usually he takes the bus but tonight he can't handle the slow lurching ride so he gets a cab. Harp shares it—too cold tonight to walk, he says—and they drop Sonny off first though it's really out of Harper's way. "You want me to walk you up?" he asks; Sonny says no, he can make it. "Okay," says Harp. "See you tomorrow. Now you take care."

"Yeah," says Sonny. "I will. You too." Harp nods, and Sonny baby-steps from the curb to the door, unlocks it and goes in. While he waits for the elevator he looks out. The cab is still sitting there. He waves as the elevator door opens. The cab drives away.

Inside, he puts down the sax, takes off his shoes, gets water and takes a pill. He looks at his watch: 3:40 on Saturday morning. It's been less than two hours since the last one and he's feeling dizzy and tired as well as being stabbed again and again from the inside. Still dressed, he lies down in the dark and breathes, in, out. In, out. Slow, slower. In, out.

He does fall asleep but the pain jabs him and wakes him up. The clock says 4:32. He waits and the pain goes away, mostly. He can just feel the little jigger of the knot twisting his innards.

He hasn't eaten in a day and half, but he's not hungry. He does have a headache. Maybe he can keep something down, a slice of bread, some soup. He warms a can of beef consommé on the stove, dips bread into it and swallows a couple bites. His stomach doesn't like it; he stops so he won't throw up.

Sonny drinks more water, and goes into the living room. He sits on the sofa, looks out the window at the flashing neon sign. "You broke like me," he murmurs to it. The sign keeps flashing.

He sits that way, listening to the silence, a long time, thinking, deciding. Finally, he shakes his head. Then he gets up, gets the sax case and brings it back to the sofa. He opens the case, takes out the sax, wets the reed, blows. Long, legato lines rise from the bell: 'Smile,' in a slow, lilting plaint that sounds like all the tears in the world. It's hard and it hurts, but he plays through the verse, the chorus, the verse, modulates and plays the chorus one last time. Then he removes the reed, holds the sax in front of him, looks at its bright and curving beauty, replaces it in the case and takes out the gun. He lays that on the arm of the sofa, beside the reed.

The Jack is still on the side table and he takes a long swallow—'bout half of what's left in the bottle; it burns goin' down and like hell in his stomach, but, though it takes a long time, it settles. He sits and waits for it, breathing shallowly so the pain won't expand with each breath. Sonny grins. Stomach don't mind good whiskey; that's good. Once he's sure it's all right, he goes to the record player, kneels and withdraws Bird: *Now's the Time. No blues tonight*, he thinks. He puts the album on, then he goes back to the sofa and sits through the tracks, listening carefully in the darkness to each one and letting the memories flow with the music—Norma, his Mama, Maryjane, Paris, Los Angeles, Harper and the feeling of standing with his horn, eyes closed and his breath coming furious and easy, the reed soft on his palate, the keys moving magically under his fingers, Norma again—"The Song is You," "Lairnd Bairnd," both takes of "Kim" and "Cosmic Rays." He turns the record over. All three "Chi Chi"s, "I Remember You." When that ends, his stomach doesn't hurt anymore. He smiles—sofa needs replacin' anyway—and drinks the rest of the bourbon. "Now's the Time" begins. Sonny listens, long and hard. He picks up the gun. He brings it to his temple. He closes his eyes.

TIO'S BLUES

1957

Blue. Blue of the sky, of the sea, of an infant's eyes. Blue of the night, of the venous blood, of the soul in its nether-land. Blue, the languid, slightly seamy sound of a tear made music, of an ache bent from the soul through brass and breath...

Blue, lustrous as sapphire, cool as autumn rain, warm as sleep, as dreams. Blue of the light at sunset, of the smoke of the incense and the candles, of the faces of the near-death. Blue of our darkness, our lust, our losses...

It's fall, but you wouldn't know that in this part of the city. For one thing, it's still hot—maybe even hotter than it was last month, when it was *hot*. Summer: an excuse for the sun beating on the heads and necks of the people who brave it, and on the sidewalks where grass grows, and dies, in the cracks. Too little rain. Too much heat, too many people sweating and swearing in it.

There are almost no fallen leaves along those sidewalks, because there are almost no trees lining them. Most of the trees (and their cooling shade) are in the park, away from the traffic; they're still in full bloom, bright, rich green. *The only green, and the only rich,* I'll *ever see; in this city anyway* Matt thinks when he walks past them on his way to work, the days he goes to work, that is.

The days he doesn't? Well, he leaves the apartment at seven-thirty anyway, before the heat has had the chance to really kick in, hangs out on a park bench catnapping, or reading in a discarded newspaper about what Ike and Nixon're up to, or looking at girls, and waits till he knows Gillian will be gone. Then he goes back to the crowded row of brick six- and eight-flats, concrete steps and porches, no lawns or open space between them where a tree *could* grow, he lies in his room, dreams, paces, listens to Tio listening to his records or, more often, practicing. Or he wanders, looking at the well-dressed men and carefully appointed women, buys a quart of beer, peers in store windows at all the things he'll buy *someday* as he treks through the city he has trekked through a couple thousand times; until it's time to go home and eat lunch, until he knows Tio will need something, until he just can't stand the heat any more. The apartment isn't cool, but at least it has fans in every room except the living room, where there's an air conditioning unit. And where Tio spends most of his time.

This particular day, however, he went to work, washed the few cars that came in early, pumped some gas, smiled at the ladies, rubbed their windshields with the chamois in a slow, powerful, hip-driven motion—they gave him tips sometimes, and a lot of 'em smiled back. By lunchtime he was wet and beat and the thermometer that hung below Ike and Mamie's picture read eighty-two degrees, so he grabbed a burger and a soda 'stead of walking the ten blocks each way, went back to work and sweated through the afternoon. He'd have left early, but he needed the money: The retard's record was supposed to be in; he had to pick it up on his way home. Three fuckin' ninety-eight! Well… At least, tonight, he could see Maeve.

He was late getting home—the coon at the record store couldn't find the damn album, took him twenty minutes of lookin' and *then* he told Matt it hadn't come in, something about the warehouse not shipping the whole order, he'd have to come back Tuesday. He was steamed, but he sucked it in and slammed the door on his way out. By then it was after six and he knew Gillian would be p.o.ed 'cause he was late for dinner—not like she ever made anything that made you wanna be on time anyway—so he ran in and upstairs, washed his face, wiped some Brylcreem in his hair and Old Spice in his pits, changed his clothes. Maeve would wait, but she had to be in early—*man, who ever heard of a twenty year old girl havin' to be home at nine!* He checked his hair, ran downstairs and past Tio (sitting in the living room, eyes closed, trumpet on his lap, listening to music—Clifford Brown of course—instead of playing it), into the dining room, mumbled "Sorry I'm late" and saw the empty table, Gillian adjusting the waistband of a skirt.

"Where's dinner?"

Gillian scowled. "What kept you?" she asked tersely. "Not work."

"Yeah, work!" he grumbled back. "We got busy. Lot a cars get dirty when it's this hot out." He looked at the wall clock. 6:40. He had twenty minutes. It would only take ten to get to the park; no, fifteen. He'd stop for the beer on the way. And Maeve *would* wait.

"*I* had a conference all afternoon. And I've got the first half of the fifth grade class giving their book reports for the parents and teachers tonight. I told you! I just got home and I have to leave again."

"Hey. I forgot, okay?"

"Tio hasn't eaten."

Matt shrugged. "This girl's waitin' on me."

"You know, it wouldn't hurt you if you stayed with him just *once* this week—"

"Jesus, Gillian"—he pulled out his comb and looked in the mirror—"you do it—"

"*Aunt* Gillian."

"—for a change, huh? I gotta go, she don't—"

"*For a change?*"

"—*Aunt* Gillian, she don't have a phone, I can't just leave her sittin' there."

Gillian blanched. "I'm here with him *ev-er-y*, night. If I didn't have twenty fifth graders waiting to—." She stopped and saved her breath. "Ohh—Never mind." She picked up her purse and pulled out a compact. "Tio?" she called.

From the living room he called back, "Yes, Aunt Gil?" Matt heard footsteps, cautious and methodical, and then Tio stood in the archway.

"I have to leave now. I'll be back pretty late. There's peanut butter and jelly in the fridge, if you get hungry before I get home."

"Hi, Matt," Tio said happily.

Matt nodded. "Hi, big brother," he said, gently, cheerily. "How y' doin'?"

"I'm doin' *good*. How are *you* doin'?"

He smiled. "I'm doin' good, too, Tio."

Tio's face lit up. "Matt can do it, Aunt Gil. Matt can make dinner."

Matt shook his head. "Jesus, Tio. 'Matt can do it.'"

Tio smiled. Tio always smiled. "Matt can. Matt's a good cook."

"Yeah, right."

Gillian looked at him. "Matt has other things to do tonight, Tio. He has—."

"I don't need you to make explanations for me." Matt ran the comb through his hair. "I'm goin' out in a couple minutes."

"Oh," said Tio. "I can wait."

Matt shook his head. "I'm gonna be out—real late."

"Oh." Tio nodded.

"*Real* late. Y' know what I mean?"

"You'll be out. Real late."

"Yeah." Matt returned the comb to his pocket.

"You'll be back to read to me?" Tio asked.

Matt sighed. *Jesus.* "Not tonight. Tio, I—I gotta meet somebody."

He brightened again. "Can I come?"

Matt laughed. "It's a date, Tio. With a chick?"

Tio's smile broadened. "Oh," he said. "You're gonna do hugging and being alone stuff."

"I'll read to you, Tio," Gillian interjected. "I'll be back about n—when the little hand is on the nine. Okay?"

"Okay." Tio nodded and smiled. "Can I practice?"

Gillian sighed, wished he could find something else, anything, besides the trumpet.

"Until… eight o'clock. Matt, will you set—"—Matt gave her *that* look—"*I'll* set the alarm so you'll know. All right?"

"All right."

"All right." She tossed the compact into the purse and took the alarm clock from the sideboard. "Matt?"

He focused on the breakfront. His hair shined in its glass. "What?" He patted it, made a small adjustment, examined his thin, lithe body. He was short, maybe, but he was lean. Wiry. Strong.

"Please don't stay out all night."

"Hey, I c'n take care of myself."

She watched him primp. It had been nine years now since she'd "adopted" him. Them. Matt'd been fourteen; difficult even then. Smart but, even before Lupe died, difficult. Both of them were, of course, in their own ways. Tio? Well, *his* difficulties weren't of his own making. But Matt… "Then why don't you?" she said. He jerked his head toward her.

"What?"

"Then why *don't* you? Get a job and take care of yourself."

He shrugged. "I got a job."

"Pumping gas and wiping a squeegee across dirty windows. You could do so much better for y—."

"Hey. I like it." He nodded approvingly at his reflection.

"Sure you do," Gillian said. "That's why you show up there half the time."

Matt smiled, a taut smile. His voice was brittle. "Screw you," he said.

Gillian did not smile. "You know, Matthew, one of these days I may just forget you're too old to punish."

"*Yeah?*"

"*Yeah!*"

Tio looked at her. "Please?" he said softly, "don't fi—."

Matt whirled on him. "Please *what*, retard?"

Gillian swallowed hard. Then she slapped him. For a moment, there was complete still.

Matt touched his face. "God damn you," he said quietly.

"When did you start using *that* word?"

"That's, what, he, *is*, goddammit," Matt insisted. He looked at Tio. His big brother smiled back. *Jesus.* Matt lowered his voice. "He oughta be in a hospital."

Gillian raised hers in response. "He *ought* to be in this house!" she shouted. "He is your brother, Matt, and if I ever hear that come out of your mouth again, *you* will leave this house. I mean it. You understand? *Do* you understand?"

Matt released a burst of breath. "Yeah," he said, "yeah, yeah, yeah, yeah."

Gillian looked at Tio. At twenty-eight, he admired Matt the same way, as a child, he'd admired Dave. The same look on his face: a perfection he aspired to. Even if he had no idea what it meant to aspire. "I mean it, Matthew. Or to put it in terms you'll comprehend, I damn well mean it." She looked at him, direct and hard. He shook his head and muttered something she couldn't make out.

She turned to Tio. "I'll see you later, Tio," she said, forcing the smile.

Tio smiled back. "I'll see *you* later, Aunt Gil. I love you." She hugged him, gave him a kiss which he returned, picked up her purse, glared at Matt and walked out the front door. Matt watched her go, then opened the fridge and pulled out a hunk of cheese. He closed the door and bit off a piece. "See you, Tio," he said, and started out.

"I'm sorry, Matt. I didn't—."

"Yeah, forget it." He stopped, looked at Tio: the smile was still on his mouth but the eyes were downcast.

Hell. Well, Maeve would wait. He sighed. He could stay a couple minutes.

"Who's your date?"

Matt grinned. Tio's favorite subject: Matt's social life. "A chick, re—. A chick." Tio's smile changed to a mirror of Matt's: eyes narrowed, nostrils slightly flared; the corners of his mouth turned just up. He spoke in a conspiratorially soft voice. "I had a date," he said. "This afternoon. In the park."

Matt took another bite of cheese and raised his eyebrows. "Yeah?" he said.

Tio's entire face lit up, and his grin stretched. *Looks like something out of a comic book*, Matt thought. "With a chick," Tio confided. He giggled. "I didn't tell Aunt Gil yet. It's a secret."

"Okay, it's a secret." Matt gave him the code: thumb and little finger of his right hand, extended upward. Tio repeated it and Matt nodded. Honest to God, Tio was funny. But, like, it wasn't like he was ridiculous. Sometimes, he wanted to know just what Tio *was* thinking, if he was *trying* to make jokes. Christ, the retard must think *some*thing. "Who is she?"

"Her name is Kerk."

Matt stifled his laugh. "Kerk? What kind of *girl* is named 'Kerk?'"

"She's pretty," Tio said. "I told her she was pretty, just like you said to."

Matt clapped him on the back. "Way to go, big brother!" Tio laughed, and Matt did too. "It work? You get into her pants?"

Tio whispered. "She wasn't wearing pants. She was wearing a dress. With flowers on it."

*

People called it The Pond, though it was more than a hundred yards across and in its deepest places—where the catfish swam (something only people unfamiliar with The Pond would do, even in its more accessible waters)—it dropped almost thirty feet to the murky bottom. Old men and children trolled for the catfish. Near the shore, ducks abounded. So did beer and soda bottles, candy wrappers and the assorted debris of picnics, parties and, here and there, forgotten articles of clothing shed in the heat of a moment.

Around The Pond, there were trees interspersed among large flat rocks that rose almost immediately from the water's edge. The rocks were where sunseekers congregated. In summer, girls in their bikinis (the more modest ones in one-piece bathing suits) and boys in their swim trunks sprawled on them and soaked up the rays while their transistor radios blared Pat Boone or the Everlys or "Tammy." A few beats, smoking cigarettes or the increasingly popular sweet-smelling weed, frequented them too; they read, talked, played their guitars or recorders or bongos; sometimes they kissed, boys and girls, sometimes boys and boys, now and then girls and girls, clutching each other with an urgency that amused their peers and appalled their elders.

The wind blew the disparate sounds along the shore, and the old folks and the mothers with the strollers and buggies who sat on the shaded benches along the walkway that ran The Pond's circumference fifty feet from its edge listened and watched and shook their heads, wondering, sometimes audibly, what the young people were *com*ing to these days.

Tio usually sat on one of those rocks. The one he particularly favored was away from the most popular, partly shaded and too small anyway to accommodate the sprawl of either sunbathers or passion; but it was perfect for one slight, quiet young man to sit watching the ducks that waddled up seeking the bread he always brought from home to tear up for them. And perfect for him to close his eyes, feel the sun on his smiling face, and blow the trumpet. Its sounds filled the air around him. He breathed them in and his lungs filled with them; sometimes he found it hard to breathe, the music filled them so completely. Some days, he'd come to the park—one of the few places Gillian would let him go by himself—right after she left for the school, and sit on his rock all morning. He could see the clock from there, hear its chimes, and when the little hand and the big hand both pointed straight up and it rang, he'd go home and eat the sandwich or the soup she'd prepare for him, and for Matt too if he was there, and he'd tell her about the music, and she'd smile. She didn't really love the music the way he loved it, or understand it the way Matt did, but he liked telling her about it: It was sort of a way to tell her he loved her like she loved him. Which felt so good.

That day, though, he'd spent the morning practicing in his room and when he got to The Pond after lunch there was a girl sitting on his rock, strumming a guitar, so he sat on another one, a dozen yards away. There were some ducks near it, too, but it was too noisy: Nearby, a bunch of boys and girls were having a picnic—he liked picnics—and playing a radio. Elvis. He *didn't* like Elvis. Elvis was too loud, there were too many words he didn't understand, and the music didn't sound like the music he loved, the sultry blue he heard in the sounds of the great trumpeters, especially Clifford Brown, and in the sounds he could make himself, that he could watch float out of the bell of his horn and, like blue smoke, embrace him, choke him, then slowly rise, to dissipate in the air above.

He tried to play, but the other music interfered and so he fed the ducks and watched the girl. He'd seen her here before—she usually sat way away from his rock, though, by the part of The Pond where there were lots of ducks. She was big—bigger than he was; burly, with close-cropped hair, almost as short as his—with muscular arms. Her dress, that was the only way he knew for sure she *was* a girl. It flared out on the rock and fell over its edge, where one leg dangled. She held the guitar across her chest—no strap—and he watched the fingers of her left hand make the chords while she picked awkwardly with her right.

He could make out the tune: "I'll Remember April." Brownie

played that. Brownie played it better than the girl did. He'd tried to play it, too; it was a hard song to figure out. But he kept trying and now he could play it better, so it sounded pretty. Not as pretty as when Brownie played it, but pretty. Aunt Gil said you *had* to keep trying if you wanted to get better at something.

The girl wiped her left hand on her dress, replaced it on the neck of the guitar and began again. She was concentrating hard, the way he concentrated when *he* was learning a new song. Her dress was pretty: sleeveless, pale blue with green and yellow flowers. *She* was pretty.

After a while, he decided to talk to her. He'd only done that, talked to a stranger, a few times. Aunt Gil said it wasn't a good idea, but Matt said: You wanna do hugging and being alone stuff, too, don't you, Tio? But how are you ever gonna get to *know* a girl *unless* you talk to one?

She played music. He played music. *There* was something to talk about.

He waited until she finished "I'll Remember April," then stood, brushed off his pants and walked uncertainly toward her. She began another song, one he didn't recognize, singing it too. When he reached the rock, he stood there. Finally, the girl looked up at him, squinting a little in the sunlight. He smiled.

"What're you playing?" he asked.

The girl looked back at the guitar and muttered, "A guitar, stupid."

He was used to that. People called him stupid sometimes, but he wasn't. Aunt Gil said so. It was just harder for him to learn things. Except the trumpet. He'd learned to play that, and he hadn't even had a real lesson, ever! "I'm not stupid," he said evenly. "I play this. It's a trumpet."

The girl kept strumming. "I c'n see that," she said. "*I* ain't stupid."

Tio listened a long moment. The chords were easy ones; he could hear that. "What's that song?"

"'Motherless Child.' 'Sometimes I Feel Like a Motherless Child.'"

"Oh." He listened again, working the valves on his trumpet with one hand, as the girl began the chorus a second time. "What's motherless?"

The girl looked at him and kept playing. "It's, you don't have a mother." She muttered: "Asshole."

"Oh," said Tio. He continued to work the valves.

The girl closed her eyes, strummed more assuredly, as if she could feel the chords better than see them. She sang: *"A long way from home, Lord./ A long, long way from home…"* Then, eyes still shut, she picked the notes between strums.

Tio thought about it a moment. "I'm motherless," he said.

"So'm I," said the girl. "So what."

He thought a moment more. "And fatherless."

The girl played louder; a look of anger crossed her face as she returned to the verse for the third time. "Lucky you."

Tio smiled. *The whole thing, twice. That was enough.* He lifted the trumpet, closed his eyes, and blew.

"Hey!" she said, "what're you…" Her voice trailed away and her fingers stopped. She sat, and she listened.

The notes purled from the brass bell, pure, clear, articulated like the languid-but-richly precise speech of an English gentleman's voice in some movie she'd seen: smooth, soothing. It was, she thought, maybe the most beautiful sound she'd ever heard.

He played the verse, the chorus, then stopped and looked at her, smiling. "I play this," he said.

She nodded in wonder. "Yeah."

He cradled the trumpet. "I saw you here before," he said. "Lots a times."

"Bullshit."

"I sit right here; you sit way over there, on that rock. Where all the ducks go."

"Yeah," she said, surprised, and shrugged. "I felt like sitting here today."

Tio nodded. "You played 'I'll Remember April.' Brownie played that. Clif-ford, Brown." He said the name carefully, reverently. "I play it too, on this. Brownie's my favorite. He played the trumpet, too, but he's dead. That's like being asleep, only forever."

She nodded. "Uh-huh."

"I like to play in the park. The way the wind blows the sound, it makes it prettier."

The girl looked out, across The Pond, beyond the perimeter of trees and clouds. "Yeah. Like it's goin' somewhere so people all the way at the end of the world'll hear it."

"Uh-huh. At the end of the world…" He took a step closer; she looked up. Her shoulders clenched. He stopped and smiled. "What's your name?" he asked.

She hesitated. "Kerk."

"Kerk," he repeated. "My name is Tio."

"*Tio?*" He nodded. "What kind of name is *that*?"

He shrugged. "It's *my* name."

Kerk nodded.

"You're pretty," Tio said.

Again, she clenched. "Bullshit."

"You are."

She looked at his face. Unlike most of the faces she knew, it was open. His eyes were wide. He was smiling, and it was really a smile. She laid her guitar across her lap. "Play somethin' else," she said.

"Okay." He closed his eyes, raised the trumpet; the sad colloquy of "Willow Weep for Me" flowed from it in the same clear and warm voice.

Shit! she thought. She said, "You play—good."

Gillian thought of her brother each time she looked at Tio: He looked so much like Dave she sometimes forgot. So, for that matter, did Matt, except for his build. But Lupe's features were nowhere to be found on either of her sons, except perhaps in the deep brown of the almond-shaped eyes. Dave had died, twelve years ago, at Iwo Jima. Gillian thought he was a brave man, however, not because he was a good soldier—there were a lot of good soldiers in The War—but because he married the woman he loved. Her name was Guadeloupe and she was poor, and she was uneducated, and she was pregnant. And she was Mexican; in 1929 that was a courageous thing for a white man to do. (Now, almost thirty years later, it still was, she thought.) Their parents—hardy Irish stock who'd picked potatoes in the ould country, and peeled them for a living in the new—called Lupe a spic whore and wouldn't let her in their home. But Gillian stayed close; they were each other's support, the three of them. She was excited when Tio was born—she was, after Dave (Lupe, utterly exhausted, slept for hours after the birth), the first person to see the newly named Echevarria—for Lupe's favorite uncle. But that was a mouthful for most everybody, so he just became "Tio"—uncle in Spanish—and she baby-sat for him, and for Matt after he was born five years later, whenever she could. And after Dave died she just moved in: *The maiden librarian aunt without prospects and nowhere else to go*, she often thought.

Then Lupe had died, nine years ago. No death is ever pretty, but hers had been particularly unlovely: quick and painful and full of rank smells and ugly memories. And so, for those last nine years, Gillian worked at the school library, took dutiful and loving care of her nephews, and watched her future become her past, everywhere surrounded by other people's children.

In the living room, "Willow Weep for Me" was playing for the dozenth time that afternoon, its trumpet lead so familiar she could hum it as well as Tio. He sat by the record player listening, eyes closed as always, fingering the valves in what she was sure was perfect unison with the recording's "horn man," as Dave had called trumpeters. She didn't mind, was used to it, in fact. She'd have chosen something baroque, but music was recreation to her. To Tio, it was Life.

"Willow," and the album side, ended. The needle *clicked* in the groove until Tio lifted it, careful not to scratch the record. Carrying the trumpet, he came into the dining room where she sat, paging through a necessary evil of her profession: this month's *School Library Today*. She looked up and smiled at him. "Aunt Gil?" he said.

"Yes, Tio?"

"I want to play like Brownie. He's my favorite. Clif-ford, Brown."

She put the magazine down. "You have to practice."

Tio nodded, and laughed. "I thought of something today."

"Oh? What?"

"Isn't his name funny?"

"Funny?"

He lifted the instrument and waved it for emphasis as he explained: "His name is Clif-ford, *Brown*. His music is all *blue*."

Gillian laughed. "I see what you mean," she said.

He laid the trumpet down carefully onto a placemat on the dining table, and looked at it. "Sometimes it's hard to listen to," he said, seriously, his smile vanishing behind the concern.

"Why?"

"'Cause Brownie's dead," he said, "and he don't want to be. He wants to make more music, so he reaches out, from the record... I can feel it."

Gillian nodded. Tio looked at her—longingly, she thought—and, dolefully, picked up the trumpet and returned to the living room. She heard him open the cover of the record player, then the needle clicked in the between-song grooves, and the slow, blue, "Willow Weep for Me" with a trumpet lead began again.

*

Gillian would be out late again—the third night this week; something *else* to do with the PTA—but this time he'd remembered and made sure he got home in time to make Tio dinner before he left to meet Maeve: alphabet soup (he loved to spell his name with it) and a couple hot dogs in buns and smothered in mustard, ketchup, piccalilli ("lilly," Tio called it). And potato chips. Matt didn't know how he could eat the things that way but hey, Tio loved 'em and that's what mattered. He even put the dishes in the sink—one less thing Gillian could complain about—before he changed into clean chinos and a fresh shirt, the red one with a button-down collar; Maeve liked it.

He came downstairs, whistling. He heard "Willow Weep for Me," again—*Jesus, didn't the retard* ever *play anything else?* but he smiled—and called "Hey, Tio! I'll be back late. Remember, Gillian'll be home when the little hand's on the eight" on his way to the living room. There was no answer. He stepped through the archway and said "Tio, I'm leav—" and stopped.

Tio lay on the living room rug, gasping and gurgling as though the room was without air, trying to say something but unable to. Matt sucked in his own breath. "Christ, what're you—oh, Jesus, you—." He bent down and raised Tio's head. "Hey," he said softly, "it's okay, big brother, take a breath."

Tio whimpered "The record."

"*The record?*"

"The music, it's, I can't breathe."

"Here," Matt said, and turned off the phonograph. "Willow" slowed to a crawl and stopped, while he hugged Tio to him and watched the struggle for breath. The attacks happened regularly; they weren't as serious as they seemed: The doctor said they'd end of their own accord. But while they happened they were painful to watch. And scary as hell: Tio curled up, small and taut, his face red-turning-blue, his eyes and hands squeezed together as though he'd never be able to open them again.

Slowly, his breathing eased and first his eyelids, then his

hands, unclenched. He lay against Matt's chest, sniffling, eyes leaking, taking in small gasps of air. Matt reached into a pocket and pulled out a tissue. "Here," he said comfortingly. "Your face's all wet."

Tio took the tissue and wiped his face.

"C'mon, blow your snot."

Tio did, weakly.

"Again," Matt commanded.

When he'd finished, Matt balled the tissue and dropped it, then took out another and dabbed Tio's eyes. Tio looked up at him, tried to smile.

Matt nodded. "C'mon, you're gonna be okay."

"I'm gonna be okay," Tio said, between sobs. "Thank you."

"Hey—that's what little brothers do, they take care of their big brothers. Right?"

"Right."

"Well, then?"

They sat that way for a while. Matt rocked him. Tio sobbed, then sniffled; then he was quiet. The clock chimed: 6:45. He was gonna be late again. Shit. But Maeve would wait.

"Matt?" Tio said finally. "It was choking me."

"I know, I know."

"It comes right out of the record player, and, and it was so pretty. I could see it, the notes, they were blue, and it was like his hands, Brownie's, it comes all around me and it holds me very tight, tighter than anything, even you, ev'rything was turning all blue, and, and I couldn't breathe."

Jesus. He dabbed Tio's face again. "Can you breathe now?" Tio nodded. "Okay. Maybe you better not practice tonight. You c'n - look at the TV till Gillian gets back, I think *Circus Boy's* on, she'll be—."

"Can you stay with me?"

"*Tio*"—*Jesus!*—"I got things I gotta do, I gotta meet this girl, she'll be waitin' on me, I—..." He grimaced. "*Damn it.*" He wadded the second tissue and threw it across the room.

"What's wrong?"

"*I wish just once in my goddam' life I could do somethin' I wanted t' do without having t'—.*" He shook his head and murmured. "Damn it."

Tio pushed himself into a sitting position and, somberly and soothingly, laid a hand on Matt's shoulder. "I can touch you," he said.

"*Just—.*" He shrugged off the hand. "I got a girlfriend now, Tio."

"I know. It's a secret." He gave Matt the code. "I don't tell secrets. Ever. Just like you said."

Matt looked at his brother. Tio smiled benignly; his eyebrows were raised, his eyes hopeful. And yet there was something there Matt *didn't* trust. Maybe it was just that he *was* a retard. He said things and didn't even know what they were, what they meant, what they... "Yeah," he muttered. "Okay. Okay. I'll stay."

At once, Tio brightened. "Okay," he said.

"*For a while,*" Matt said quickly. He leaned against the bulky lounge chair. "You want the music back on?"

Tio nodded, and leaned against the chair beside him.

"You sure it'll be okay?"

Again, Tio nodded.

"Okay." Matt turned the phonograph back on and restarted the side.

They sat and listened, Matt with his eyes open. "This the record I just got you?" he asked. "The Clifford Brown one?"

"Yeah," said Tio.

"You play it all the time you're gonna wear it out."

"It's beautiful."

Matt looked at him. Tio's breathing was regular again, one hand rested on the trumpet beside him, the other had fallen onto Matt's leg. The room was dimly lit, mostly the early evening light filtering through the white chintz curtains, but Matt could see his eyes move beneath the lids. "I got another one of his for ya," he said. "On order."

Tio opened his eyes and sat straight up. "C'n I have it now?"

Matt laughed. "It's on *or*der, retard."

Tio furrowed his brow. "What's 'on order'?"

"I don't have it yet. The store's gotta get it in first."

"Oh." Tio leaned back. Again they sat, listening. "Matt?"

"Yeah?"

Tio sat up and looked into Matt's eyes. "It's okay when you call me retard. I love you."

"I - love you, too, Tio."

Tio moved his hand to Matt's knee. "Can I touch you?"

"*Tio*, I—." He backed away. "I don't have time."

"I won't tell anyone. Just like you said." He gave the code.

Matt stood. "*I gotta be someplace*," he said, and pulled out his comb.

Tio looked at the music, and said "Oh."

"Hey, you feelin' better?" Matt said, "'cause I really gotta go."

The music filled the room, merging with the softly falling blue seeping in. Matt tapped the comb nervously against a palm.

"Matt?" said Tio.

"*Yeah?*"

Tio looked at him, his smile gone, and said gently: "Why don't anybody love me like the music loves me?"

Matt shut his eyes. When he opened them again, Tio was still there, looking up at him. He sighed deeply. "*Christ*," he said, and sat down. "C'mere, Tio."

Tio's smile returned. He slid against Matt's chest and held to him as Matt folded him into his arms, rocking him, lulling him. Matt closed his own eyes, sang with the record; Tio hummed.

They sat that way a minute or more, then Tio dropped a hand to Matt's leg and, slowly, slid it up, down, along his thigh. Matt opened his eyes, started to say something. Tio looked up at him, eyes wide, eyebrows raised. He moved his hand up, and left it there, squeezing gently.

Matt took a deep breath. He closed his eyes and nodded.

*

Away from The Pond, she saw the park as an enchanted forest. A spell of slowly falling darkness was beginning when she got there: The twilight was filled with the calls of birds, the chitter of squirrels, and the chirrs of crickets and beetles all diffused by the occasional radio and, at various places discreetly just far enough apart, rhythmic sounds and labored breathing punctuated with cries or groans.

Maeve sat on an old brown sweater, knitting. She'd wanted to bring a blanket, like last time, but Da had been in the living room when she left and he would have wanted to know why. As it was, he looked at the sweater with narrowed eyes: "It might get cool," she told him, rubbing her thin, freckled arms that matched her tiny, freckled face. "I'd need it," and she hurried out. Ever since he'd found Colleen and her boyfriend in the living room, lips locked and arms surrounding each other at God-knows-what-hour of the night, he'd not only been suspicious of anything either of his daughters did but careful to prevent anything that might justify those suspicions.

She held up the scarf. It was coming along nicely and she'd soon finish it. That pleased her: There'd be plenty of time, even with the increased requests the holidays would bring for her work, to make a matching cap, something to cover Matt's ears when winter came. *Oh, and please God, a better winter than last year's*, she thought, and made the Sign of the Cross. Da still wasn't used to the cold, though he'd been here almost since the war ended and, really, it wasn't that much colder than it had been in the ould country. But every year, he coughed and sneezed through the cold months, and drank tea and Guinness constantly; a cup of one or bottle of th' other seemed always to be in his hand.

She'd worried she'd be late and ran out directly after supper, leaving Colleen to wash the dishes, and arrived moments before the clock rang the hour. Now, at half past, Matt still wasn't there. Well, he often was late; but never terribly. Almost never, anyway. He *would* come; he always did. It was just that he worked hard, and there *was* his brother. *He must take so much time, bein' slow and all.* She'd wait. She had her knitting. Really, she didn't mind, except she *did* have to be in by nine.

She listened to the night around her. It sounded—private: the birds and bugs, a faint horn from the boulevard which lay, invisible, beyond. She liked coming here, both to be alone with Matt, and for that privacy; it was part of the enchantment. At home, she was assailed with sound and sweat and scent and it felt like there was no place to be by herself. Home was never quiet, she and Colleen shared the little room where neither of them could turn without bumping into the other. Da smelled of oil and grease and Ma (and the entire flat) of onions and potatoes and whatever she'd boiled with them for that evening's supper. There were only the four rooms, plus the bath, which it seemed someone was always standing outside of, waiting impatiently.

She heard footsteps and looked up from her wool. Through the trees, she could see the faint lights that ran along the roof of the old fieldhouse, its doors and windows boarded; where kids hadn't pulled them off, anyway. The steps came nearer and she saw Matt. Instinctively, she smiled, put the needles and yarn into her bag, stood up and waved.

He was carrying a brown paper sack—the beer she'd have to wash from her breath before she went home—and he wasn't smiling. He stopped, looked at her, nodded and sat. She sat as well, facing him, and reached for his hands. He gave her the right and kept the sack in his left.

"I was afraid you weren't coming," she said, the soft lilt in her voice musical and slightly quivering. "It's so late."

"There was some things I hadda do."

"Oh…" She lifted his hand and kissed the fingertips. They smelled of soap. She liked that; he was, always, freshly showered. And he was wearing her favorite shirt; that was nice of him to think to do, with all the rest he had to think about. "I'm glad you're here. I like your shirt."

He grunted, lifted the brown bag and swallowed from the bottle inside, then offered it to her. She shook her head. "No. Thank you," she said. He drank again. They sat in silence.

"Is everything all right?" she asked finally.

"Yeah, sure, everything's fine." Matt's face, so handsome, was clouded. *I've done something* she thought, and prayed she was wrong.

"Is it something at work?"

"Hey, I said everything's fine. Okay?"

"Okay." She nodded, let go of his hand and picked up her knitting. "The park is so empty tonight; I'd have thought there'd be a million people out on a lovely night like this. Takin' advantage of it. Especially since they say there'll be rain tomorrow."

He snorted. "Everybody's doin' somethin'. Seein' somethin' b'sides this crummy city. *Livin'*."

"*We* can go somewhere."

Matt snorted again. "Yeah; sure." He took a long drink, shook the bottle, and tossed it away in the bag. "As soon as the retard dies or somethin'."

The word shocked her. "*Matt…*" she said, harshly.

"*What?*"

She took a small breath and looked down. "Nothin'…" He leaned against a tree. She touched his leg. "You, you'll do something, Matthew. *We* will."

"What? Wash some more rich guys' Cadillacs?"

She laughed, hoping it was a joke. "No!" she said brightly, "something wondrous. I said a prayer for it at Mass this morning. You'll see."

"A prayer. Sure. I'll see. When Christ comes back again.

When *you* get a job."

"That's not fair, Matthew!"

"No?"

She put the scarf in her lap and shook her head. "My Da won't let me. You know that. *I* want to."

Her Da. Jesus. The "ould man" kept her on a fuckin' leash. Well, at least she strained at it, slipping away to meet him, not acting the good little girl "her Da" was so sure she was. Hell: She even bought him a bottle of whiskey for his birthday and sipped a capful while he got drunk. The other girls he'd gone out with, most of 'em wouldn't touch the stuff. Or let him touch their stuff, either. He sat a moment, then slid next to her and kissed her cheek.

"I know," he said gently.

She wiped an incipient tear and forced a laugh. "I'm afraid sometimes I'll just end up another old maid, like my sister. Still livin' at home when I'm thirty, sneakin' t' see—anyone, and workin' in the kitchen at the rectory. I'll never get to do anything in the world, never *see* anything grander than the vault of St. Timothy's." She faced him and took his hands in hers. "If I hadn't met you I…"

He shrugged. "Yeah," he murmured.

Maeve lifted his hands to her chest and held them there. He liked touching her, and they felt so—good, *there*. The first time he'd done that—just a few weeks ago—she was startled, not that he'd done it, but by how much *she'd* liked it. She'd gone to Mass the next morning, sure, but she hadn't made Confession. God would still hear her prayers, she was sure. It was a small sin. Everything they did was a small sin, because they *were* going to … She was sure of that, too. He'd ask her and she'd accept at once, never mind askin' Da. They'd run away somewhere. Elope. *Live* … It was just a matter of the money, so Matt could live out his dreams. And, once they were married? She'd *get* a job. And she'd make a home for him he'd be pleased with, proud of. He'd be proud of *her*. She *could*. He'd see.

In the meantime she prayed for small things, dreamed of small things, did small things. Now, she squeezed his hands tighter to her breasts. "Da says we're going to get a television," she told him. "I prayed for *that*. For Christmas. We'll be able to see the Tournament of Roses parade."

Matt let her grip hold him to her. "Yeah," he said, noncommittally.

She almost-whispered, "You could come watch it with us."

"A parade? Jesus."

"Yes."

He pulled away, leaned back and folded his arms across his chest. "Fat chance," he said and sat, sullenly, watching her. Nearby, an unseen man and woman laughed; the woman said "Don't *do* that!" but laughed again. Then there was silence. Maeve picked up the knitting.

"You're awfully quiet."

"Can't I just not want to talk? I mean, Jesus."

"Sure. I'm sorry."

He watched her hands, her narrow fingers maneuver the needles. They clicked. *Like the grooves on the retard's records* he thought. Tio had washed his hands, like always, and then taken Matt's advice: He sat in front of the television, smiling, while Matt washed. "Thank you, Matt," he'd said when Matt came back into the living room and gave him the peanut butter, jelly and potato chips sandwich. *Dessert*. Jesus. But he was smiling when Matt left the apartment.

Maeve worked quickly, concentrating, though she could knit practically in her sleep: The bag was her constant companion. It was how she earned the little money she had, making custom sweaters, mittens, hats, for friends and neighbors and the members of St. Timothy's congregation.

He leaned forward and looked. "So," he said, "what're you makin' this time?"

"Just a scarf."

"A scarf. In September?"

"It'll get cold soon enough."

"Yeah, I guess."

She held it up. "You like the color?"

"Yeah."

"Good! I *thought* you liked red. It's for you."

"Yeah?"

"Yes." She smiled.

"How come?"

Maeve's laugh, as musical as her voice, was triumphant. "Because I want it to be, silly. It'll be for Christmas."

He shook his head. "*Chris*'mas. Jesus."

"Matthew?"

"What."

She replaced the scarf in her bag and moved toward him, laying her head carefully onto his shoulder. She hesitated, then undid a button of his shirt and rubbed his chest lightly. "I don't mind so much, really; I mean, I know you don't mean it in any hard or disrespectful way, but me Ma and Da"—she hesitated again, then added coaxingly—"they're likely to be upset at hearin' the Lord's name in vain."

"So what?"

She laughed uneasily. "I want them t' like you," she said, and squeezed his shoulder. "I mean, if we're goin' t', you know…"

"Mm."

"And they do want to see you again soon. They don't approve of my seein' a man as often as we do, when he's only been to the flat a few times." She looked at his eyes staring into the night, wondered what he saw there, what he wanted, what she could do to help him find it; without pressing him. "I'd… I'd like to meet your family, too."

"It's just my brother an' Gillian." He snorted. "*Aunt* Gillian."

"I know. But I'd still like to. Sometimes—sometimes I feel like you're—… I don't know…" She undid a second button and continued to stroke his chest. He liked that.

He nodded. "Yeah, okay..." He lifted her hand away from him, held it, and her other, by the wrists, then brought her face to his. She felt his breath, smelled the beer. "Hey," he whispered, "Your folks approve of this?" and kissed her gently. As always, it took her breath away.

"No," she murmured.

He wrapped his hands around her face. "Or this?" he said, and kissed her deeply, opening her mouth to his tongue. Urgently, she returned it, wrapping her arms around him. He pushed her right arm with his hand, slid it down until her hand settled between his legs. She felt his erection and gasped slightly, as she had the first time she'd touched him there. He pressed on her hand, then reached for his zipper.

"Matt! Not here." She held to him.

He moved away. "Where, then?"

If only we could go somewhere, quiet, nice, cool and all alone. "I don't know—where, where we went last time? Oh, but there's no blanket" she fretted, silently cursing her own inability to escape with one.

Suddenly, Matt grinned, slyly, and ran a hand slowly across her chest, stopping to squeeze just long enough, just hard enough that she felt the wetness beginning. "Never mind," he said. "I know where."

"Where?"

"Just come *on*," he insisted, and got up.

She grabbed her knitting bag and the sweater. "All right," she said breathlessly. "All right."

*

There was thunder, rain poured onto the roof and dripped through the occasional cracks in the ceiling, puddling in the pits in the floor. They were dry though. She knew the cubbyholes in here like she knew the corners of her own room, maybe better: Here, she didn't have to keep one eye on the door, wonderin' if somebody was gonna bust in, unannounced, uninvited. She came to the old fieldhouse to get away from there, from *them*. A lot of people knew the ways in but few bothered, except when it rained (and even then, rarely; it was way too dark if you didn't bring a flashlight—she brought a lantern one—and there were - things. Crawling things, skittering things). For her, though, it was sanctuary, rain or shine. Usually she brought the guitar; sometimes she read comic books or looked through old magazines. But she had never, before today, taken anyone else into it.

Now they sat listening to the rain, lit mostly by her flashlight, ghosted by the faint gray afternoon light that leaked between the boards on the windows or through the broken panes where the boards had been torn away. She played a while, then listened to him blow his "horn." *Shit*, maybe he wasn't all that smart, but he could *sure* as shit play the trumpet. He'd finished, then sat there smiling, working the valves like they were three extra fingers, magic fingers. *Shit*.

"I like to play," he said with a smile, and laughed. "A lot."

She laughed with him. "I guess you do," she told him. "I never knew anybody who played as good as you."

"I practice," Tio told her.

"Me too!" she said indignantly. Then she laughed again and shrugged. "I guess I gotta practice more, huh?"

"Aunt Gil says all I ever do at home is listen to music or play it."

Kerk ran her fingers roughly across the sound board. The steel strings twanged in inharmonious protest. "I can't practice there. My old man don't like it."

"Oh."

She reached into a pocket of her dress, took out a half-smoked cigarette and lit it. "Only place I can play is the park; I

come ev'ry day, when it ain't too cold. Even when it's like this."
She gestured upward. "Then I come in here. Last week, we had
that big rainstorm? Time I got *here* I might 's well have jumped
in The Pond, I was so wet. Good thing I got a bag for this." She
tapped the guitar and laughed; Tio laughed. She dragged deeply
on the cigarette and blew out the smoke in small rings. He
poked a finger into each one. "I just stay in here," she went on.
"Nobody cares. Hell, practically nobody's ever in the fieldhouse
since they closed it up."

There was a peal of thunder. Tio shivered. "I wish the rain
would stop. We could go outside again. It's dark in here."

"Yeah." Kerk blew another smoke ring. "He's a fucker. My
pa. They're all fuckers."

Tio put two fingers through the ring, and giggled. "Aunt
Gil's nice," he said. "So is Matt."

"Yeah?"

"Uh-huh. I'm his big brother so he takes care of me. He gives
me Clif-ford Brown records."

Kerk took a last drag and flicked the cigarette toward a
shallow puddle. It sizzled and went out. "Only things *my*
brother ever give me was these. Him an' his 'friend.'" She lifted
the lantern with one hand, and with the other, she pulled up the
hem of her dress. High on the inside of her thigh, there was a
large, fresh black and blue mark.

Tio stared. "Does it hurt?" he asked.

"Na." She lowered the flashlight but left the hem where it
was. "Not as much as the one I give him. Pow! Right in the gut."
She swung her fist toward Tio. He flinched, but she stopped
before it reached his stomach. "Made 'im barf. Both of 'em." She
laughed. Tio laughed.

"Pow!" he said.

"Yeah!" Kerk reached into another pocket, held her hand
there a moment, then withdrew a slender object. She flicked her
wrist: a long blade snapped open and gleamed in the flashlight
beam. "So I got this an' I told him, I told him if he ever touches

me again I'll stick *it* in him. I will, too. Him *and* his fuckin' homo friend." She jabbed the knife, as into a body, fury driving it through the imagined flesh. "*Fucker*," she spat.

Tio looked at it wonderingly. "It's sharp," he said.

"Fuckin' A."

He stroked his trumpet. It was smooth, warm. "C'n I touch it?" he asked.

Kerk waved the knife. "What? This?"

He shook his head and pointed at the bruise. "Your leg."

Kerk extended the blade between them, jiggled it in her hand. "How come?" she asked, warily.

"To see what it feels like. I never touched a girl."

She moved the knife to his shirt, holding the tip firmly against a button. He continued to smile. "Never?" she said into his eyes.

He shook his head.

She looked at him hard. She figured he hadda be twenty-five, twenty-six; maybe more. *Nobody that old's never* touched *a girl*, she thought. *Except maybe a homo*. But his eyes were wide, just like they'd been yesterday. Hell, maybe it *was* true. "Yeah," she said slowly, and closed the knife. "Okay."

He reached over and laid his hand on the bruise. He ran his fingers lightly up her thigh, and down, feeling the fine hair, the warm-smooth skin. "It's soft," he said.

She let him go on. Hell, way he was doin' it, it felt kinda good. "You, uh, you like doin' that?"

He continued to stroke. "Uh-huh," he said.

She slipped the knife back into her pocket. "And you really never done this? Anything?"

Tio shook his head. "No."

She waited, carefully, wondering, as he moved his hand in the same slow pattern again and again. Finally, she said: "Can I touch you?"

His rhythm didn't change. He nodded and said "Uh-huh."

She reached to his thigh and began to rub it, through his jeans, the same way: slow, even strokes. Each one just a little firmer. "You like that?" she asked. Tio nodded. She coughed. "It's not real fair, y' know."

"What's 'not real fair'?"

"You're touchin' my *leg*. All I c'n feel is your *pants*."

"Oh. I can take them off."

Kerk whispered. "What if we gotta leave, quick?"

"Oh," said Tio. He continued to rub.

She moved her hand up, just slightly, and pressed harder. "Maybe, maybe you could just kinda—undo 'em. A little."

"Okay," said Tio. He undid the button at his waist and reached for the zipper. "Will you hug me?" he asked.

Kerk watched as he lowered the zipper and tugged the pants down and sat, looking into her face. She looked back. Then, very slowly, she put one arm around his shoulder and pulled him toward her, gently. With the other, she reached into his underpants.

"You're nice," she said and closed her eyes.

Tio resumed stroking her thigh. "*You're* nice," he said. "Kerk?"

"Yeah?"

"Is this a date?"

She felt so goddam good! *This* felt so good. Not like... "Yeah," she said. "I guess."

Tio giggled. She opened her eyes and whipped her hands, her leg, away from him. "*What?*" she hissed.

Tio reached for her leg and tried to rub it again. "Matt does hugging and being alone stuff on his dates, too. With his girlfriend. *He* says it's nice, too."

Kerk nodded. She sniffed once, then moved back toward him, lifted her hem higher and put his hand in the cotton-covered "V" of her legs. He rubbed, as he had before, slowly, evenly. She replaced her hand between his legs and stroked. "You, uh," she said softly, "you—wanna be my boyfriend?"

Tio smiled. "Okay," he said brightly.
Kerk squeezed gently. "Okay," she said. "Okay."

*

Dave and Lupe had known, early on. Gillian, then thirteen, had come over when Tio was barely a week old, and Lupe told her: He was a punishment from God.

She loved him desperately and guiltily, but she never stopped thinking that, even after he discovered music. They got him a trumpet—a little toy—when he was five and he slept with it, the way most kids slept with a teddy bear. Dave loved jazz, he took Gillian, and Tio—carrying his toy trumpet—with him to the clubs to listen; he was a strictly for-the-living-room tenorman but he had friends in the business who welcomed him cordially. They sat at a table, smoke, noise and alcohol all around, and Tio was entranced. Horn men stopped by, spoke to him, smiled; *played* for him. And Tio played for them, on his trumpet. And then one day, Dave's friend Trumpy traded eights with Tio, and laughed, not unkindly, at the sound of the little boy's instrument. Tio asked Dave if he could "blow on the *man's* horn." The "man" smiled and gave it to him.

He blew. It was like magic.

*

She came home exhausted, and her head was killing her. She'd slept badly last night, the library smelled of fresh paint and she hadn't stopped running all morning: The first month of school was always that way. Lunch wasn't a "break." It was just running someplace else.

Gillian came up the back steps, dropped her briefcase on the kitchen table and took two aspirin, heated water for tea. The phonograph was on, louder than usual; it annoyed her. She just wasn't in the mood for music. Or to eat. Or to go back to the school. Or for Tio. She wanted—*something*; *any*thing. That wasn't this life.

She sighed and sat down. Well, at least she could have a few minutes to herself, then she'd make Tio's lunch. She closed her eyes and tried to let her mind wander, but everything got in the way. The water finally boiled. She got a cup, carried it to the stove, and dropped it. It shattered on the floor. "Damn it" she said under her breath.

From the living room, Tio called. "Aunt Gil?"

So much for her privacy. She smacked her lips. *Okay. He doesn't understand, and* you *have to.* "Yes, Tio. Turn the record down, all right?"

Instead, to her surprise, he turned it off, came into the kitchen smiling and said "Hello, Aunt Gil."

"Hi, Tio," she answered, sweeping up the broken china. "Do you want a glass of milk?" She sighed. "I'm sorry. Lunch'll be ready in a minute. Tuna salad."

"Okay," he said. "I like tuna salad. With lilly."

She smiled at him. "That's how I made it!" He giggled. "What."

"Aunt Gil? I met a girl."

She stopped sweeping. "Oh?" she said, and started again.

"She's real nice."

"I'm sure she is," she agreed carefully. "Where did you meet her?"

"In the park. She plays a guitar."

"I see." She dropped the shards into the garbage, took another cup from its hook, and a teabag, and poured water. Her head throbbed.

"Her name is Kerk. She's pretty." Tio sat at the table. He cocked his head. "You look pretty too."

"Thank you, Tio." She took the bowl out of the fridge, and the bread and the chips from the cupboard. Tio liked chips on everything. "I have to talk to some teachers about the books for their students, after school. But I'll be home in time for dinner."

"Okay. Aunt Gil? Is it okay if Kerk comes here?"

Mentally, she breathed a sigh of relief. "Of course it is. I'd like to meet her." She made two sandwiches, poured milk for both of them, then wondered if Matt would be home for lunch. Well, he could make himself a sandwich, if he wanted one. "Would you like to invite—Kerk to dinner on Saturday?"

"Okay." He looked at her as she set the plates down, and giggled.

She sat and smiled. "What?"

"She's my girlfriend."

"Oh." She chewed, thoroughly and thoughtfully, swallowed, then said: "Tio? Do you know how - boys are - different? From girls?"

"Uh-huh," he said, and drank half of his milk in a single swallow. She got up and went to the fridge. "Matt told me. It's so they can do *different* hugging and being alone things."

She was reaching for the milk bottle and didn't see Matt, a burger and a bottle of soda in hand, step into the archway. "That's what Matt told you," she said.

"Uh-huh," said Tio, and took a large bite of his sandwich.

"Did he, did he say anyt—" Gillian began.

"What did 'Matt tell you,'" Matt asked.

Tio swallowed and smiled at his brother. "About boys and girls. You said girls get st—."

"I know what I said, Tio," he interrupted. He smiled and held up his right thumb and little finger briefly. Tio nodded eagerly.

"But *I'd* like to know," said Gillian, refilling Tio's glass. She stood beside the table, intently focused on Matt's leaning figure.

"No big deal," he said. "I just figured he oughta know about that stuff."

"What *stuff*?"

Matt laughed and clapped Tio on the shoulder. "Birds and

bees stuff. *Right, big brother?*" he said.

Enthusiastically, Tio nodded again, and, mouth full, repeated "Birds and bees stuff."

Gillian took a slow breath and set Tio's glass on the table. He reached for it at once. "Just what—exactly—did you say, Matthew?"

Matt sat, took a bite of his burger and looked at Tio's plate. "Tuna salad?" he asked.

Tio nodded. "It's good," he said. "Aunt Gil made it with lilly."

"Mm," said Matt, and turned to Gillian. *She looks good*, he thought. *For once. Somebody might actually think she's a girl.* "Just—stuff. So he wouldn't get into any..., y' know, with his girlfrie—. Oh, sorry Tio. I forgot."

Tio said "It's okay" and washed the tuna salad down.

"Forgot *what?*" said Gillian. "*What?*"

"It was supposed to be a secret, Aunt Gil." He clapped Matt on the shoulder and said cheerfully, "But it's okay 'cause I already told her. Aunt Gil said she c'n come over. Kerk wants t' meet you, too."

"Yeah." Matt finished his burger and licked his fingers. "Where *you* goin'?" he asked Gillian.

"I have an after-school meeting. I'll be home early, if you'd like to join us for dinner."

Matt snorted. "Fat chance."

Silently, Gillian returned the milk to the refrigerator. Matt sat, scatting softly and tapping his fingers to a song she didn't know, while Tio finished his sandwich in two large bites. "It was good," he said. "Thank you, Aunt Gil. I'm going to listen to music now. Clif-ford Brown. Isn't his name funny, Matt? Clif-ford *Brown*. When his music is all *blue*." He giggled.

"Uh-huh. That's funny," Matt said, watching Gillian.

"You're welcome, Tio." She stood by the refrigerator door, watching Matt watch her. "Tio?" she said. "Would you take the record player upstairs? To your room? You can listen to it there, okay?"

"Okay."

"Okay," said Gillian, and kissed his forehead.

He got up, and clapped Matt on the shoulder. "See you later, little brother," he said, and laughed.

"Yeah," said Matt as Tio walked away. "I'll see you later."

"I'll be home before the little hand is on the five," she called after him.

"Okay." In a few moments she heard him on the stairs. She sat across from Matt and looked at him.

"What?" he said.

"I—we need to talk about some things."

Matt finished his drink and started to get up. "I gotta go back to work. I only came home to change this." He touched his wet t-shirt.

She grabbed his wrist. "It will only take a few minutes."

"Jesus. What?"

Gillian leaned forward, willing her voice to remain calm. "Do you have any idea what it's like, for me? Raising him. Y' know you might help me a little. I *could* use it."

"Hey! I take care of him all the time. And *you're* always goin' t' meetings and sh— places."

Upstairs, there was trumpet music from the record player. "*I* am home almost every night, Matthew," Gillian began. "Do you think—"

"Okay, okay, okay, you don't go nowhere."

"—this is where I *want* to be; all the time, instead of—going out like you do, wherever it is you go. For *nine*—"

"Where I go is my—."

"—*years* I have *been* home almost every night. *Every time* he nee—."

"*Okay! I said, You're home. Okay?*"

Gillian swallowed. "I *am*."

"So what. He don't need a watchdog."

"No," she said. "I don't think *he* does."

"What the hell does that mean?"

"It means—." She stopped. This was *not* something she wanted to talk about, at least, not when she wasn't completely in control. Her head still ached. The unfinished sandwich sat on her plate, the glass of milk beside it. She took a deep breath and began again, slowly and quietly. "It means, there are some things *you* shouldn't be—instructing him in."

Matt grinned. "Oh? Some things?"

"… I need to know what you told Tio."

He pursed his lips and looked down. "I told him"—he looked at her, squarely—"I *told* him about sex. *You* know what that is?"

She blanched. "*I*—" she started, and caught herself. "I think you should be a little careful, about discussing—certain things."

"'Certain things'?"

"You *know* what I'm talking about!"

"Hey," Matt said. "He's my brother."

"But he's *my* responsibility."

"Jesus; he's old enough t' know. You think he don't ask?"

Gillian shook her head. *Dave should be here*, she thought. *Someone should be.* How do *I* tell a twenty-eight-year-old retarded boy about… "I'm sure he does. But *you're* old enough to realize he doesn't understand!"

Matt grinned. "Oh, he understands," he said assuredly. "It ain't like his *body's* retarded."

"He doesn't know what it *means*, Matt. What could happen."

"So who's gonna tell him? You, *Miss* Librarian?"

"I— …" Gillian stood up and went to the stove. She retrieved the tea and drank it in one swallow. It was tepid and too strong.

"Fat chance," said Matt, and got up.

"*I'm only saying he*—he doesn't understand the consequences!"

He dropped the soda bottle in the wastebasket and walked up to her. Swaggered up to her, his hands in his back pockets and a smirk across his face. "Oh, he does. I think he does. What he—"

"Matthew, *he's* not ready f—."

"—understands, I think he under*stands* it'll feel good. Real good. Course, feelin' good, that's somethin' *you* wouldn't know anything about."

He stood there, poised like a boxer about to come out of the corner while his opponent rose slowly after a nine-count. She moved to slap him, then stopped. It wouldn't change anything. Instead, she laid the teacup on the counter, carefully. "Matt," she said, her voice perfectly even, "pack your things. Tonight, because tomorrow morning—*tomorrow* morning—I am going to find an apartment, a furnished room in a boarding house if that's all I can get on short notice, and I am going to take anything of yours I see in this house, put it in a taxi and have the driver *leave* it there for you."

He didn't bat an eyelash. "Screw—you," he said.

She dropped the sandwich in the garbage and put the the rest of her milk into the fridge, then she picked up her briefcase. Her head pounded. "Tomorrow morning," she said. "Good-bye."

"Yeah, yeah, yeah, yeah, yeah."

Gillian walked out the back door.

Upstairs, "Brownie" was playing something; Tio had joined in. Matt listened, until the song ended. Then he went upstairs and quickly changed his shirt. He'd be late, but as he stepped out of his room he stopped, thought a moment, and called "Hey, retard!"

From his room, Tio answered "Yes, Matt?"

He knocked on the door. "You okay?"

Tio opened it. "Uh-huh," he said. "I'm okay."

"Mm." He smiled. "Can I come in a minute?" he asked.

Tio's smile expanded. "Sure!" he said, and opened the door wide.

Matt stepped through. Except to read to him now and then, he rarely came into his brother's room and, when he did, he didn't look around much: There wasn't much to see. Now, he took it all in. Like his own, Tio's room was small and spare: a twin bed, neatly made (unlike his own); an empty bird cage, the residue of Tio's pet parakeet that escaped when Tio left both the cage and his window open; a few pictures on the wall: their parents; one of Tio with their father in uniform, taken just before he left the last time, when Matt was eight; Clifford Brown, Louis Armstrong, Harry James, all cut carefully from magazines and taped above the bed with just as much care; one of a smiling, youthful Gillian, holding Tio's hand with baby Matt in her arms. A couple of books of fairy tales on a shelf and music magazines, with lots of pictures. A chest and closet, clothes hung neatly, shoes carefully arranged. The trumpet on the bed, its case at the foot. One wood chair and a small desk, where a small whirring fan and a stack of records were, next to the record player. "Turn that off?" he said, and pointed. Tio did. "Thanks," Matt said.

"You're welcome," Tio said, and sat on the bed.

Matt sat on the chair, ran a hand through his hair. "Your record's still on order," he said, "the new Clifford Brown one."

"The store's gotta get it in first!"

"Hey!" Matt said. "You remembered. Good for you!" Tio shrugged happily.

Matt looked out the window, then crossed to it. Tio's view was the same as his: Nothing but another brick wall. He could prob'ly touch it if he stretched his arm. He shook his head and murmured "Shit."

Tio's face darkened. "What's wrong, Matt?"

"I'm, mm, I'm sorry. About tellin' your secret. Y' know."

"It's okay."

"Course, I mean, I know *you* don't tell secrets. Ever. Right?"

Tio gave him the code. "Right."

Matt returned it. "Ever," he said.

"Ever."

"Right." Matt smiled and sat down again. "So," he said, "when's your girlfriend comin' over?"

Tio picked up the trumpet, worked the valves. "I don't know. I didn't ask her yet. Aunt Gil said I could. For dinner Saturday."

"Ohhh." Matt grinned.

"Matt? What's birds and bees stuff?"

Oh, shit. "Oh, it's…" *What?* "It's like hugging and being alone stuff. Only better."

"Oh," said Tio, sagely. "Do you do it?"

Matt grinned again. "Sometimes."

"With your girlfriend?"

"Sometimes."

"'Cause you love *her*?"

"Yeah. And 'cause it feels good."

Tio smiled hopefully. "Can *we* do it?"

"*It's*—." Matt took a breath and looked outside. Still nothing but wall. "Ya gotta have a boy and a *girl*, Tio."

"Oh." He nodded thoughtfully. "Can you teach me about it?"

"Tio, I… I don't know if—it's—somethin' you'd like."

"Why not?"

Jesus. "'Cause—I don't *know*, I mean, you don't hafta like somethin' 'cause I *do* it, just…" Under his breath Matt muttered "*Jesus.*" He stood. "Anyway, look, I gotta go back t' work now. I just came home for a minute. Maybe I'll tell you about it later. *May*be. Okay?"

"Okay." Tio took the cloth from the case and began to rub the trumpet. "Matt?"

"Yeah, retard."

Tio grinned ear to ear. "I got another date with Kerk. Tonight." He giggled and lowered his voice. "After dinner. I'm gonna tell Aunt Gil I'm going for a walk."

Matt laughed softly. "It's gonna rain again," he cautioned.

"That's okay," Tio said. "We can go to the old fieldhouse."

"How're you gonna get in? It's all closed up."

"Kerk knows a way." He wiped the mouthpiece. "That's what we did yesterday when it rained. It was dark."

"It's *real* dark at night. Darker even than when it rains."

Tio shrugged. He didn't like the dark but it was okay. If Kerk was there. "We can play in the dark. And she said she can bring a big flashlight."

Matt chuckled. "Is that what you do with her? *Play*?" On his bed, Tio squirmed and giggled. "What?"

He bent forward and whispered. "We, we do hugging and being alone stuff, too."

"Yeah?" *Gillian'll love* that.

"Matt? Maybe we could do birds and bees stuff. After you teach me."

"I said 'maybe,' Tio." He squatted by the bed. "Hey," he said with a twinkle, "*you* wanna know a secret?"

"Uh-huh." He gave the code.

Matt returned it. "*I'm* goin' there with somebody tonight. There's all kinds a—little places in it." He stood up. "Maybe I'll see you there."

Tio smiled. "Maybe."

Matt walked to the door and opened it. "Yeah," he said. "Maybe."

*

She wasn't sure exactly where it was coming from, but she heard a faint voice—a girl, singing "Greensleeves"—accompanied by a guitar. *It's pretty*, she thought, and lit another votive. The "room"—that's what Matt called it; she thought it more like a stall—brightened a little, though she still didn't like it: Darkness always unnerved her; invisible strangers made it worse, and it wasn't a very comfy space. But it *was* comforting to know there was someone about, even a stranger, who sang nice tunes, and sang them nicely.

Tonight was Da's dart night at the pub. He'd left directly after supper. She and Colleen had cleaned everything quickly, while Ma sat for a change, next to the radio; then they'd both gone out. Maeve easily slipped the flashlight, the blanket and candles into her knitting bag and, anyway, Ma was sitting there, eyes closed, listenin' to John McCormack's warbling tenor sing "When Irish Eyes are Smiling," and hummin' along! If she knew the girls were leavin', she paid no heed.

Still, Maeve was uneasy. Whatever else, she didn't understand "why." She'd probably misunderstood, at least, she was *sure* she must have; but they had been so clear, so—certain. She'd been a little embarrassed and more than a little hurt, but, mostly, she'd been confused. *Matt* must *have told them*. He'd said so. He *said* so.

She sighed and laid out the blanket carefully, being cautious not to let it touch the small flames. Outside, she heard the clock chime the quarter hour: when Matt had said he'd be there. Well, she'd ask him and he'd have an explanation. Still, Maeve couldn't help feeling disappointed. And afraid. He loved her! How could he not tell…

She heard steps. "Matt?" she whispered. "Is that you?"

He whispered back—"Yeah"—and appeared, in his red shirt and, to her pleasant surprise, without a sack. He put his arms around her. Surprised again, and happy, she held him to her, despite her unease. "There's somebody else in here," she said, louder than she'd intended.

Matt shushed her, and listened. Then he laughed softly. "I think it's the retard's girlfriend."

Maeve looked up at him. "He's got a girlfriend?"

He shrugged, and sat on the blanket. Maeve followed. "He met this girl by The Pond, a couple days ago. So now she's his girlfriend." He listened again. "She sings okay."

"Yes." She put her head in his lap and closed her eyes, and then he began to stroke her hair, something he'd done before, but always—*after*. The fear vanished, and there was only his warmth and the loveliness of the music. She felt dreamy; this, *this* is what it would be like, when … He'd come home, she'd greet him at the door, they'd embrace, kiss, even before they spoke.

It was a spell she was afraid to break. But she *had* to ask. She snuggled into him and said "How was work today?"

He curled her bright red bang around a finger. "Okay. I, uh, I was thinkin' about you."

"Really?"

"Yeah, really." Matt leaned over and kissed her cheek. The perfect kiss. She sighed. "What'd *you* do?" he said, then continued but with a hint of sarcasm, "Pray?"

"Yes," she said, uncomfortably.

He kissed her again and laid a hand on her breast, squeezing gently. "Me too," he said, and grinned.

She opened her eyes and looked at him. "Matt," she said quietly. "This evening, I, I met your Aunt."

His hand stopped. "You what?" he said.

*

He still didn't like the dark and he was glad he could hear her singing; that made it easier to find her. He crept anyway, afraid of stepping on something, or tripping. He knew he wasn't very graceful. That's why he always walked slowly when he was by himself. Aunt Gil said that was fine, though: A lot of people walked slowly, and it was a good idea to be careful. He liked having good ideas. Brownie had good ideas, too. He must've. You had to have good ideas to play music as good as him.

Kerk's voice grew clearer, and he could see her outline in the dim light. She sat, her broad back to him, the guitar across her chest. He didn't want to scare her, so he called "Hi" quietly, then took the last few steps toward the flashlight beam.

She laid down the guitar and smiled at him. "Hi," she said. "Siddown."

He did, and opened the trumpet case. "That's a pretty song."

"You know it?"

He shook his head. "But I heard it." He pondered a moment. "I think Aunt Gil sings it. Around Christmas. I don't know the name."

"'Greensleeves,'" Kerk told him and picked up her instrument; she strummed a chord. "Think you c'n play it?"

He smiled. "Uh-huh."

"C'mon, then," she said, and began.

"Okay," Tio said, and raised the trumpet to his lips, closed his eyes, and blew.

*

She'd told him. Now there was no turning back. "I—met your Aunt," she repeated.

"How'd that happen?" he said tersely.

Maeve sat up and reached for his hand. He kept them clasped. "I—found her name in the telephone directory, and I was passing nearby and decided to stop." She tried to look at him but couldn't. Instead, she looked at her lap. "She—she was surprised. So was I." She waited, but he was silent. "Why?" she asked, finally.

"Why what?"

"Why didn't you—tell her about me?"

Matt sighed deeply. "Christ, I just never, I don't know." *He should've stopped for beer. Damn it*! He scratched his cheek. "It was none of her business."

She tried not to make it sound like an accusation, but it still felt like one. "You said you had."

Matt sighed again and tried to lean back, but there was no wall. He shrugged and stretched. "Look, I forgot. Okay?"

She turned toward the music; the guitar was barely audible under a beautifully played trumpet. "I don't know," she said, "if it is okay, Matthew."

*

They played "Greensleeves" twice, then Kerk floundered her way through "Time," listening to the clear beauty of Tio's horn more than playing. They finished that. Tio lowered the trumpet and smiled. "That was pretty," he said. "Do you want to play 'Motherless Child'? I practiced that."

Kerk shook her head. "Let's stop a while, okay?"

Tio said "Okay" and put the trumpet into its case.

They sat that way, Tio just smiling, Kerk randomly plucking guitar strings. There were soft sounds, both from the outside—laughter, dogs barking, thunder. *Shit*—and from another part of the fieldhouse: voices, too soft to hear their words. Pretty far away, she guessed. Whoever it was, though, could probably hear them, or their playing, anyway. She spoke in a whisper. "You wanna like sit and, you know, like we did yesterday?"

"Uh-huh," he said.

She pulled him toward her so they were facing, and leaned against the wall; then she hiked her dress and casually opened her thighs. Tio sat and watched. "You gotta get ready too," she told him.

He said "Okay," undid his pants and pulled them to his knees. They sat that way, just breathing. Then Kerk reached for his hand. "I didn't put nothin' on underneath this time," she said, and slowly put it between her legs. "Feel?"

"Yeah." He rubbed. She closed her eyes, reached for him and squeezed.

Oh, damn, she thought. *Oh, goddamn.* She smiled. "That

feel good?"

"Uh-huh," Tio replied. "It feels good. Kerk?"

"Um?" she murmured.

"Aunt Gil said you can come for dinner on Saturday. She wants to meet you."

She only half-heard. "Yeah?"

"Uh-huh. Do you want to come?"

Eyes still closed, she gasped slightly and said "Yeah."

*

Matt didn't move. But he looked at her, so hard she could feel his eyes. "Look," he said. "I—I'm sorry. I just forget. I mean, I *mean* to tell her, just—I get pissed at her and forget." He half-laughed. "I told Tio."

She turned to him. "You told Tio?"

"Yeah. I told him I had a girlfriend. All about you."

Maeve shook her head, sadly. "I met him tonight, too."

"So?"

"He didn't know who I was either."

"Jesus. He's a retard." Matt started to touch her but this time she pulled back. "He can't even tell time, Maeve; he—forgets things all the time, 'specially names."

"He was very nice," she said. And he had been, nice and polite—she wished Matt was that polite, especially around Da and Ma—except that she caught him staring at her a few times. But he was always smiling. "He told me I was pretty." Matt laughed. "Don't laugh."

He stopped, but his face remained lit. "Just, *I* told *him* you were pretty. I told him—you were the prettiest girl in the world."

Well. Tio *had* repeated some of the things his aunt had said. Maeve *thought* that was strange. Well. "Really?" she said.

"Ask him."

"What?" she said, confused.

"Go ask him. I heard him—his trumpet. *You* heard it—a minute ago. He's here. He said he was meetin' *her* here."

She listened and realized the music had stopped. "It's quiet now—Oh!" she exclaimed and brought her hands to her face. "Do you think they're …?"

Matt grinned and put his hand on her arm. "He was tellin' me about what they did. '*We* do hugging and kissing stuff, Matt. We go on dates.'" In spite of herself Maeve giggled. "Ssh. They don't know we're here, they'll leave us alone."

"I thought you wanted me to ask him what you said."

Matt shifted. His arm fell across her lap. "Later."

"When?"

Jesus. He reached to her face and touched it, gently. "Saturday," he said. "At, um, dinner. You, you c'n come over and we'll—talk."

She looked at him. Yes, it *was* okay. At least it was *going* to be. She was sure. "Really?" she whispered, but there was no doubt in the question.

He smiled and brought her face to his. "Sure," he whispered back, and kissed her. "Sure."

*

She lit a cigarette, a fresh one, and offered it to him. He smiled but shook his head, then poked his fingers through the smoke rings as she blew them. He liked doing that; she liked doing something to amuse him.

She felt good. Goddam good. *Fuckin'* good. He was nice. *This* was nice, even if it was a crap-filled dark corner of a place her pa, and her brother, would've said was a shithole. And they'd laugh at *him*.

She started as she heard something scurrying. Then, distracted from her reverie, she heard the rain pounding down and looked up. "Hey," she said. "It's rainin'."

Tio listened. "Uh-huh."

Kerk eased back. Suddenly, she felt chilly and spread her dress over her legs. That warmed them. Warmed her. She smiled. *She felt good.* "I'm glad we're in here. I like doin' this."

"Me too," said Tio.

Kerk drew on the cigarette, blew out the smoke, and watched him poke at the rings. "I ain't had a boyfriend before. Not a real one, anyways. I mean, there've been some guys I - you know, kinda liked and that. But they were mostly rats."

Tio giggled. She sat up and reached into her pocket. "*What?*" she said.

He smiled at her and pulled up his pants. "Rats. I was seein' rats with you." He giggled again.

She watched him carefully. He continued to laugh, but gently. "Yeah..." she said finally, and snorted a laugh of her own: one note. "Yeah." She touched his crotch. "That felt good."

"Uh-huh." He touched hers, and rubbed.

"You like it?"

"Yeah," he said, "It's real dif'rent. From Matt."

"Matt?" Her hand stopped.

He continued to rub. "You feel dif'rent. Down there. He don't get all sticky till after."

She sat up, pulling her hand and his away. "Whatta you mean?"

He was surprised *she* didn't know, but happily explained. "He's a boy and you're a girl. Girls get sticky *first*. Matt said."

She tossed the cigarette and stood up abruptly, brushing off her dress. "You said you never done this."

Tio stood as well, awkwardly, and zipped his pants. "I didn't never with a girl," he said. "Except yesterday."

Her voice darkened. "You done this with Matt," she said, jabbing a finger into his arm.

He giggled. "You're silly. Matt's not a *girl*. He likes me to, 'cause he loves me."

Her teeth clenched. Just like her brother. *Just like her* fuckin' *brother!* "You're a homo" she yelled.

Tio's brows furrowed. "What's a homo?" he asked.

"What you are." She raised a fist. *"You're a fuckin' homo!"* She swung; Tio flinched as she hit his stomach. He gagged and gasped for breath. She shouted *"Homo. Fuckin' homo pansy queer"* and swept the back of a hand across his face.

He looked up at her, eyes wide, and did not move.

*

They heard the girl yell and Matt looked up. He couldn't make out the words, something about homos, but they came from the direction where Tio's trumpet had been a few minutes before. "What the hell?" he said, and stood up quickly.

He heard a grunt, then a strained "Please." Tio's voice. He moved hurriedly toward it.

"Matt!" Maeve called after him, then stood, reflexively grabbed her knitting and followed.

"Tio?" Matt called, and saw the light leaking from a cubicle a dozen yards ahead. He ran toward it, almost tripping on debris and the wet floor.

"Please, don't," Maeve called from behind. "You'll—be careful."

*

"*Homo!*" Kerk bellowed, and slapped him again. He grunted "Please" and crumpled to the floor in a fetal ball. "You fuckin' ..." She spat, and drew back her foot.

Matt dove into her, shoulder first. She was almost half a foot taller and weighed fifty pounds more than he did, but she was off balance and his momentum drove her backward; she fell against a stanchion as Matt tumbled to the ground. He saw Tio, struggling for breath, and got up before the girl regained her bearings. He lashed out at her with his fists, swinging blindly. She blocked him easily, kicking and scratching, then brought her knee up, connecting with his thigh and barely missing his crotch. He groaned and stepped back.

As he did, Maeve grabbed at Kerk from behind. Kerk swung around and knocked her away with a forearm. "Matt," Maeve shouted, and he lunged again. Kerk turned back and threw him off her.

"Matt" gasped Tio. "Please don't fight. I'm sorry. I can't breathe."

The girl reached into her pocket. "Matt," she said. "You're the *other* homo." She took out the knife, looked at his face, deeply shadowed in the pale light, and flicked her wrist. The blade sprang open. "Fucker," she said. Matt, breathing heavily, froze. She stepped toward him, her face set, her eyes fixed on his, the blade extended. "You fucker."

"No!" Maeve screamed, and leapt at Kerk's back again. She plunged her knitting needles at the bigger girl. The steel hit below her shoulder blade, puncturing the skin. "What the fuck" she shouted. She dropped the knife and whirled, reaching for Maeve with one hand and her wounded back with the other.

"No!" Maeve screamed again. "Matt. *Matt!*"

He saw the knife fall and searched the ground for it. He found it quickly and picked it up. "Please," Tio rasped, "Matt." Matt looked at the knife, then reached for Kerk, pulling at her as she choked Maeve with one hand.

"*Matt*" Maeve coughed, and began to scream.

Kerk dropped her and turned to face him, her face contorted with fury. "You fuckin'—" she hissed, and raised her fist.

He stabbed her.

It was as though time slowed. He felt the resistance as the knife hit her stomach, broke through the flesh and into her, deep, deeper, until the entire blade was buried. She was beside him, almost in an embrace, breathing on him, her dress against his hand and her blood beginning to flow over it. She looked down, with startled bewilderment, started to reach for the knife, changed her mind, looked up and raised her fist again.

He pulled the knife out, then stabbed her again, pulled and plunged, into her, out, again, again, again. He heard her groan, and wheeze, and cough, and felt the blood on his arm and chest and spread through his chinos, felt it surge, and spurt, and flood. She looked at him, eyes wide and glazed. Then she fell, an arm flailing into her guitar and cracking it. The strings rumbled.

Matt stepped back, panting. Her eyes were open; he could hear her breathe. He took the knife and drove it into her heart and held it there, gulping air.

She stopped breathing.

Tio gurgled, his eyes and fists clenched tightly. Maeve stopped screaming. She did not move. For what seemed to Matt like forever, everything was still. Then, at last, he lifted his hands. "Oh, Jesus," he whispered.

Maeve took a tentative step toward him. He looked up at her, then stood. "Jesus," he said. "C'mon, let's go."

Maeve looked down. The girl lay there, unmoving except for the blood spreading across her body. "Matt, we—." She looked at him. "Is she—?"

"Fuck it," he said. "Let's go!"

"What about Tio? He's chokin' or some—."

"Let's go!" he yelled.

She looked quickly at Tio, lying there, rocking on his side. "Matt…" she began.

He grabbed her hand and pulled. "Goddammit. Let's *go!*" As they ran out she looked back and saw Tio, rocking slowly, and trying to breathe.

He rocked and rocked until his breath began to return. It was like when the music held him. It was hard to breathe, but it always let him, after a while. He was okay now. He sat up slowly. It was dark. He didn't like that. "Matt?" he called, and reached for the lantern and moved it around so he could see. Matt wasn't there but Kerk was, lying down. He wiped his nose and looked for his trumpet. It was there, too. He picked it up and blew a short note: all he had breath for. Kerk didn't move. She was prob'ly asleep, but he was glad she was still there; she hadn't left him alone in the dark. He smiled and called to her. "Kerk?"

He waited, but she didn't answer, so he reached over and touched her leg, rubbing it. It was wet and sticky—different sticky than she had been under her dress. He shined the flashlight on her face. Her eyes were open. "Are you sleepy?" he asked. She didn't move.

He put the light down, sat in the near-dark, the trumpet in his right hand, working the valves with his left. He blew another note, this one was a little stronger. He smiled and shook her leg. "I was scared," he said. "I couldn't breathe. But I'm okay now." He laid the trumpet in his lap. "Kerk? We can touch some more. It's nice." He reached under her dress. She was sticky all over; too sticky. Matt never said girls got *so* sticky, everywhere, or stayed sticky so long. He wiped his hand on his pants. "*You're* nice" he said, and smiled. "It's okay you hit me."

In the dim, he saw her guitar. "You want to play some more now?" he asked. "I can teach *you* a song. Brownie plays it. Isn't his name funny? Clif-ford *Brown*? When his music is all blue."

He picked up the trumpet, closed his eyes, and blew. The notes purled from the brass bell, pure, clear, warm, floated like languid blue smoke all around him, embraced him, then, like drying tears, rose and dissipated slowly into the air.

NIGHTHAWKS

Hold fast to dreams
For if dreams die
Life is a broken-winged bird
That cannot fly.

Langston Hughes

The   light from the globed streetlamp crept through the heat
and the haze. In it, the diner was an oasis, isolated by the vague
pallor b_____ Th___ seemed to fade. Scrimmed by shadows
_____ the moon, it resembled a backdrop, not
_____, not a world. The aura hovered, circling
_____ow and lonely blues in the dark.
_____urch clock chimed once, a long chime,
_____ gotten used to it, the brief *clangs* at
_____, the longer ones marking the hours in
_____ife. Now and then Jimmy really heard
_____ed. He'd furrow his brow and look
_____oment of reverberation to remind him
_____.
_____the diner's white light, he continued to
_____ The price of peaches was down. That
_____ches. His ball team was in last place,
_____—and it was only August! No news
_____ovie was at the Alhambra, with the first
_____-Secret Service in Darkest Africa. That
_____d—plus a Daffy Duck cartoon. And
_____d too, the newsreel. Not that it could
_____war the radio didn't, but they showed
stuff that wasn't about the war, too, about Hollywood and horse
racing and pretty girls.

The radio played something familiar, just music, no words.
He preferred that. He couldn't quite place the tune's name—
something by Glenn Miller—but it, too, was background.
Words were okay. Mostly, though, they got in the way. They'd
replay themselves in his head and sometimes he couldn't get
them out. When that happened, he just shut the radio off.

He looked up at the abrupt sound of loud voices outside the

window, glimpsed a shrouded couple, phantoms hurrying past. Like dreamin', he thought. Except for the streetlamp itself that cast the same ghostly light on the gas station across the street, the world seemed almost vanished.

"Hey, buddy, get a refill?" The man in the dark blue suit and gray fedora at the far end of the long side of the curved counter lifted his cup. Jimmy nodded. "Sure thing," he said. He folded the paper carefully and walked over. "Good coffee," the man said.

"Made just before you come in," he replied. "Any other night, this time?" Jimmy laughed, "it'd be staler'n yesterday's doughnut. But Saturdays're usually pretty busy, startin' right about this time. All night. Guess the weather's keepin' folks away t'night. Hot."

"Yeah," the man said.

"That's August for you. And they say it's gonna rain."

"Yeah."

"Course, it's still early. Half the places, they don't let out till two. Guess you folks're the early birds. You catch any worms?" he said and laughed again, then shrugged at their silence. "How 'bout you, ma'am? 'Nother cup?" he asked the redhead in the red dress on the next stool. Pretty girl, he thought; *looks a little like* ... someone he couldn't remember. The girl shook her head—her pageboy flared attractively—without glancing up from the matchbook she opened and closed, opened and closed. "Okay," he told the man. "Comin' right up."

The song changed—The Andrews Sisters crooned "God Bless the Child"—as he set the cup beneath the tall urn's spigot, and the bell over the door rang. He looked back. A youngish colored man stood there, paused in the doorway. He was thin-faced, and thin-bodied, even gaunt; close-cropped and -shaven, wearing dark pants and a jacket, and a white shirt whose collar showed sweat. His eyes scanned the diner carefully. One hand stayed on the knob, the other held a cane. He looked up, surprised by the bell or maybe just wanting to stop the attention it might cause. The girl glanced briefly; so did the man in the gray hat, staring a moment longer.

"Evenin'," the colored man said. "You still open?"

Jimmy smiled. "All night, every night. Even Christmas."

The colored man didn't move. "Sure ain't much like Christmas out there." He wiped his cheek with a sleeve.

Jimmy laughed, a short, inviting laugh. "Nope. Gonna rain though, they say."

"Yeah, feels like it."

"C'mon in. Be with y' in a sec." The colored man limped in tentatively, looked for a place to sit. The diner was empty except for the couple. He chose a stool on the counter's short side, well removed from them, and stood behind it, leaning on the cane. Jimmy refilled the waiting cup and served.

"Thanks," the man in the hat said.

"Anything else? We got some good pie."

"Nah," the man said. The girl shook her head.

"Well," said Jimmy, "just say the word 'f you change your mind."

The colored man stood a moment, listening to the music: some white women singin' the blues. He shook his head. *Damn white women can't sing blues, least not like Billie sings 'em. Don't know why they bother.*

"Evenin'," Jimmy said.

"Evenin'," the colored man said.

"Hot out there."

"Yeah."

"Not too bad in here. Boss just put in the air conditioning. Picked the right time, I guess."

The colored man nodded. "Yeah. Be okay I have a cup a coffee? An' maybe a glass a col' water?"

Jimmy slapped the counter. "Set yourself down," he commanded. "Have it right up."

"Thanks." Slowly, the thin man laid the cane across the

counter and sat, manipulating his right leg into a bent position. "Ah, damn," he murmured.

The man in the blue suit was slight. Despite his build, an incipient paunch and thinning hair, he had a swagger about him that, he felt, was most notable in the jaunt of his hat— lowered slightly over one eye which, he thought, made him look like Bogie—and the way he held his cigarettes, between the tips of his unexpectedly long and graceful fingers. His name was Gil, he was thirty-three years old, possessed by his wife and by his ulcer, which he credited silently with keeping him out of the Army and damned loudly for interfering with his taste for whiskey and fried food.

He sat, eyes half closed, with the music of the earlier evening running through his head, where he still danced to it. This song, the one on the radio?—he wished they'd play something else; he'd heard it a thousand times. Lousy dance music, and the words were depressing. Yeah. You got money, ev'rybody's your friend. Empty pockets, you got *nothin'*. Well, someday he'd have money. Then let 'em ask. Let *Leslie* ask. Let Leslie beg.

The smoke from his cigarette enveloped him. His eyes watered from it, and he wiped them with a hanky. Donna looked up, then down again; he smelled the strong perfume on her neck.

She stirred her coffee with her finger, sucked it clean.

Gil glanced at his watch. "One," he said.

She nodded without looking at him. "Uh-huh."

"Ought to be gettin' home. Don't you think?"

She looked straight at him, hard. "I'm drinkin' my coffee."

"Okay, okay. Don't get sore." Christ, he thought. Women.

He watched the counterman approach the colored boy with a cup and a glass, set them down, then lean in to talk. He *was* a talker, that was for sure. Well, he was old: looked fifty, at least— too old for the Army, too young for the grave; and doin' this kind a work, late at night? He prob'ly needed to talk, just so there'd be a voice to hear.

The colored man sat stiffly, hands clasped before him, but his eyes continued to dart between the diner and, at each sound from it, the street. Jimmy put the coffee and water down, smiled and rested a hand on the counter. "Got to get a chair back here. Feet get tired, spendin' all these hours standin' on 'em, and the stools? they're okay for a while, but ..."—he tapped his lower back—"*after* a while ... Y' know?"

The customer nodded. "Yeah. Thanks," he said.

"Anything else? We got some good pie. Home-made ice cream."

"Naw."

"'Kay, then. Let me know, you want a refill." Jimmy stood up full and took a step toward his paper.

"Wait a sec. You got ice cream?"

"Choc'late, vanilla an' strawberry. Made fresh this morning."

"Vanilla," the colored man said. "Couple scoops."

Jimmy leaned in again. "You want a sundee? Got some nice peaches."

The colored man shook his head and pulled a folded newspaper from his jacket. "Okay," said Jimmy. He watched while the man took a stubby pencil from his shirt pocket, licked the tip and began to make notes. He looked up. Jimmy smiled. "Comin' right up," he said.

"Hey, mister," the girl called. The colored man ignored her and reached again into a pocket, withdrew a cigarette pack and tapped it. Nothing came out.

"Yeah?" said Jimmy.

The redhead raised her cup. "'Nother one now?"

Gil pursed his lips. "Another cup? I—it's gettin' late."

"You got one. And we got time. It ain't like we *got* to be someplace. Nobody's... expectin' you." She snorted a laugh. "Or me."

"Sure thing. One sec," Jimmy called.

"Hey, mister?" said the colored man. "You got a cigarette?"

"Sorry," Jimmy said. "Don't smoke." He refilled Donna's cup, then headed toward the kitchen.

Gil dragged on his Chesterfield. "Well…" he said.

"Yeah," said the girl. "Well."

The colored man rummaged through the empty pack once more, then crumpled it and put it back in his pocket. He sighed. "You spare one?" he called across the counter. "I'm out."

"Me?" Gil said. The colored man nodded. Gil lifted his hand. "Last one. There's a machine, 'crost the street. In the gas station."

The redhead looked at Gil squarely, then took a package of Lucky Strikes from her purse and slid it along the counter. "Here," she said. "Help yourself."

He waited a moment, unsure of the invitation, but the girl waved at it and so he pulled it to him with the crook of his cane. "Thanks, lady." He tapped one out and, sure-handedly, lifted the pack to toss it back.

"Keep it," Donna said. "I'm quittin' anyway."

"Thanks." He lit a match, then the Lucky. It tasted good.

She lifted a delicate silver Zippo from her purse and cradled it in one hand. Gil watched; she laid it on the counter and twirled it once. "Might 's well keep this, too," she mumbled.

"Thanks, I got matches," the colored man said.

Gil covered her hand with his. The girl just stared at it.

The colored man was poring over his pencil and paper when Jimmy returned with the tan porcelain bowl; the white light reflected on its glazed surface. "Here y' go," he said. "Be no trouble to squeeze on some syrup, case you changed your mind about a sundee."

"Jus' the ice cream." He laid the paper to one side and picked up the spoon.

"Okay."

"How much?

Jimmy checked it off. "You want refills on the coffee, 't's a dime. Twenty for the ice cream. Two bits an' a nickel altogether." The customer reached in a pocket, pulled out coins, laid them on the counter. "Even," Jimmy said.

"Uh-huh." He picked up his pencil and turned to the newspaper again. Handicapping, Jimmy noted. He picked up the three dimes and silently added them up. "You, um, y' got any hot—*tips*?"

The man looked at him and sighed. "Tips? Yeah, I s'pose: Don't bet on any horse I bet on. That's the best tip you ever gone get, mister."

"Rough night, huh?"

"Los' ev'ry race. Ev'r' one." Jimmy whistled. "Yeah," the colored man said.

The man in the gray fedora kept his grip on the redhead's hand. He meant it to seem both affectionate and insistent, but she wasn't interested in his affection at the moment and struggled against his insistence. She yanked. He let her hand go. She rubbed it and he picked up the lighter.

"Hey," he grumbled. "I gave you that."

"That makes it mine, don't it?"

"Yeah…"

"Then I c'n do what I want with it." Donna blew on her coffee.

Gil nodded, crushed out the cigarette, pulled another from his pack. "You had fun tonight, didn't you?"

"Yeah."

"I mean, you had a good time, right, Donna? Dancin's your favorite thing, ain't it?"

"Yeah."

"So, so what d' you wanna do something like that for?"

Donna slurped; a thin caramel stream dripped down the side

of her cup. She blotted it with a napkin. "I dunno," she said. "I just... leave it be, huh?"

"I mean, this ought to *mean* something to you. Got your initials on it and—ev'rything."

"You, d'you give Leslie stuff like this? With her initials on it?"

He sat up abruptly. "Leslie?"

"Yeah, Leslie."

"What's she got to do with it?"

Her nostrils flared. Though she passed for mid-twenties—nobody ever asked *her* for ID—she was almost nineteen, and being the other woman was, even after a year, something she couldn't get used to. Or be happy about. Even if it was because of the damn war and all the guys her age were off gettin' killed, or their arms shot off, or whatever. "Just, she's... I keep thinkin' about her. All right?"

"Well, don't," Gil said.

"*Don't*? How *can't I*?"

"Hey," Gil whispered. "Keep your voice down, huh? Just—don't. She ain't here."

"Yeah," said Donna. "I know."

Gil opened the Zippo and flicked the wheel. It sparked; a small flame engulfed the wick. He lit his cigarette and flipped the lid closed. "B'sides," he said, "she don't smoke."

Donna's head snapped toward him. She snatched the lighter and threw it into her purse.

He ran a placating hand through her hair, along her neck, and rubbed gently. "Honey, we got the next two days all to ourselves. Let's have some fun, huh? Tomorrow we can... go to the beach. How 'bout that, huh? And then we'll have supper somewhere quiet, maybe go to a movie..." He looked around, then whispered into her ear. "Out to the drive-in movie?" He blew gently and nipped her lobe; she loved that. "Huh?"

She didn't move. "I don't know."

"C'mon, don't spoil it."

Donna shook him away. "I just—just get… tired of this."

"Of what? Y' mean me?"

She sighed. "I mean, of—*this*. Sometimes. When you're—When you ain't around. Y' know?"

"Yeah," said Gil. "*I know.* I get tired of it too. I *been* tired of it, of her, for eight years."

"Oh, yeah? So why don't you do somethin'?"

He swiveled on the stool to face her. "I can't. You know I can't. Christ, if I was even to try…"

"Yeah. You can't." She sipped her coffee. Just her luck. Yeah, there was a war on; yeah, she was one of the lucky ones. Yeah.

"I can't. That don't mean I don't want to. It's—it's real hard, and I *do* get tired of it. And every night I get home an' see her there I get more tired of it."

An ash fell from his cigarette. She brushed it off the counter and looked around: The scrawny waiter and the colored man were both looking at papers. The radio played "I Can't Get Started." That was the damn truth! "Y' know what I get tired a, Gil?" she said quietly. "I get tired a not bein' able to *say* nothing. I mean, I get up in the morning and I go to work and a lot of the girls, the ones who *got* somebody still over here, they're talkin' all the time, about their husbands 'r their boyfriends, how they did this, how they're *gonna* do that." Donna shook her head and laughed, a choked, throaty laugh. Gil lowered his forehead into his hands. "'What're *you* gonna do this weekend, Donna?' I bet I been asked that a thousand times. I don' know, I always say, I gotta see what happens. An' then *I* go home and one of my girlfriends calls? What'm *I* doin' to*night*? *Her* boyfriend's comin' over, she's cookin' somethin' and then *they're* goin' someplace, how come *I'm* just sittin' at home all the time? And, an' what'm I gonna say to her? What'm I gonna say to any of 'em? I gotta sit here 'cause if Gil c'n get out he'll call me? Or, maybe he's gonna come by for a couple hours 'cause he's sup*posed* t' be workin' late? or, 'r: We're gonna go dancing over to The Paradise Club come Friday and then he's gonna spend the night, 'cause his wife's out a town? Am—"

"Aw, Christ—."

"—I gonna say that?" she went on, and laughed again. "So all I can do is think about it, I can't say nothin'—"

"F'r Chris' sake, Donna—."

"—*And so I think about those things*," she said, loud enough that Jimmy and the colored man glanced up at her. She ignored the glances but lowered her voice. "And I think about her. And, and it, I get—tired."

"Christ!" Gil swallowed his coffee, one large gulp. The heat seared his stomach. It twitched.

"You, you shouldn't oughta say that all the time."

"Yeah?" he said, not-quite slamming the cup into his saucer. "What should I say?"

"I don' know. Not that." Donna swirled the contents of her cup. *Mud.* Well, she was gonna sit here and drink ev'ry drop. *Yeah. I'm lucky.*

Gil sighed. Jesus. What did the girl *want* from him? Even after a year he had no idea. Hell, even after eight years he had no idea what his wife wanted either. No, he *did* know that. Maybe he was a fool, but he wasn't *that* much of a fool. "Look," he sighed, "she's got me by the—."

Donna turned her head sharply. "She'd get everything, Donna. Not that we got so much, but she'd get all of it. And a ton of alimony besides. The wife always gets it all."

"Oh, yeah?" she said acidly.

He hesitated. "Most of the time. If they been married a while, unless—. Most of the time."

"Yeah. Most of the time," she repeated. "Unless."

Gil dragged on his cigarette, took off his hat and wiped his forehead. Despite the air conditioning, he was sweating. He stretched on the stool. "I just, should just never've married her," he said, and snorted: "'Are you sure?'" he asked the cup.

"'Oh, yeah, I'm sure,'" he answered on its behalf, in falsetto. He sighed. "So I said okay, we'll get married... I shoulda known, right then. But I'm so—dumb."

"No you ain't!"

"Oh, no," he went on. "I ain't dumb. 'The doc says I lost the baby and I can't have no more...' Christ. Two weeks after we're married," he mumbled. "And I be*lie*ved her! Till I got the note, anyway."

"What note?"

"I never told you?" Donna shook her head. He leaned toward her and lowered his voice. "Well... I'm sittin' at home this one Saturday when the mail comes, and there's something from the doctor, a bill, I figure. So I open it, and there's a bill, all right. And a note, and *it* says he con*firms* she ain't ever been pregnant, but she's in perfect health... She can be a mother ten times over. 'S many times as she wants. ... I never said nothin' about it. I *should* of said something, then. But I was too... dumb." He pursed his lips and looked to her, whether for confirmation or denial she didn't know. She gave him neither. "Real dumb. I just paid the bill—like I paid all of 'em—an' threw the note in the drawer, made out like nothin'd happened." He sipped his water. "Eight years, just like nothin'd happened. Eight years and no kids. ... Always wanted a kid. ... Christ..."

Gil shook his head. *Well, that's done. She knows now. But Christ.* He waved away smoke, took a deep breath, let it out slowly. "Well," he said, "you ready yet?"

"In a minute. It's hot."

"We only got the two days."

"I know." She sipped the coffee.

"I mean, you have coffee ev'ry day. It ain't like we can do this all the time."

"Yeah," said Donna. "It sure ain't."

Gil stretched again, adjusting himself on the stool. "Christ," he said. "What's got into you tonight?"

"Nothin's got into me. What d' you mean?"

"I don'now. You just been actin' strange."
"I told you. I been thinkin' about some things."
"Yeah. You told me."

Jimmy read his paper between trips to the kitchen, carrying bus trays or garbage cans and returning with platters of clean cups and plates, glasses, silver, and empty trashcans that smelled faintly antiseptic. Now and then he smiled or whistled. The colored man looked up each time. Couple times, he heard the counterman murmur something he couldn't make out. Each time Jimmy finished with a sigh and a shake of the head.

He listened to the music—first time in a while he'd heard any. Wasn't no radio in his hotel room, hadn't been one in the hospital, leastways not where he could hear it good over the constant noise: people coming and going, sobs and moans and the clatter of metal against metal. He sipped his coffee, ate his ice cream. *Good.* He hadn't ice cream in a year, 'cept for once, when the girl who kept the garden wrangled some and gave him a scoop. There hadn't been no other ice cream in Africa, not even for Christmas. Wasn't no place to keep it froze, the Major said. Hospitals didn't have it neither.

Periodically, he looked around, saw the man in the gray hat and the redheaded girl, watched him light up, draw, exhale, watched them talk, watched their faces: trouble there, he noted. *Hell: There's trouble everywhere.* He went back to his paper. There was something familiar about the girl, but just what he couldn't place.

Gil reached for his cigarette, then, suddenly, clutched his stomach. "Oh, God," he rasped.
"What?"
"My stomach."
Donna put down her cup. "'S matter?"

He winced at the pain. "Must be the coffee."

"The—." She shook her head. "What'd you drink it for?"

"I didn't know it was gonna do this to me. It's been okay." He squeezed himself together. "Hey!" he called, his voice strained.

Jimmy looked up from the funnies. "Yeah?" he said.

"You got - facilities in here?"

Jimmy pointed. "Through the door, go down the stairs and turn left."

"You gonna be okay?" Donna stood up. "I mean, should I—?"

"Yeah, I'll be okay, just… I'll be right back." He started away.

"Yeah," she said.

"And when I get back, we're leavin'." He rushed through the door; his hurried footsteps resounded on the wood stairs.

The colored man set his paper down, tucked the pencil back into his shirt pocket, lit a smoke, and dipped his spoon into the ice cream. It was good, and smooth, a taste he could hardly remember. He licked the spoon.

"He *must* be in a hurry," Jimmy said. "Steps don't make a sound if you walk slow."

He looked at Donna. She still stood, watching the doorway. Then she shrugged, picked up her cup and eased herself back onto the stool.

"Somethin' wrong with the coffee?" he asked.

She shook her head. "Nah. He's just—there's this problem with his stomach. It's pretty bad. The Army wouldn't take him or nothin'."

Jimmy nodded, knowingly. It'd been the same during the First, only it didn't last long enough for it to matter. Lotta guys had "problems." He'd had a problem too, but he'd made it in. Wasn't nothin' gonna stop him from makin' it in, he told his family. And nothing did; but… "Umm," he murmured.

The colored man licked his spoon again. "He always that nice?" he said.

"Gil? Oh, he ain't so bad. He's just a little—impatient, that's all."

"He your husband?"

Donna looked hard at him. He looked back without expression. She sat upright, hands folded before her. "Now don't you be gettin' any ideas, mister," she said.

"Wasn't." He dipped the spoon.

Donna slumped gently, and sighed. "No," she said, "he ain't my husband ... I'm—not married."

"I see."

"*What* d' you 'see'?"

The colored man swallowed his spoonful. "That you ain't married."

"That's all?"

"Uh-huh. That's all."

Her coffee had cooled, but she added another dollop of cream. She should've ordered Sanka. But, then, she hadn't expected she'd want to just go home and sleep. That *sure* wasn't the plan, not for *this* weekend. She looked at the counter guy; he'd gone back to his newspaper. He laughed, and turned a page. "Love that *L'il Abner*" she heard him murmur.

"I was," she said. "For a while."

The colored man put the spoon down. "The war?" he said gently.

"Yeah," she said. "The war."

"Sorry. I didn't mean..."

"Yeah. Okay. Okay." She turned toward the window. There was nothing much to see: barely visible outlines of buildings across the street, the full moon between passing clouds, here and there a flash of neon or a pair of headlights. She wondered about Bill. Not that it made a difference anymore.

His favorite subject broached, Jimmy broke into the silence. "You in the war?" he asked enthusiastically.

"Me?" said the colored man. "Yeah."

"You, um, y' see much—action?"

"Some. Some." *Some.*

Jimmy sauntered over and leaned against the counter. "I was in the first one," he confided. "Least, I was in the Army, then. Enlisted, day we got into it." Oh, he'd looked good in his uniform! He stood in front of the tall mirror in their apartment, and his parents, his sister, even her girlfriend (who he'd always thought of as *his* girlfriend, since they'd gone to the pictures together—twice) all told him how good he looked. "But it was over by the time I was ready to go."

The colored man tapped his ashes into the ashtray. "You was lucky then."

Jimmy sighed. "I guess so." He sighed again. "Um, how's the, the ice cream?"

"It's good."

"Made fresh this morning."

"Umm," the colored man said, and dipped his spoon. Jimmy watched. *Boy don't talk much*, he thought. *But not ev'rybody does, I guess.* "How 'bout some more joe, huh?"

"Sure." He swallowed the rest of the cup.

Jimmy took the empty. "Comin' up," he said, and moved away.

The colored man watched him, a hand clutching his cane, as though wondering if, maybe, the counterman'd suddenly turn, the cup in hand and poised to hurl at him. Then he got up, carefully, took off his jacket, and laid it on the counter beside the cane. A twinge shot through his leg; the knee ached. They said that would happen, 'specially when it was gonna rain. Hurt like hell. He muttered "Ahh. Damn it!" and, gingerly, sat again.

Donna looked at him. "'S wrong?"

The colored man rubbed his knee. Six surgeries, that was what was wrong. Seemed like it was worse than when it happened, sometimes. "Nothin'. My leg."

"What'd you do to it?"

His expression—in his voice and in his eyes—was brittle. "Just—it got hurt," he said. "Okay?"

Donna shrugged. "I was just askin'."

He thought a moment, looked at the pack of Luckies on the counter. "Yeah, I—Sorry."

"'S okay." She walked to the window and looked out. *Nothin'.* Just clouds, the moon, the haze.

Jimmy brought the coffee with a "Here y' go" and set it before him. Steam rose. "Mm," the colored man said, and blew on it. "My leg?" he said, loud enough for her to hear. Donna turned. "I—it was over in Africa." She nodded. "They sent me home. Hey, listen, thanks again for the smokes."

"Yeah," she said, and sat again, watching him.

"Y' know," said Jimmy, "I always wanted to go to Africa. Think it'd be kinda innaresting, t' see all those things. Pyramids, the Sphinx. They're in Africa, ain't they?"

The colored man nodded. "Yeah. They said."

"You didn't see them neither, huh?"

He snorted. "Unh-uh. Didn't see much a anything excep' mud in the winter and sand in the summer, few A-rabs and a lot a shootin'."

"Mm," Jimmy said, and smacked his lips sadly. "I never knew nobody who did. See that stuff, I mean. But I bet they'd be innaresting. Don't you think?"

He nodded again, sipped his hot coffee. "Mmm."

"*Lot* a things to see there, I bet."

"I hear."

"You were in Africa? Fightin'?" Donna said.

The colored man cleared his throat before he spoke. "Yeah. Fightin'."

Donna looked toward the door that led to the staircase, then back. "That's—where Bill was," she said. "My husband. Near— Algeria, it was called. The place where he g—, where he - was."

"Yeah?" he replied, with a faint note of curiosity.

"Uh-huh. He wrote me a couple letters from there. He thought it was a kinda interesting place."

"Umm."

She swiveled on her stool to face him. The pageboy flared. "'D you think it was? Africa, I mean?"

It was her hair. Yeah, her hair. "I guess."

"With all those wild animals and elephants and snakes and ni—Africans, I mean."

If he noticed the correction, he chose to ignore it. He smiled, just a hint of a smile, revealing perfect teeth through his thin lips. "Animals an' snakes? That's what he wrote you about?"

"No, they were just short letters, he never said nothin' about any a that. Just, I know there's a lot of them, in Africa."

Now, he smiled unmistakably. "Not up north, 'round Algeria," he said. "There's a lot of birds. No animals. 'Cep' camels and chickens."

"Oh." Donna seemed disappointed. "I thought there was. You know, y' see in the pikshurs..."

Jimmy leaned back against the counter, arms folded, listening.

The colored man shook his head. "Unh-uh. Not no wild ones, anyway. Not 'round Algeria."

"But that's where you were?"

"Yeah," he said, his smile falling away. "Algeria."

"Bill was there till Feb'uary. Then, I mean, that's when..."

So. "How long were you...?" He held up his left ring finger, rubbed his right thumb and middle finger up and down around it.

"Oh, not real long. I, I never even really—felt like we really was married, I mean, I only knew him a couple weeks before." Donna sat up and smiled; her eyes were bright and young. "I was workin' at Woolworth's and he came in sometimes an' smiled at me, and then he started sayin' things like, like how I'm pretty and I could be in pikshurs." She giggled. "He was jokin', I mean, I knew that—but he wasn't—*lookin'*, like most guys'll say that." Idly, she twirled a lock of the pageboy's roll. "He was just a nice guy, three 'r four years older 'n me but real good looking. We went out a couple times, and then right after Pearl he said he was gonna enlist and would I marry him, so there'd be somebody back home thinkin' about him, he said..." Jimmy nodded. *Somebody thinkin' about you, that's what they all, we all, wanted. Well.* "I didn't wanna say no," she went on, "I mean, he was a nice guy and everything, and there were all these guys who weren't gonna come back, an' I was seventeen, I mean, there wasn't gonna be a lot a guys around... An' I couldn't think why not. So I did.

"And then he went over, an' all I got from him was a couple letters, I didn't know what'd happened. And I met Gil... and then in Feb'uary, Bill just—." She stopped, stared into her coffee, shook her head. "Gil—doesn't like to talk about it. I mean, he doesn't like *me* t' talk about it. It upsets him."

"Gil ain't here," the colored man said.

"I know but, it's, it's just— ... nothin'."

He nodded. "Okay."

On the radio, Frank Sinatra's silky voice bemoaned the hour and the end of a brief episode, and asked for one more for the road. The song ended; there was a silence. Jimmy sighed into it: sounded like a good story, but if the girl wasn't gonna tell it, well... He couldn't just ask a *girl*. Now if it was the boy tellin' it, he—.

"He... This one day," Donna interrupted his thought. She spoke slowly, hesitantly. "He—came back. ... He wasn't, I mean he just got, not *just*, but his arm, they had ta—." With her left hand, she sliced at her right arm, just above the elbow; then she raised her eyebrows and looked at them. Both men nodded. "— And then, he—came back. Didn't call 'r nothin, just walked inta the apartment one day, 'surprise,' big smile on his face an' everything... and Gil was—there. ... So he got a divorce. Last spring." She shrugged. "Just, Gil—doesn't like for me ta talk about it."

"Yeah," said the colored man. "I see."

"It wasn't *Gil's* fault," she said. "It—just happened. Y' know?" She looked down, into her nearly empty cup.

"Uh-huh." He drank his coffee, took a spoonful of the ice cream, let it melt in his mouth. He swallowed it slowly.

"Anyway," Donna said. She looked back up; both men looked at her. "I think it'd be pretty there. In Africa. If it wasn't for the war, I mean. I seen in this pikshur once, there's a lot a mountains and jungles, with all kinds a flowers growin' wild and trees and things, like you don't see here. Like orchids. Y' ever see an orchid?"

"Unh-uh," the colored man said.

Her voice brightened. "They got 'em at this place uptown, I forget what it's called, but they grow 'em there an' anybody can walk in and look at 'em. Bill and me went there, once. They're pretty, and they smelled so good. And he gave me one, the day we got married."

Jimmy perked up. "Corsage?"

"Yeah," said Donna, "that was it. A corsage."

Jimmy smiled. "I gave one a them to somebody once," he said softly. "Long time ago." In a hush, he saw her: dressed in red, like the girl here, with her brown hair all done up, tied with a pink ribbon. "Well…" he whispered.

The air conditioner hummed. The radio played. A car horn blew a long, fading note.

The colored man stretched and rubbed his leg. "Hey," he said, "I'm gone kinda stretch this out. Locks up on me if I keep it folded too long. Okay?"

Jimmy nodded. "Sure, go 'head. Ain't nobody here 'bout to trip over it." He laughed.

The colored man let the leg out. "Ahh, damn," he murmured.

Jimmy stood straight up, poured himself a cup of coffee, added cream and sugar. "So," he said. "Africa's where you got that."

"Yeah," the colored man answered, slowly.

"Shrapnel? Knowed a couple guys, from the First, got their

legs busted up in France that way."

"Unh-uh."

Jimmy smiled. "Combat, eh." That was the best, that was where heroes got made, got their legs or their arms busted up. Even maybe got killed.

The colored man stared at him and again spoke slowly, a drawl of bitter reverie. "I—got hit," he said. "Broke my knee, an' the bone down here, eight diff'rent places." Jimmy whistled. "Yeah ... Didn't get a doc for it till the next day. Set real funny. What's left 'f it."

Poor boy, Jimmy thought. Tough enough bein' colored, but a colored cripple? Too bad. He seems nice enough. "But y' still got it," he said cheerily. "Least they didn't cut it off."

The poor boy said "Yeah. I guess I'm real lucky."

Donna reached out, as though to touch him, although she was too far away. "Some guys, they come back missin' somethin' altogether," she said. "Like..."

He looked at her. "Ain't no diff'rence, lady. Losin' it, bein' like this: Ain't no diff'rence at all."

She drew her hand back. "I'm—sorry."

"Yeah. So's everyone else. But you got to get on with your life, boy. They al'ays tellin' me that. Got-to-get-on-with-your-*life*... Yeah." He closed his eyes a long moment and breathed, deeply and slowly. *Got to breathe deep and slow.* They were tellin' him that, too, at the hospitals.

"You will," she told him. "People'll help you."

"Sure they will. Sure."

"They will. I would. If there was anything..."

He opened his eyes and looked at her, trying to figure something out. "What's your name?"

"Donna," she said.

"Donna." She nodded. "Well, Donna, you're real nice." He pointed at the Luckies. "An', you *are* real pretty. Jus' like he said."

Noiselessly, the staircase door opened. Gil stepped through and stood silently, watching.

"Yeah?" Donna said.

"Yeah," the colored man replied, and smiled again. Then he added, gently, "'Specially your hair. Girl I used t' know had hair like yours. Same color, even wore it the same way. She liked flowers too..."

"Your girlfriend?"

No, sure *not his girlfriend.* "Jus' a girl I knew," he said, a small strain to his voice. "Nurse. Liked t' watch me play ball. We was—friends. In Africa. For a while... She tried t' keep a garden, in Africa in the middle of the war, she kept this garden!" He laughed a tight, single note. "She kinda looked like you, a little. And her hair was real pretty. Just like yours."

"You like her hair," Gil said.

The colored man looked toward the voice. "Yeah," he said calmly. "I do."

Donna leaped in. "You better?"

Gil lit a Chesterfield, sauntered back to his stool and dropped the matchbook on the counter. "You havin' a nice chat?"

"We was just talkin'."

"Umm." He sat.

"How's it feel?"

He rubbed his stomach. "Still queasy. What I need's a good night's sleep." He looked into her eyes and put a hand on her thigh.

"You want some milk?" Jimmy asked. "That'll help settle you."

"Naw," Gil said. "We're going." He moved his hand up.

Donna looked back at him, then picked up her coffee. "I ain't done yet."

"Well, f'r Chris' sakes." He pulled the hand away and, just above a whisper, asked: "You want t' stay here an' 'talk' with your new friend? That it?"

She looked at him again. "*We was just talkin'.* Killin' time. Y' understand?"

"Yeah. Well, *we* ain't got no time t' kill."

She took a tiny sip, felt his breath on her face and put the cup down. "If you're so—anxious t' go," she said, "then go. I c'n get home on my own."

He leaned in and murmured. "I want t' go home with you."

"In a couple minutes."

Gil straightened, lifted his hat and wiped his hairline again. "Christ" he said, and took a long draw from the cigarette. He looked at Jimmy. "You got any vanilla ice cream?"

Jimmy shook his head. "Sorry." He nodded toward the thin man, who had just dipped his spoon into his bowl. "This fella just got the last of it. There's still some choc'late in the freezer, little bit a strawberry."

"Nah," said Gil, and followed Jimmy's nod. "I got a taste for vanilla."

The colored man lifted the spoon and put it into his mouth, then returned Gil's look. "Y' know," he said, "the gas station 'cross the street's got a machine. It's just brim-full a vanilla ice creams."

Donna's head turned toward him sharply. Gil's eyes narrowed. "What 'd you say?"

"I said there's a machine, 'cross the street. In the gas station. Full a vanilla ice creams. They keep it right next to the cigarette machine."

Gil grunted a laugh, then beckoned to Jimmy. The counterman came and bent toward him—unnecessarily: Gil's low voice was clear to all of them. "You must need business real bad," he said, "servin' niggers."

Jimmy jumped back. "Now, ain't no call—" he began, as Donna said "Gil, he just—."

"*What?*" said Gil.

The subject of Gil's remark spoke almost as quickly. "Somethin' you want to say, mister?" He half stood, without moving from his place. "Somethin' you want me to hear? 'Cause if there is, don't you be *sneakin'* on me, you say it good and loud and *right* to my face so I don't make *no* mistake 'bout what you sayin'. You unnerstand?"

"Please. He didn't mean nothin'," Donna said over him. She grabbed Gil's arm. "C'mon, let's get out a here. Please, I wanna go—."

But Gil stood, hands clenched, ready. "You want me t' talk to you, boy?" he said, the words clipped and deliberate. "That what you want? Aw right. Aw right." He shook Donna's hand off. "*You* wait a minute." He set himself, adjusted his hat, and stared at the boy. Who stared back. "What, 're you, lookin' for, boy?" Gil said.

"Gil, *don't...*" Donna looked to the slender man, half risen, one hand on his cane, the other squeezing the edge of the counter. "Mister..."

The slender man looked back at her, at Gil, then again at Donna. Then he sat and lifted his spoon, licked it. "Nothin'," he told Gil. "Just t' finish my coffee, eat my vanilla ice cream. Have a little peace and quiet."

Gil snorted. "Then maybe you better be a little quieter."

"Yeah," said the colored man. "Maybe we both better be. Boy."

Gil slammed his fist. "Why, you—" he hissed.

"*Gil.* C'mon, I'm ready." Donna grabbed her purse. "How much we owe you?" she asked, but Jimmy was reaching beneath the counter. He came up holding a baseball bat.

"Hey! you two," he shouted. "Don't you get into nothin'. Not in here."

Gil and the colored man stood, eyes locked. "*How much?*" Donna said.

"Two coffees, with refills. Twenty cents," Jimmy said without looking at her.

She dropped a quarter on the counter. "C'mon. Let's go." Gil didn't move.

"Wait a minute," he said.

"You said you wanted to get some sleep. Let's go. Right now."

"I said wait a minute!" He took off his hat and set it on the counter, loosened his tie. "Boy," he said, "you want to step—"

"I mean it!" Jimmy shouted, moving from behind the counter.

"—outside with me?" Gil continued. "That what you want?"

"Boy" breathed, deeply and slowly. "Like I said: I just want some peace 'n' quiet." Without taking his eyes from Gil's, he added quietly: "'Less *you're* wantin' somethin' else."

Gil looked at him, cocked his head and looked toward Jimmy, who held the bat in both hands, at ready. He snorted again. "You're just lucky my stomach's actin' up. Damn lucky."

The colored man's eyes smiled; his mouth did not.

Gil straightened his tie. "Siddown," he told Donna. "I'm gonna have a glass a milk."

"I thought you wanted ta—."

"*I'm gonna have some milk.*" He sat, beside her, and put on his hat, slouching it over one eye, looking out the corner at the boy, who had returned his focus to the ice cream. "How 'bout it?" he said to Jimmy.

Jimmy watched him, and the colored man, for a long moment, then went behind the counter and replaced the bat. "Sure," he said. "Comin' right up."

Gil smoked with a fury. Donna reached over, touched his hand. He allowed it but stared ahead. "You got antacids?" she said.

"Took a couple. Downstairs. They ain't helpin'."

"I got milk at home."

"You got coffee at home, too."

"I—."

"Yeah? Yeah?"

"Nothin'." She wrapped her hand around his. "I, I just don't want anything to happen. T' you."

He smirked. "Nothin's gonna happen t' me."

Jimmy placed the milk before him. "Thanks," Donna said.

"That's thirty-five cents, altogether."

Gil reached into his pocket. "You want somethin' else? While I'm drinkin' this? I ain't gonna gulp it down, y' know—that's no good for the stomach neither."

Donna sighed. "No," she said.

"Okay." He dropped another quarter on the counter. It clattered. "Keep it."

Jimmy nodded. "Thanks." He rang the sale, dropped fifteen cents into the glass next to the register, took his coffee and walked over to the colored man, who sat unmoving except to raise and lower the spoon or his cup. "Don't let him get you upset," Jimmy said confidentially. "Prob'ly just had a little too much…" He tilted a hand to his mouth. "We serve ev'rybody in here. Always have." The colored man nodded. "So. So y' didn't see much a Africa?"

He spoke softly. "Not much."

"Y' got any stories?" Jimmy asked. *The boy* needs *to talk; 'bout somethin'.* Sometimes, he felt like the bartenders in the movies and on the radio: listenin' to ev'rybody's stories. But he liked stories, and he liked listening. It was something he'd always been good at. "'Bout the war, I mean. Most guys, they come back from the war, they got nothin' *but* stories t' tell. Y' know?"

The colored man nodded again. His voice remained low, but grew harder. "Yeah, I know. In the hospitals, they all told stories. 'Bout when they could see, 'r sit up straight. Or walk right."

"Umm. Y' figure a man goes to war, he's gonna see a lot a things. Have a lot t' tell about. Y' know?"

"Yeah."

Jimmy took a slurp from his cup. "I know this guy," he said, "comes in here all the time? I know this guy, was in the First, got stories about ev'rything. French guy, got a name a mile long. We call him Louie." He laughed. "He was a hero, in the First.

Got a bunch a medals f'r savin' some guys from the Jerries. Moved here when they went inta France this time, said he was too old to fight 'em again and he couldn't stand not fightin' 'em. Him 'n' me, we got to talkin' this one night, though, 'bout the wars, and what it was like t' face the enemy. He said the same thing you did"—the colored man looked up—"that I was lucky, I mean, 'cause I didn't have to"—and nodded.

Jimmy frowned. "I don't know though. I just think maybe a lot of things'd've been—I don't know. Diff'rent. If I'd of been a soldier boy. I mean, I done a lot a things before here, maybe I would've done a lot of other things instead. Maybe I'd've saved some guys, too, ended *up* doin' something—else, 'stead a slingin' hash an' cuttin' pies. Not that this"—he made a small sweeping gesture at the diner—"'s so bad. Just..."

Trouble everywhere, the colored man thought. *Ev*'rywhere. "Wha'd you wanna do?"

Jimmy shrugged. "Oh, I don't know, just, somethin' a little more—innaresting. Important. Or maybe, just've got married, have some kids," he laughed, smally and ruefully; "come home at night 'n' put my feet up, read *Smilin' Jack* an' listen to *Gang Busters*..."

"You never been married?"

"Unh-uh. You?"

"No. Moved aroun' too much. More'n half a ev'ry year."

"Mm," Jimmy commiserated. "I come close, once. 'Bout twenny years ago. Girl—didn't think I had a future, she said. I was sellin' shoes, then." He stood straight up; a look of wonder crossed his face. "I don't know what she meant. 'I don't know what you mean,' I told her. 'If I'm good at it,' I told her, 'they'd make me assistant manager, maybe even the manager one day.' Good job, sellin' shoes."

"Yeah?" The colored man almost smiled.

"Uh-*huh*. People'll always need to buy 'em. Best to sell somethin' people always need t' buy. I was pretty good at sellin', too, once I learned. Still do it, right here. That ice cream? I sold it to you. You didn't just happen to think of it, y' know."

Now, he laughed. "You're right. You're right."

Jimmy laughed, too, then leaned against the counter. "Never could understand why she didn't think there was a future in it," he said, the wonder returning in a shake of his head. "Some people... They're just—crazy."

"Yeah," said the colored man, without changing his expression. "Some people..." He swallowed coffee. The radio began "That Old Black Magic," a slow instrumental. He smiled, shook his head. "I like that song."

"Yeah. Me too."

"Girl I knew in Africa sang it. Ain't heard it in a while, but I like it." He stirred his coffee slowly, thoughtfully. "Y' know, there *was* this one thing I seen there."

"In Africa?"

"Yeah. These—birds."

Jimmy looked confused. "Birds?"

"Uh-huh." The colored man leaned in toward Jimmy, steepling his fists beneath his chin. "Like I said—there was a lot of birds. And there was these, these *crazy* ones, there was these crazy birds we used to see all the time. Near the desert. I don't know a lot about birds, but these, I think they were some kind a hawks, y' know, they were big, and kinda gray lookin'. I seen hawks at a zoo once, that's how they looked. Excep', except these, I only used to see 'em at night." He looked away, out the window. "I'd be on guard duty, or I couldn't sleep so I'd be settin' up smokin'. It was so dark, even with the moon, but you could see miles aroun' because there wasn't no trees, and it was so clear. And I'd look up, and they'd be there, six, eight, ten of 'em, just floatin' in circles, smooth and dark, like, like they were lookin' for something, they were tryin' to figure somethin' out, maybe... Just circling aroun' and aroun', lookin' and circlin', lookin' and circlin'...." He looked back at Jimmy, shook his head.

"What d' you suppose they were lookin' for?"

He shook his head again. "I don't know. Food, I guess, but I don't know. Sometimes I wondered if they even knew, the hawks I mean. They just kept flyin' aroun' in circles, never landing, never—goin' *after* nothin'… All night long. And then, before it got to be morning? They'd jus' fly away, wherever."

Jimmy laughed lightly. "Crazy birds," he said. "Crazy birds and crazy people."

"Yeah," the colored man agreed. "Crazy."

The church clock clanged twice briefly. The thin customer looked out again, toward the sound. There was the cloud-masked full moon, the blink of neon, headlights moving slowly; some vague silhouettes of places where people worked or lived or played. *Where white people worked and lived and played.* Jimmy followed his gaze.

The colored man looked back and pointed to his cup. "Y', um, you got some more…?"

"Hmm?" Jimmy said, listening to the chimes resound through the night. "Oh, sure. Comin' right up."

Gil stared at the glass of milk, now and then tilting it to his mouth. He looked up as the chimes rang. "One-thirty," he said, and lit another cigarette. "Christ, I'm tired."

Donna laid her hand softly on his back. "That helpin'?"

"I don' know. It's still kinda…" He gestured: *topsy-turvy*.

She rubbed, beneath and between his shoulders, one eye on the counterman and the colored guy; *they* seemed to be havin' a good time. "You wanna go now? I'll rub your back, that'll relax you."

"I better let it settle a little more. Eight, nine blocks, I ain't ready to walk that far yet."

"We could take a cab."

Gil coughed to clear his throat. *The damn smoke.* It was making him tear again. "I shoulda drove." He wiped his eyes, sighed, rubbed his stomach. "Christ."

"What?"

"This stomach. My pa's sixty-seven, he's got a gut like a steel trap. I'm thirty-three and I got this."

She rubbed a little harder. "You got a lot worryin' you."

"Yeah. Yeah." He looked at her; she smiled and he smiled back, tentatively. "Look, I'm—sorry I got ... you know. Before."

She kissed a fingertip, touched it to his cheek. "It's okay."

"Thinkin' about Leslie, I get so—aggervated."

"I know."

"I know you know." He patted her hand. "You're real good to me."

She smiled again and leaned against him. He put his arm over her shoulder and, awkwardly, held her. "Gil...?"

"Yeah?"

"Maybe, maybe we could go to Reno. We could even stay there. I heard it's nice."

Oh, Christ. "What'm I gonna do in Reno?"

"They got stores and things. Factories. Don't they?"

"I don' know. I guess so."

She sat up and faced him, her hands holding his in her lap. "We could be together. All the time."

"I don' know, Donna. Maybe after the war."

The war. The g.d. war. It spoiled everything. "After the war. When's that gonna happen?"

Gil shrugged. "I don' know. I don' know."

She turned back to the counter. "Seems like it's always been goin' on. Like it always will."

"I know." Suddenly, he turned her to him; his face lit up. "But it won't," he said energetically, "and then we're gonna go somewhere, honey. You'll see."

Donna smiled anxiously. "Yeah?"

Gil took her hands and brought them together against his heart. "Uh-huh. We'll ditch this place, get on a train and go— anywhere you want: Reno first, then California, New York,

Chicago. Florida if you want," he added, intimately. "You name it."

She giggled. "Florida? How come Florida?"

Gil narrowed his eyes and did his best Groucho. "Thought you might wanna rassle an alligator 'r somethin'."

Donna laughed. Jimmy and the colored man looked toward her briefly, but she didn't notice. I *am* one of the lucky ones, she thought, and squeezed her hands inside Gil's grip. "C'n, c'n *we* have kids?"

"Yeah." His excitement grew. He'd *have* a kid—*no, he'd have* "Three, four, *five* kids, 'n' a house 'n' a yard 'n' a dog. The big shaggy kind. And I'll mow the lawn an' you can—grow veg'tables—"

"Yeah."

"—and at night we'll just sit around and listen to the radio, an' if we want"—he heard "That Old Black Magic" and smiled —"we c'n dance right there, in our own living room. Hey! C'mon. This's my favorite song." He lifted Donna from her stool, pulled her close and they danced. "How's that sound, huh?" he murmured to her.

"Yeah," she whispered. *Yeah!*

"You'll see," he said, "someday we'll have all a that. Okay?"

She stopped and frowned at him. "'Someday.'" ... *Yeah.*

Gil let her hands go; they dropped to her sides. Her eyes emptied. "Yeah," he said, trying to comfort. "Someday.... Someday."

The colored man relaxed on the stool. "This's good coffee," he said, as Jimmy poured the refill.

"Thanks. Guess y' get tired a that imitation stuff in the Army."

"Real tired. Real quick. Least in the hospital here they got real coffee. And real food."

"How long you been home?" He set the cup on the counter.

The colored man added a dash of sugar and drank: a long, hot swallow.

"I ain't *been* home, yet," he said. "Been here a month, in the hospital. Jus' got out this mornin'. First time I been out in civilian clothes in almos' two years. Feel funny."

"Yeah, I bet they would."

"Docs said I needed t' get used to 'em." He added another dash of sugar and stirred. "Got to go walkin' aroun', *do* things. But I got t' stick aroun' 'nother week 'r two. They still got some stuff they need t' do 'fore they let me go. Meantime I got a room at a *ho*tel. Twenty-third floor."

"High up!"

"Yeah." He drank. "And they got maids an' ev'rything."

Jimmy nodded. "Nice."

The colored man shook his head. "Too quiet. I ain't used to it. Lotta noise at night back home, in the War. Even in the hospitals, sounds always comin' through, nurses goin' in an' out, ambulances, people talkin' in their sleep. Hotel, that high up, can't even hear the wind with your window open. I was jus' lyin' there an' sweatin'. Couldn't sleep. Felt like I had t' go someplace, see somethin', hear some *sound!*" *Like the desert. No sound at night, 'cept, maybe, the wind and the birds cryin'. Not even the sound of people walkin', real careful, on the sand.* He slapped his hand on the counter. It made a dull *crack*. "Ever get like that?"

"Oh, yeah," Jimmy said. "Times, I just stand behind this counter, ain't no one else in the place, and I think: got to be somethin' out there. Got to be somethin' else t' do, some other place t' go…" He laughed softly. "But there ain't. This's it. But like I said, it ain't so bad. Ain't so bad…"

"Long as there ain't somethin' else y' wanna do."

"I suppose." Jimmy drank from his cup, looked at the couple and, amused, shook his head: they were dancing. *Some people.* He pointed discreetly. The colored man smiled too. "So," he said, "you just got out the hospital today, huh."

"Uh-huh."

"Well, that's why I ain't seen you before. I remember faces pretty good and when you come in, didn't think I'd seen yours."

"Mm. You here all the time?"

He laughed. "Feels like it. But I'm just the night helper— here eight in the p. m. till eight in the mornin'."

It felt good, the younger man thought. Ain't had a real conversation in a long while. Just small talk, I guess. Don't *mean* nothin', but... "Long day," he said, to keep it going.

"Yeah. I don't mind it though. Keeps me busy. It's somethin' t' do. 'f I wasn't here I'd prob'ly just be out gettin' in some kind a trouble. Y' know how it is."

"Uh-huh."

"What kind a work you do? B'fore you went in?"

His jaw tightened. "I played ball," he said slowly.

Jimmy whistled. "No kiddin'?"

"Center field. With the Monarchs."

"Yeah?" The thin man nodded. "You must've been pretty fast, playin' there."

"Yeah. Pretty fast." He laughed—a small, sharp laugh; then, gradually, his eyes looked away, away from Jimmy, away from the diner, from the city and the night. "Wasn't like runnin'. Like *fly*in', like bein' all in the sky and the wind and the sunlight. ... Best feelin' in the world. Was like my whole life, ever since I was a boy, only thing I *wanted* t' do, only thing I was *good* at. An' I was good." He paused a moment, a man returned to earth against his will. "Was. Real, good." He looked away again. "I *was*... Better'n anybody. ... Jus' like—flyin'..."

Jimmy looked with him, into the sky and the sunlight. "Yeah, must a been somethin'," he said, filled with the wonder. He looked back, into the colored man's face, and saw the rest: unavoidable truth. He cleared his throat. "Guess, guess you can't play ball no more."

"No," he said, "guess not."

For a moment, Jimmy thought of placing a hand on his

shoulder. Instead, he said "Too bad" and shook his head.

"Yeah," said the colored man.

Jimmy took a deep breath and smiled at him. "I saw a couple games, few years back. Forget which teams, but they were all colored boys. Lot of 'em played pretty good."

The colored man seemed buoyed. "We came here, two, three times a season."

"Maybe," Jimmy remarked, "I saw you."

"Maybe."

"I kept the programs. Still got 'em at home. I could check. What's your name?"

"Wray Grubbs," Wray Grubbs said. "Wray's with a 'W,' after my daddy."

Jimmy stuck out his hand. "Jimmy Ringstad." Wray Grubbs took it. "Mr. Ringstad," he said.

The sky lit suddenly with lightning; a soft thunderclap followed it.

"Oh!" said Donna.

Gil turned to look. "Great. Rain."

"It'll cool things off." Jimmy walked to the window, cupped his hands against it and peered out. The street was still obscure, but the haze was gradually disappearing under a light mist.

"Till morning, maybe. Then it'll be like a steambath," Gil said sourly.

"Maybe we ought t' try t' get a cab now, before it starts, we could—." Donna stopped. "There a 'phone in here?" she asked Jimmy.

"Unh-uh. Gas station's got one"—he gestured across the street, then returned to the counter—"if they're still open."

"I'll go look." Donna started toward the door.

Gil stopped her. "Nah," he said. "They're closed. Look, you c'n see ain't nobody there. Christ. Station's closed, there ain't no cabs on the street..." He winced and rubbed his stomach.

"C'mon. We c'n walk."

"In the rain?"

"It ain't really started yet," she insisted. "Maybe we c'n beat it."

He shook his head. "You ain't got no coat on 'r nothin'. Your dress'll get ruined. So'll this." He touched his lapels.

"Okay" she muttered and picked up her cup. It was empty. "C'n I have some more a this?" she asked Jimmy.

"Sure thing." He turned to Gil. "You want anything? Else?"

"Nah. I'm gonna…" Gil pointed toward the downstairs door, then looked at Wray. "Just for a minute," he said, and started away.

"Gil?" Donna called after him.

He stopped. "Yeah?"

"Gimme a cigarette, okay?"

"I thought you were quittin'." He snorted, but reached into his pocket.

"Just, can I have one?"

He opened the pack. "I'm out."

"Oh," Donna said.

He crumpled the empty and left it on the counter, saw the Lucky Strikes lying there and picked them up. "Here," he said, and tossed the package to her. "These're yours, anyway."

Donna caught it. "They ain't," she said. She looked at the colored man.

He glanced lazily at Gil. "Go ahead."

She took one.

"Gimme one, too," Gil said.

Wray braced himself against the counter, and took the half dozen steps to where Donna sat. He picked up the package. "Unh-uh," he said, and made his way back to his stool.

"What?" said Gil.

"You want one, you ask me."

Gil sniffed. "I ain't askin' you for nothin'."

Wray lit a cigarette and put the rest into his pocket. "Okay," he said, evenly.

"They're his, Gil," said Donna. "I gave them to him."

Outside, the rain began in earnest, a soft drumming growing louder.

Gil sniffed again. "You really do want trouble, don't you, boy?"

"Your stomach feelin' better? That it?"

Jimmy took a step toward the hidden bat. "Hey you two. I told you."

"Boy," said Gil, "you must really like bein' a cripple—"

Donna started. "Gil, what're you—don't say that."

"—'cause it's like you're askin' t' have your other leg all busted up too."

Wray stayed on the stool. He drew on his cigarette, and nodded calmly. "Oh yeah," he said. "I like that jus' fine. *Jus'* fine. An' I'll tell you what else I like, mister. I like people who when they say somethin' ain't gonna complain about their stomach hurtin' too much to back it up. That's what I like. Now, you want a cigarette, you ask me f'r one. Or"—his voice rose—"you want t' step outside with me, you ask me *that*."—and lowered— "Or, I'll tell you what, you c'n jus' walk right on over to that door an' I promise, I'm gone be jus' one step behind you. Rain or no rain, don't matter *none* to me."

Jimmy leaned between them, the bat in hand. "I mean it, both of ya. There ain't gonna be no trouble in here. I'll use this. I will. Y' understand?"

Wray looked at Gil. "*I* understand," he said.

"How 'bout you, mister?"

Gil's eyes stayed on Wray. "Yeah. Yeah, I understand," he said. There was another thunderclap; he turned to the window. "Christ. Look at that. Listen to it."

"Yeah," said Donna. "Good thing we didn't…"

"Yeah." He started past Wray. "I'm goin' downstairs," he said, and kicked the boy's extended leg as he passed.

Wray screamed. "You don't want it hurt," Gil said stopping only long enough to glance back, "keep it out a the way."

Wray grabbed his cane and lunged after him, catching Gil's ankle in the crook. "What the—" he yelled as he tumbled.

Jimmy's shouted "Hey" and Donna's cry of "Gil" got lost as the crippled man limped the few steps to Gil and grabbed him by the lapels, lifting him from the floor. "*Now!*" he shouted, "You got something—"

"I told you there wasn't gonna be no—." Jimmy lifted the bat.

Wray yanked it away and shoved Gil to the floor. "—you wanna do," he went on, "you do it, mister. Here." He stood over Gil, the bat clutched between his hands, raised, his wiry arms taut.

Donna stood frozen. "No," she said, "please. Don't. Let 'im go ... Let him *go*."

"You think you c'n do it," Wray said, ignoring her, ignoring Jimmy's reach and Gil's efforts to slide away, "you go 'head an' we'll git it over with 'cause I ain't lettin' nobody do nothin' t' me no more. It been done t' me *good* in the Army, and it ain't bein' done by *you* 'r nobody else ever again. You got that? Huh? *Huh?*"

"Leggo a me!" Gil shouted.

"Oh, yeah, I'm gone let go a you," Wray said, his voice softer but his face set, the bat poised. "I'm gone let go a you an' then I'm gonna take this an' y' know what I'm gone do with it? I'm gone smash your leg, same way those boys did mine. Wasn't no war did this, wasn't no bullet, jus' these four, five white boys. An' y' know what they wanted? They wanted t' beat us at ball so bad and they couldn't. They couldn't beat *me*. I was too good, an' they didn't like no colored boy playin' ball better th'n a white boy and they *es*pecially didn't like no white girl, no *pretty* white girl, bein' my friend, and *root*in' for me against them, so, so one night, they come sneakin' inta my tent, carryin' one a these, an' one of 'em puts his hands over my mouth so couldn't nobody hear me scream, couple of 'em hold me down, and t'other, he says 'we gone show you a ball game we play back home, we

call it nigger-ball,' an' he went SMASH with it"—he brought
the bat down hard on the floor beside Gil's face—"SMASH,"
he repeated, "on my knee, I don't know how many times, I
r'member the first one, I think I r'member the second. After that
I don' know. So the po' little colored boy got sent home wit' a
cane an' a medal, s'posed t' git on wit' his *life*, 'cept he ain't got
no kind a *life* lef' t' live, thass all. But you gone be all right, they
tell me, it's only a leg. You c'n still walk. You gone be *all—right*.
An' I been rememberin', all this time, I been thinkin': Oh yeah.
Oh, yeah. I'll be all right the someday I git me some wise-ass
white boy an' I do it t' him, an' maybe knock his pecker off f'r
good measure."

Breathing heavily, he took a step back and lowered his voice,
let the bat, still tight in his hands, ease onto the counter. "Only,
only I ain't gonna sneak up on him. I'm gone *tell* him, *jus'* what
I'm gone do. So now—boy—you jus' go on out that door and
you git ready, 'cause I'll be there, and *I* will be *good* 'n' ready.
You wanna do that? Huh?" He raised the bat again and stared
into Gil's eyes. "That what you want?"

The rain pounded the window. Outside, a honk sounded and
faded away. On the radio, "In the Blue of the Evening" ended,
"Juke Box Saturday Night" began.

Donna took a step toward the colored man. "Please…" she
said softly. Wray stared into Gil's eyes.

"No," Gil whispered.

Wray nodded. "No. I didn't think so." He looked at Gil
another long moment, then slammed the bat onto the counter
and left it there. He picked up his cane and walked back to his
stool, took a swallow of water, sat and stared blackly into the
glass.

Gil got up slowly. Limply, he picked up his hat and walked
to his stool, glancing toward but steering clear of the nigger. He
sat, wiped his face, put his hat on.

"Gil," Donna said gently.

"Don't you say nothin'," he barked. "*Nothin'*."

Jimmy picked up the bat and turned it in his hands, as if examining every inch of the grain. "Jesus," he said quietly, and looked at Wray. "Jesus. They did that t' you? *Soldier boys* did that?" Wray just breathed, slowly, deeply. "You, you—okay?" He laid the bat down. "Jesus," he murmured.

Wray looked up, into Jimmy's eyes, as though the word had been prayer he knew would not be answered. "Yeah," he said hoarsely. "Okay."

Jimmy nodded and looked at Gil. "You okay, mister?" Gil waved him away. Jimmy sighed and slid the bat under the counter. "Jesus," he repeated softly, and stood up. "Listen, I'm, uh, now I'm gonna get everybody some coffee—'r some milk—and we're gonna wait here real quiet till the rain blows over. Shouldn't be too long. Don't usually rain this hard but a short time. But *anybody* makes any trouble...?" He waited, but no one moved.

He refilled their drinks as the rain roared into the quiet. Donna broke it. "You gonna be okay?"

"Yeah," Gil mumbled. "I'm gonna be fine. Just fine."

She nodded. "Mister?" she called softly.

Wray replied without looking up. "Yeah?"

"C'n I"—she picked up the cigarette she'd taken and pointed at it—"I mean, can we have another...?"

Wray looked up; her eyes were filled with hope, with sorrow, with unknowable trouble. *Trouble, everywhere.* He tossed the pack.

"Thanks." She took one and—"Here."—tossed the package back. It landed on the counter beside his cane. "I'm—I'm..." She looked at Gil, then back at Wray and shrugged sadly.

"Yeah," Wray said.

She put both cigarettes into her mouth, struck a match and lit them. The smoke rose and circled her head. "Here" she said, and handed one to Gil. He took it, in silence.

They sat that way several moments, then Donna turned and

looked out the window. The rain had cleared the haze; down the street, she could make out neoned words, see through the windows of the cars that drove by: men, women, together, alone. People going places.

She got up and walked to the glass that ran the diner's breadth, looked up, into the rain. Across the street, above the building, something moved. She smoked and stared at it.

Jimmy watched her. "Somethin' out there?" he asked.

She tapped the ash. "I don'now. Just—it looks like there's these..." She pointed. He walked to the window and looked out. "Y' see 'em?"

"What?" He cupped his hands against the glass.

"Right over there? Above that buildin'?" He looked up and caught the movement. "Just goin' 'round and around."

Yeah. Sure—'round and 'round. "Huh," he said. "How 'bout that."

"Think they'd—*do* somethin'. Y' know?"

"Yeah, y'd think that, wouldn't ya?"

Donna sighed. "Yeah... Yeah, y' would."

She walked back to her stool and sat, picked up the matchbook and opened it, closed it, opened and closed. Jimmy looked a moment longer, then went behind the counter, flicked off the radio—the words were getting in the way again—and took a swallow of coffee. It was cold. He debated getting a warm up, decided not to, and bent to dump the cup into a bus tray. Wray glanced at him, then picked up his water glass. Gil smoked.

Outside, the rain pummeled the pavement. The diner was silent, except for the rain and the distant cries of birds.

ANIMATION

Tuesday afternoons, he discovered some weeks before, there is nothing on, not even on cable, but he doesn't feel like reading or going for a walk and it's too early to eat. If he eats now, he'll only do it again, late, and that'll make it harder for him to sleep. He has enough trouble sleeping anyway.

So Aggie takes a drag on his cigarette and leans back on the sagging, faded-floral-pattern sofa, waving the smoke out of his eyes. It stings and they're watering, which makes it hard to watch the TV screen, where an animated cat is chasing an animated mouse.

The TV is on mute, so he'll hear the phone in the bedroom if it "rings." The ringer's broken: Only a soft ratchety squeak lets him know someone's calling. Merilyn tells him he should get a new one. They're only twenty dollars. He could get one used for even less at a resale shop—that's where she got hers and it works fine, she says. But he doesn't want to spend money on a phone. Not now, when he's drawing unemployment and hoping he won't have to dig too far into his savings. He could give out the cell number, but he's changed his plan to prepaid minutes: another economy measure. At least Merilyn's agreed to forgo her alimony. She doesn't really need it; she doesn't make a lot but she can live on it and anyway, she's getting remarried in a couple of months. Aggie knows the guy makes a good living, and Oliver and Penny like him. At least, they don't *dis*like him, Penny says.

He's putting out the cigarette when the phone squeaks. The cat, now being chased by a dog, is still chasing the mouse. He goes to the bedroom to answer the phone and gets there on the third squeak. "Hello," he says into the receiver.

"You're home," says Merilyn.

"Uh-huh," Aggie replies.

"I thought you might be out. Job hunting."

He shrugs. "I went to the unemployment office today. I looked on the computer. And through the paper. Nobody's hiring fifty-three year old accounting clerks."

"You're not a *clerk*, you're an assistant accounting manager."

"Was," Aggie says.

"Did you send out your résumé to those places I gave you? Bartlett's pretty well connected. He said you can use his name," she reminds him. Bartlett is her fiancé; she announced that last week. He's about Aggie's age, half a foot taller and he looks like Kevin Kline; Aggie's been compared to Joe Pesci. Bartlett's condo—soon to be Bartlett-and-Merilyn's condo—is barely a mile from Aggie's apartment, in the same building as the one he and Merilyn owned before the divorce. She got that as part of the settlement, and now it's up for sale. He's met Bartlett a few times—both of them were members of the Condo Association's board, although Bartlett joined just a month or two before Aggie moved out, and he co-hosted the going-back-to-college party Mer threw for Penny last month in the community room. Aggie was a "guest."

"Not yet," he says.

"I'm not nagging, but you should do it," she says. "Sitting around the apartment isn't good for you."

The "apartment" is the three small rooms—living room; kitchen/dining room-cum-office; and bedroom, all frayed like the furniture—he's lived in the past eighteen months, since the divorce. Merilyn's never seen it. It's crowded with the debris of their marriage: basically, everything Mer didn't want. He can't stand the place, but he's got a kid in college and—till recently—alimony to pay, and it's what he can afford.

"I don't sit around here," he says.

"Okay," says Merilyn. "Look, I know you're—well, Bartlett isn't something you're used to yet," she says, "but he really is a nice guy, very understanding. We're having some people over

Friday evening, nothing fancy, just drinks and a buffet—all very casually soiree-ish. Oliver's coming, he's bringing Moli; and there'll be some people you know: the Smiths, the Cullinans. He'd—we'd—love to have you come too."

"I gotta go now," he says. He looks at his watch. "I'm supposed to call somebody at three-thirty."

"About a job?"

"Yeah."

"Okay, I'll let you go. You'll think about Friday?"

"I'll think about it."

"You don't have to RSVP. You can just show up. I'll e-mail the info. He's in 28-D."

"I know."

"Well ... Good luck with the call."

"Yeah," he says, "thanks." He says "'Bye" and hangs up without waiting for her reply, then returns to the living room, where, in silence, the dog chasing the cat is being chased by a bull, while the cat is tiptoeing toward the mouse, carrying a sledgehammer. He sits, presses the "mute" button on the remote; sound erupts as the cat brings the hammer down, just missing the mouse. He lights another cigarette and watches.

By 5:30 he's channel surfing and feeling restless. He checks his voicemail just in case: no calls. He sits at the computer in his "office"—the tiny dining table in the kitchen; he eats in the living room, when he cooks, but most of the time he goes to the fast food place on the corner—and checks his e-mail: just some spam and a message from Merilyn formally inviting him to Bartlett's soiree. He goes to a porn site and looks at pictures. They don't *do* anything for him, just two-dimensional images of women he can't have in three dimensions and couldn't even if he had the money. He's fifty-three, well into middle-age, balding and overweight (though he's not *fat*) and, since the divorce and especially since his unemployment, everything reminds him how the world is geared toward slim, pretty people who have twice his money and are half his age. Except for his kids, Aggie doesn't *know* anyone half his age. Their friends—his and Merilyn's—were really her friends. He didn't mind them, they didn't mind him, but he wasn't really close to any of them. Nor to his co-workers of as many as fourteen years (not one of whom has called since he was laid off). There are men he knows well enough to play bridge with, even go to a ball game, but the only person he was, *is*, close to, really the only one he's ever been close to (besides, he supposes, Merilyn), is Penny who's a thousand miles away, in California where she's studying physics, of all things. She calls him every week and e-mails him regularly. Oliver's busy making his first million with his stocks and his golf and his law-student fiancée who calls herself Moli ("it used to be M-O-L-L-Y, but there are *so* many M-O-L-L-Ys" she says). He can't remember the last time Oliver called him. Or that he called Oliver.

He picks up the phone and calls Penny. It's the middle of the afternoon there but they haven't talked, just short e-mails, in more than a week—it's a new semester and she's immersed in schoolwork, and she and Brady are at odds, the way they always are when they're under pressure. If they're having this much trouble when they're just living together, he wonders how they'll cope with married life. If they *get* married. He and Merilyn coped with it better when they were young; it was after the kids grew up, after he started asking What Is My Life About, that trouble set in. He still doesn't know the answer. And, he feels, every day of his life is peeling away, like the calendar pages in old movies.

Penny answers on the first ring. She sounds chipper. "Hi, sweetheart," he says, and she replies with an enthusiastic "Daddy!"

"How y' doin'?" he asks.

"Okay," she says brightly. "Just, Brady's being a pain in the ass and I just wish this damn month was *done* with!"

"Wish you were here. I'd drag you away for couple of hours. Get you a good dinner."

She sighs. "I wish!" She laughs. "Anyway, I couldn't. I've got a Soc paper due Friday and a Chem quiz tomorrow—at eight!"

"So?" he says. "You gotta eat."

"I wish I had time. Honest. We've got leftover pizza in the fridge, that'll do if I get hungry. I probably won't even eat."

He laughs. "Butterflies playing ping pong with the pepperoni?"

She laughs too. "Something like that."

"Well. Take care of yourself, okay?"

"Okay," she says. "Thanks. Um, how are *you*?"

He shrugs. "I'm okay. Getting through the days."

"Good! Well; I'm gonna go study."

"You'll ace it, sweetheart."

"Mm. From your lips to God's ears."

"'Bye," he says.

"'Bye," Penny replies, and hangs up.

He goes to the fast food restaurant, Express Ribs, orders the plate of rib tips and fries and a large Pepsi. Merilyn (and his doctor) would cringe, but never mind them, he wants comfort food and this qualifies. While he's waiting, he stands at the counter and glances through the tri-fold take-out menu for the hundredth time. They've added new items, he notices: lamb chops with mint jelly, Greek-style chicken (*with lemon juice and dill butter sauce!*).

"Here y' go, Aggie," says Enriqué, the swarthy Dominican counterman who always seems to be there.

"Thanks," Aggie says. He puts the menu back on the counter.

"Hey, take one with you," Enriqué says. "We're gonna be delivering; starting next Monday. You live in the neighborhood, right?"

Aggie nods. "Yeah."

"You can call, we'll send it over. Twenty minutes tops."

"That's good to know." He puts a menu in his pocket and starts toward a booth.

"Get you a plate of hot rib tips even if it's raining *gatos y perros*." Enriqué laughs.

"Yeah," Aggie says with a smile, and sits. He doesn't bother lifting the plate from the tray. He's hungry, hungrier than he should be probably since he had a big lunch, and he just dives in.

He knows eating out is expensive: If he ate at home he would save enough in a week to buy two new phones, but, what the hell, a man has to indulge in a few things he enjoys. He glances through the *News* while he eats. Just what he needs: more bad news. Unemployment's up, consumer confidence is down. When he's done he says "'Bye" to Enriqué and goes back to the apartment, but he's still restless. He checks his e-mail again, nothing, takes a shower. When he finishes it's 7:30, still light out. He can feel dinner lying heavily in his stomach; he's gained five or six pounds in the three months he's been out of work. That, plus the ten or fifteen he put on right after the divorce. When he was thirty, he was trim; that, he thinks, was a long time ago.

He decides he'll go for a walk.

It's warm but the sky is overcast so he slips on a windbreaker and a cap and, ignoring the god-awful slow elevator, takes the stairs down the four flights to the ground; then walks through the small lobby, out both doors, and stands on the sidewalk debating: north, south, east or west? There's nowhere in the neighborhood he hasn't walked during his tenancy. Most of it's commercial: small businesses, restaurants, a gym he's thought about joining a dozen times. If he walks east he'll end up in a park but, since it'll be dark in less than an hour, he decides against that. Too many people will be there who don't belong there, after dark. He sighs: life in the big city. Instead, he turns right, south, the direction he least frequently travels.

At the end of the second block there's a bar, Pancho's Villa. He's never been in it—Aggie's never been much of a drinker, particularly alone, and he's still very full, but he stops in front and decides, what the hell, he'll go in. So much for his walk. The television is on, some ballgame, there's a silent juke box, an empty pool table, six tall, small round tables, each with two or three high stools, all vacant; movie stills on the walls and pictures of sports heroes and Mexico, none of Pancho Villa, and the bar itself that looks like a thousand he's seen in movies and TV shows. Three men are sitting there (he guesses the youngest is maybe thirty-five, the others are about his age), apart from each other, beer mugs or shot glasses before them. He picks a stool near the young man, who's drinking beer. The bartender, grizzled and sixty-ish, white apron and plaid shirt, looks away from the game and waves at him.

"Beer" says Aggie.

"Draft?" the bartender asks. "We got Bud and Sam Adams on tap. Bud Light, too."

"Sam Adams," Aggie says.

"Okay. Sam you am" the bartender says and pulls a mug from under the bar. "You want a taco?" he asks. "Tuesday's taco night." He flicks his head at a glass-covered steam table filled with trays of ground beef, melted cheese, lettuce, tomatoes, jalapenos and tortillas. "Fifty cents."

Aggie shakes his head. "Just ate," he says.

"Okay," says the bartender. He fills the mug and sets it in front of Aggie, takes the five he's put there, brings back two-fifty and returns to the game.

He can't remember the last time he had a beer, and it tastes good. He sips it and looks around. The bar, he thinks, is like him, old and wearing out. The wood-paneled walls are scratched and nicked, there are burn marks on the bartop and the felt on the pool table is frayed. He's got to get a job, *something. Got to*. When he first got laid off—they said "laid off" like it was going to be temporary but Aggie knew better—he did look: Places the unemployment office sent him, that he knew from having been in the business for twenty-six years at one place and another, that he heard about through the grapevine or the web or the *News*. He'd accept a lower salary, he told them; sure, his experience was worth something but he understood, everybody was having trouble. He'd prove his worth and, when times got better, they could make it up to him. By actual count he'd gone on eleven interviews and sent another two dozen letters with résumés and references in the first month alone. Now, it's nineteen interviews and he's lost count of the letters. *Nada.* Ignored him, completely. Nobody said it, of course, but he knew: He was too old. They all wanted kids, ambitious, tech-savvy twenty-five year old sharks who were ready to chew their way up the food chain. Like Oliver. *Bunch of assholes*, he thinks and waves his empty mug at the bartender who nods.

"Pint this time?" he asks. "Only half a buck more than the mug."

Aggie shrugs. "Sure" he says, "and I think I'll try a taco. No peppers," and pulls another five out of his pocket.

While he's sitting there, the young guy a couple stools over starts talking to him. At first it's just bar talk, baseball, the weather, TV, then the guy, Guy's actually his name, says he and his wife're having some problems ("I know about *that*" Aggie says). Aggie tells him he's looking for a job and the guy, Guy, tells Aggie the company he works for is expanding, they need an accounting supervisor for one of the divisions. Aggie's never been a supervisor but what the hell, he can do that, can't be much different than being a manager, he tells Guy, and Guy says "Can't be" and writes the information on a napkin for him. "You talk to Judy Palchuk," he says. "Man, she is a *babe*, I don't care if she *is* forty." He thanks Guy and buys him a beer and they talk some more about wives and baseball and jobs and wives again.

"Hey," Guy calls when Aggie gets up to go, "Good luck. Maybe see you around."

"Thanks" says Aggie, and heads into the night. He's a little woozy but he only has the two blocks to walk—*that's good*, he thinks, and grins. He's not sure how many beers he had but they snuck up on him like the cat snuck up on the mouse in the cartoon and then *wham*, the hammer. His head doesn't hurt—now—but he's sure it's going to in the morning.

Wednesday morning he wakes up feeling bloated but, surprise, there's no headache, thank God. He showers and, nine-fifteen sharp, he calls the company, Academy Electric. The HR girl, Judy Palchuk, is cordial and encouraging. She says "We've been using a recruiting firm, but you sound like you've got the right experience," and invites him to come in for an interview on Friday. "How's eleven? In the meantime, e-mail me your résumé, all right?" she says.

So. He sends the résumé and preps a pot of coffee, lights a cigarette. He has two whole days ahead of him. To prepare. He feels okay, maybe a little sluggish, that's probably the beer. Or it could be he's been living what Merilyn calls "an unhealthy life." But he can do something about it: He can join the gym. Yeah, he knows: A couple days won't make a difference but the longest journey begins with, uh-huh, and his pants *have* gotten tight, losing a few pounds has to help. *And* he'll sleep better. The point, he says to himself in the mirror as he shaves, is to *take* the first step. Once he's got the job, he'll change his frame of mind. Answer The Question and Make His Life About Something. In the meantime, he can get himself ready. And, what the hell, maybe he *will* go to Bartlett's party, he'll be able to tell Merilyn he's started working out, he's got a job lined up, a good job, better than he had.

Everything to gain. Nothing to lose. Except that weight.

As he adds cream to his cup, he wonders what Penny had for

dinner.

He plans his arrival at the gym to miss the early crowd, so he'll have plenty of time and space to do whatever he ends up doing. He walks in at 10:30, carrying a canvas bag containing sweats and tennis shoes, and a muscular girl in black tights and a tight white tank top, maybe she's thirty, greets him with a smile and a welcoming hand. She points to a nametag just below her shoulder that reads "Riana" and says "'Rye-ana.' Rhymes with Diana." She guides him into her office, sits and asks: What are your fitness goals, Mr. Agystyn?

Aggie shrugs. "I don't know. Lose some weight. Get, you know, *in shape.*"

"Uh-huh" Riana says, smiling—she has perfect teeth—and explains to him just how the Uptown Fitness Center can help him do that, and more, just $29 a month for a one-year membership, that's on sale now, it's regularly $39. Half now, the rest in sixty days. No initiation fee if he joins this month. And six sessions with a personal trainer are included.

Riana walks him through the facility, shows him the myriad machines and explains their functions, says "hi" and introduces him to a dozen people, exercisers and staff, offers him a complimentary carrot juice from the juice bar (which he declines—*carrot* juice?), and they head back to her office where he signs the contract and gives her a check. "Great!" says Riana. "I'll get your ID made right away and then you can talk with Tom." Tom is a personal trainer, one of the staff he met. He's young, muscular, with a full head of hair. He too has perfect teeth. Aggie laughs to himself. *I should hate this guy*, he thinks.

He does a light workout, because he's winded after five minutes on the treadmill and a few more on a couple of other machines. Tom encourages him, designs a fitness plan which he enters on the computer, and shows Aggie how to enter his workout stats so he can keep track of his progress, his accomplishments. "You'll see," Tom says. "It seems hard now, but in a few weeks you'll realize just how much progress you've made. And you'll see—and feel—the results." Aggie nods. A few weeks of this and the result will be a coffin, he thinks, but he's spent the money, he's *got* to get better, *got to*, and, well... *It's that step.*

A new leaf turned, he leaves the gym, drops his bag at the apartment and goes for a walk. It's a beautiful day; he's gone a mile through the park before he even realizes it. Mid-September: The kids are back in school and the bicycle path is empty so he walks on it, smoking and watching the old men sitting on benches, who watch the young women pushing strollers and watching the babies in them. He's almost to the zoo when he realizes he's hungry, he hasn't had anything today except coffee. He leaves the park and finds a diner. There's a late lunch crowd but he doesn't mind the wait. He buys a *News*, sits at the counter and peruses the menu carefully, decides on a chef salad then changes his mind when he sees what's in it. When the waitress, forty and dowdy, comes he orders cottage cheese and half a cantaloupe, and a glass of skim milk. "Okay, Slim" she says with a grin. When she brings his food he reads and tries to eat slowly; it's hard work, doing that.

The rest of the day he spends on various forms of self-improvement. He buys some workout clothes—he can't have just two pairs of sweats!—and stops at the grocery, where he picks up milk and fresh vegetables and fruit. And a steamer—he'll steam the veggies, they'll be healthier. And a bottle of multi-vitamins at the drugstore. He calls his doctor who agrees to prescribe Rogaine. He picks up a month's supply. He needs to stop smoking, too; the druggist suggests something he says will help him. It's expensive but he's gonna feel good, and look good, too. Damn good!

He feels energized already, animated—the bull chasing the

dog who's chasing the cat who's chasing the mouse! In a burst of enthusiasm he stops at an electronics store and buys a phone. $49.95, but what the hell, it's got bells and whistles like he's never seen. The hell with the resale shop.

Aggie makes dinner, a big salad with "Lite" dressing and some steamed broccoli; he pours a little lemon juice mixed with a half-tablespoon of olive oil and a dash of pepper over it, like Merilyn did. It's good! He's been missing that sort of thing. After dinner he goes for another walk, comes home, does six pushups—all he can manage—applies Rogaine, watches a movie, has one cigarette (cold turkey usually doesn't work, the druggist said; use the aid to help you cut back, and wean yourself off them slowly) and gets to bed early, feeling good, really good—*better than a baptism*, he thinks.

Thursday morning he convinces himself not to smoke while he drinks his coffee. He's jubilant at his success, he goes to the gym, and gets on the treadmill. He's done seven minutes when Tom stops by. "Don't overdo it" he counsels when he sees Aggie striding and puffing. "Don't push yourself too hard, especially early on. Okay?" Aggie, breathing hard, nods. "It takes a while," Tom goes on. "I mean, you didn't get *out* of shape all at once and you can't get back *into* shape that way either." Aggie nods again, puffs some more and decides Tom's right. He takes a break, experiments with a glass of carrot juice (it's not too bad, he decides), then does his prescribed reps on the machines Tom included in his regimen, enters his data and does three more minutes on the treadmill, all he can handle. Then he weighs himself, as Tom did yesterday before he began his workout, and is ecstatic: He's lost three pounds! Already. He showers and smiles at himself in the mirror. *This ain't gonna be so bad*, he thinks. *In fact, it's gonna be easy.*

Lunch is another home-made salad, another splatter of dressing, some cottage cheese, diet soda. He checks his e-mail (there's one from Penny saying she thinks she aced the Chem quiz) and skips the porn, opting instead to surf through health sites. He creates a diet, looks at home gym equipment and reviews job sites—not that he needs to find something, now, but just to see what's out there. He's not surprised when he doesn't find much, but he's pumped: He'll *get* an offer from Academy Electric, so what's *not* on the web doesn't matter.

He goes for another walk in the afternoon, drops off the white shirts that have been scrunched up in the closet (he's going to need them again!) and stops at a coffee house where he sits and glances through the *News* and the free weekly paper. There are a number of attractive women, he notices, most of them reading or working on laptops. They're all college age, too young, but it reminds him he hasn't had a "date" in months. Since the divorce Aggie has had a few what he supposes were dates, women his own age he met though work—divorcées or, in one case, a widow. He had dinner with them at a restaurant, or they went to a movie, coffee afterwards, made small talk; then he'd gone home. They didn't call, neither did he. There just wasn't anything *but* small talk. Or maybe he was out of practice. Jesus. He'd been married almost thirty years, what the hell did he know about *dating*? He did place a personals ad in the free weekly once: there were two responses but when they talked on the phone he couldn't build an interest in meeting either of them.

He reviews the ads as he sips his coffee. They're mostly from men, mostly young. *Maybe it's time*, he thinks, *to try another ad. There's gotta be* some *girls out there*. Or maybe he can meet somebody at the gym. He'd noticed a few over-forties; they were in pretty good shape, too, some of them. Or through one of the internet services. Yeah. He can try that over the weekend.

He's too nervous to sleep well Thursday night. He has two cigarettes while he shines his shoes and watches some cop show, drinks two cups of herbal tea which only makes him wake up in the middle of the night needing to pee, and Friday morning he's up at 7:30, showered and shaved with a pot of coffee brewing by 8:00. He allows himself one cigarette, to calm his nerves, while he checks his e-mail, just in case there's something from the HR girl; there isn't. He dresses carefully—pinstriped navy suit, crisp white shirt, conservative tie—then prints an extra copy of his résumé just in case. He uses mouthwash after his coffee, leaves the cigarettes on the night table so he won't forget and light one, and puts a package of mints into his jacket pocket. He looks in the mirror one last time, and approves: If *he* were Judy Palchuk, he'd hire himself in a heartbeat. He's no kid. *He's* a man.

Even though the appointment isn't till 11:00, he's out the door at 9:20; he prefers not to use the car except in emergencies, and he's not sure how long the bus ride will take. Anyway, Academy Electric is in the heart of the city, and there's bound to be a place where he can wait if he's *too* early.

On the way to the bus stop he passes the gym and peers through the window. Inside, a dozen exercisers are going through their paces, including a slim, maybe-forty-five redhead he saw there yesterday. He'll go after the interview: He'll be psyched anyway, it'll be a good way to burn the extra energy before tonight, before Bartlett's party.

The girl at the reception desk says "Mr. Agystyn to see Ms. Palchuk" into her headset mike, then nods and says "Okay." She smiles at Aggie. "She'll be down in a minute," she says. "Please have a seat."

"Thank you," Aggie murmurs. He sits but he's energized and has trouble staying still.

He stands when the elevator door opens only a few minutes later and a girl gets off. Judy Palchuk is tall, slender, about forty, immaculately coiffed and manicured, and dressed in a steel gray suit. She wears small gold earrings and a watch with a black velvet strap, but no other jewelry. Guy's right, she *is* a babe though there's an I'm-all-business look in her eyes that gives her a certain severity and Aggie a certain pause: He wants her to think he's friendly but he doesn't want to seem familiar. She smiles graciously and offers her hand as she greets him in the lobby, makes small talk as they ride the elevator up to the fifth—top—floor and walks beside him as she guides Aggie to her office. "Judy Palchuk Vice President, Human Resources" is in gold-outlined black letters on the door.

"Thanks for coming," she says.

"Thank *you*, Ms. Palchuk," he answers, "for seeing me."

She says "Hold my calls, Mark" to her secretary, who nods and says "Yes, Ms. Palchuk," then she offers Aggie coffee (he says "No, thank you" and surreptitiously swallows a mint while she refills her cup—a ceramic mug bearing the corporate logo) and a seat, then sits herself. It's a comfortable office that overlooks the company parking lot and, in the distance, the city skyline. *A nice view*, he thinks. It's a big company—he looked it up on the web—but he didn't realize it had such large offices, and Judy Palchuk's is on the top floor, among the pantheon of white collar gods.

"We're a growing firm, Mr. Agystyn," she tells him. "Academy started twenty years ago as a father and daughter working out of one room with a dispatcher. Now, we have this," she spreads her arms at the breadth of the building, "and almost two hundred full-time employees plus about a hundred more who contract with us on a job-by-job basis. And," she adds with a smile, "a lot of *them* average a lot more than forty hours a week."

He nods. "Guy told me," he says.

"That's right, Guy Allen referred you. He's been with us quite a while. Have you known him long?"

Aggie shakes his head and smiles. "As a matter of fact, I just met him."

"Ah," says Palchuk.

For the next twenty minutes they talk amiably; she describes the firm, the job's duties and perks, the benefits and, although everything is pretty clear he asks questions so she'll know he's interested and paying attention: He's been through this process often enough in the past three months to have it down pat. She answers the questions pleasantly, asks him details about his experience, outside interests, salary requirements.

"I was making fifty-eight thousand at Renders" he tells her, "but I'd been there fourteen years. I know things are tough right now, for everyone, so I'd be willing to start lower, say fifty. Once I've proved myself, well, when times get better, you can make it up to me." He laughs, just to show money isn't the be-all and end-all of his world.

She nods. "Oh, fifty-eight is within our range, Mr. Agystyn. For the right person."

"Please," he says, "everyone calls me Aggie." She nods. He senses it's time to take the bull by the horns. "I think I *am* the right person, Judy," he says. "I've done everything you've mentioned. I hope you'll check my references. They'll tell you I'm reliable, I do good work, I'm easy to get along with and, and, and I'm—reliable," he says. He's afraid he sounds desperate. He smiles to show he's relaxed. "Really, I can do whatever you need me to do," he adds. "I may be fifty-three, but I'm willing to learn and I learn quickly."

Palchuk smiles, everywhere but her eyes. "I'm sure you do, Mr. Agystyn."

He smiles back. He's uneasy, for the first time since he sat down. "Well," he says. "Good!" He laughs again.

Palchuk stands up. "I have several people I have to discuss this with," she says.

"Oh," he says, and adds, "of course," trying to conceal his surprise. And his disappointment. He stands, too.

"I'm sure you understand how these things work. It'll be a week or two before we actually make an offer, and Clea

Voynovich—she's the controller—has the final say. She'll be doing the second round of interviews, but you have excellent credentials and I'm glad to have the opportunity to consider you. Assuming you'd like to be considered?" she adds with a small laugh.

He laughs with her. "Yes, I think I'd like that a lot," he says. "And, you'll find, I'm a patient man."

"Well then, Mr. Agystyn. Let me walk you to the elevators. It's kind of a labyrinthine route for the uninitiated." She leads him out, talking casually about the neighborhood, the building, the problems with the elevators. "You'd think an *electrical* firm could solve an *elevator* problem!" she says with a laugh, and again he laughs with her. As they wait for it, she says "Thank you again," and smiles. "We'll be in touch." She extends her hand.

Aggie takes it. "Thank *you*, Judy," he says. "I look forward to it."

On the ride home he reviews the interview. He doesn't know why he's tense; she was very nice, she seemed to like him; she certainly didn't rush him out of her office the way some of the HR people had. He decides he can be hopeful. He didn't say anything that might have embarrassed him, he was aggressive but not too aggressive, nervous, yes, but anyone in HR has to know a lot of people are nervous on a job interview. He did well, he thinks. Maybe not *as* well as he'd have liked, but ... he should have expected there'd be a second interview. After all, the person he'd be working for would want to meet him. Of course she couldn't just offer him the job then and there. Her job was to screen, but she'd be in touch. Probably not till next week, but he could wait. As he'd said: He is a patient man.

He works out, goes for his walk, thinks about the interview and decides, what the hell, what's done is done and he did the best he could, and she *was* encouraging. He checks his voicemail and e-mail when he gets back, nothing on either, and takes a nap—he's tired from the stress and the exercise and from sleeping badly the night before. He sleeps fitfully, half-listening for the phone, wakes up about 6:30, checks his e-mail—still nothing—and decides he'll get to Bartlett's party about 9:00— late enough that he won't be one of the early arrivals—it starts at 8:00—who'll get stuck talking to no one but Merilyn and Bartlett till the bulk of the guests arrive, but not too late: *He'll* be one of "the bulk of the guests." Merilyn's wrong, he doesn't mind the idea of Bartlett (although, truth is, talking with him isn't high on Aggie's list of priorities; the guy *is* marrying his wife. Ex-wife). He *does* like Mer, but there just wasn't anything there any more, between them. They liked each other, even during the proceedings, and still do—but love? Sometimes he wonders if they had ever loved each other. It was the late '70s, they got married because everyone else was getting married; even though they waited a few years they eventually had kids because everyone else was having kids. Now? Well, they probably talked more now—certainly more easily—than they had the last few years of their married life. But thinking about her, their marriage, is thinking about the past: it's passed. He has to keep moving forward. "Life goes on," his lawyer told him after everything was said and done. "For a while you'll think it doesn't, but it does."

He showers slowly and dresses carefully, even shines his shoes again. He's hungry—he worked out almost half an hour and all he's had to eat was a lettuce and tomato sandwich and a glass of milk—but he doesn't eat anything, figuring there'll be plenty of food at the party. He'd planned to walk but the Weather Channel is forecasting rain, so he calls a cab for 8:45. He's restless, though, can't sit still. He decides he'll go to the bar, have *a* beer, *a* cigarette—that won't spoil his progress *and* he deserves it, a reward, and damn it, he's still thinking about the interview, he's still tense, and a beer will relax him. Then he'll catch a cab on the street. If it rains he can call for one and wait inside. He cancels the time order, grabs a folding umbrella and his raincoat, and walks the two blocks.

Pancho's Villa is busier tonight and the crowd is mostly young. He should have figured: Friday. The juke box is playing music he doesn't know, some rock singer croaking words he can't make out, and a couple of couples are alternately dancing to it and playing pool. One of the girls, a slinky brunette with a chest out to here, makes a terrific bank shot and her partner, tall and dark, gives her a congratulatory slap on her ass; she smiles and slaps *his* ass. Aggie pinched Mer's ass a few times when they were kids, but he never *slapped* it, and she never slapped his. They never played pool, either. Only bridge and Scrabble.

The tables are filled but there's room at the bar and, as he makes his way toward it, he sees Guy sitting there. "Hey," he calls out. "Hey. Guy." Guy looks at him, blankly for a moment, then breaks into a big smile.

"Hey Aggie" he calls back. "How you doin', man?"

Aggie sits beside him, lights a cigarette and orders a mug of Sam for himself and a pint for Guy. He tells him enthusiastically about the interview. Talking about it, like this, he feels better. *It is going to happen*!

"Hey, man," Guy says, "way to *go*." He raises his hand; it takes Aggie a moment to realize what's expected, but then he raises his own and Guy slaps his palm. "That Judy?" he says. "Ain't she a *babe*."

"Uh-huh" Aggie agrees, grinning.

"But ya gotta be a little careful with her," Guy goes on. "I mean, man, sometimes? She is one uptight lady." He swallows half the pint. "I been there, like ten, eleven years, and at the Christmas party last year, I ask her to dance?—That's it, just: 'Hey, Judy, how 'bout a dance,' and she says, 'No, thank you Mr. Allen.' *Mr. Allen.* Like she just met me the first time. And she's like that with everybody: Mr. this and Ms. that." He laughs. "'And it's *Ms.* Palchuk,' she says to me. 'Ms. Palchuk.'"

Aggie nods and thinks to himself: *What did I call her? It was Ms. I think.* Except at the end—by the elevator. Well, she couldn't hold *that* against him, it was just a parting geniality. He laughs a little nervously. He's not sure. Maybe he shouldn't have, maybe he said something else wrong, or the wrong way. She'd been cordial but, what the hell, being cordial was part of her job. Just like being professional is; she *shouldn't* seem too enthusiastic. About anyone. But maybe she was *just* being cordial. Maybe she was just going through the motions, what the hell, he was already there, she'd set aside the time. Maybe, when he left, she stuck his résumé in the "forget about *him*" file. *No, she said she'd be in touch. And why shouldn't she be?* He *does have* the credentials, he *is* reliable. He just had to be patient, that was all. He'd be ready, when the second interview came around. But maybe he shouldn't have told her his age. Maybe he's too old, or she wants someone younger, her age, a man she can relate to personally as well as professionally; but damn it, *she can't just ignore him.* "Like all the others" he mumbles. Who the hell does Judy Palchuk think she is! "I think it went well," he says, to himself. *It* has *to have. Has to.*

"That's good, man," says Guy, and shakes his head. "She sure is a babe," he says ruefully. "Too old for me," and there's a twinkle in his eye as he adds "but maybe not for you, huh?"

Aggie laughs—*Judy Palchuk?*—and shakes his head. He doesn't have any illusions about himself. He looks and he wishes, and sometimes he's fantasized, but he knows he's not the sort of man "babes" are drawn to. He never was. He and Mer got together because, well, because they were both members of the un-smart set: not bad-looking, not poor, not dumb—just ordinary and average like, he thinks, most people. He knew even then he wasn't going to live a special life. Average was okay. Not everyone can be president. You take what life gives you and you try to be happy with it but, whatever, you get through it. Like he has the last two, three years. Like his father did. "Life is something you get through," his father told him. "Last sixty-five, seventy years, it's all you can ask." His father died at fifty-four. A heart attack.

He doesn't know why, maybe it's because his own fifty-fourth birthday is four months away, but he tells Guy about his father. Aggie hasn't talked about him in he doesn't remember how long. He had a hard life, too, never got what he wanted. Hell, he never got *any*thing, except Aggie's mother—a kind woman but a helpless one who was always sick—and her medical bills that he couldn't pay. Guy nods, sympathizes but says "At least you grew up with him. My old man, he walked out when I was five." He finishes his beer and Aggie orders another round and thinks *Maybe I should eat something*. Friday is hot dog night, they're fifty cents, but he decides to hold out. One more beer is one thing, but, he knows, he'll eat at the party.

The bar keeps filling up, the smoke has thickened and the music's constant. Aggie's had three or four beers, pints now, when he hears laughter near the pool table. He looks: The brunette and her partner are dancing, well, standing there and rubbing up against each other in time to the beat. His hands are all over her. Aggie looks away. He and Merilyn slept together but that was all for a year or more before the divorce and since it, well, he's had those dates but nothing "up close and personal," as Oliver (leeringly) describes his relationship with Moli—how can anybody look that way when he's talking about his *fiancée*! He gulps the pint and waves for another. "Make it a pitcher," he says, and Guy slaps him on the back and says "Hey." *Moli*, he thinks. *Who the hell calls herself "Moli."* He looks at the brunette and her partner. She's nibbling at his neck; he's rubbing her ass.

He supposes Bartlett rubs *his* hands all over Merilyn's ass. *Jesus*, he thinks: *She is sleeping with Bartlett. She is* screwing *him.*

149

For some reason, that hasn't occurred to him until now. The idea surprises him. He pours from the pitcher, empties his glass and fills it again. Who the hell does Bartlett think he is? Who the hell does Merilyn think *she* is?

"Who the hell does she think she is" he mutters, and Guy, whose eyes are bright and glassy, turns to him.

"Who?" he mumbles.

"Huh?" says Aggie.

"Who the hell does *who* think she is?"

Aggie just shakes his head.

"Hey," says Guy. "Let's have a real drink. What'll y' have, I'm buyin'? Hey!" he waves to the bartender.

A real drink. Aggie *used* to drink Scotch, a shot—one—before dinner, sometimes a Scotch and soda when he and Mer went somewhere. Maybe a couple every year at the office Christmas party. There's a bottle of Dewar's somewhere in the apartment, unopened. "Scotch" he says. "Dewar's on the rocks."

"Dewar's on the rocks," Guy calls, "and a Bushmill's, straight up." When they come, Guy clinks his glass against Aggie's. "To your new job" he says, and tosses it back.

"Yeah" Aggie mutters, and swallows his Scotch.

When he looks at his watch it's twenty after nine. He's late—well, later than he expected to be. "Hey," he tells Guy, "I gotta go to the party." He's had five or six beers and two shots. He's feeling no pain. In fact, he's not sure he's feeling much of anything and grabs at the bar for support as he gets unsteadily to his feet. "Whoops" he says. Guy laughs.

"Hey, man, you okay?" he asks.

Aggie's not sure, but he *is* going to the goddamn party. Soiree. Whatever. He picks up his umbrella and raincoat from the bar. He'll walk, he decides. That'll clear his head. He tells Guy good night and opens the door where he's met by a deluge so thick he can't see the streetlights until, a moment later, there's lightning. He mutters "Hell" and pulls out his cell. There are taxi company numbers on the back of the door and he dials one. A recording answers and asks him to please hold, tells him his call is important, someone will be with him soon. He waits, two minutes, three, before a heavily accented female voice says "What is your destination?" He tells her, and where he is, and his name and phone number. She repeats everything, says "Thirty minutes" and hangs up. *Thirty minutes?* Aggie calls another company. This time he's on hold nearly five minutes before a real voice answers and tells him it'll be forty minutes to an hour. He grumbles "never mind" and looks out Pancho's Villa's window. The rain's lighter. He decides to walk. Or maybe he can catch a bus, or a cab on the street. He looks back at Guy who's staring into his beer, and walks out.

There are no empty cabs and the only bus that passes him speeds by while he's almost a block from the stop. He runs after it, waving and shouting *"Hey!"* but it doesn't stop. *"Asshole!"* he yells. A woman hurrying along across the street looks at him, then picks up her pace.

The rain is steady; the umbrella's not much help and the coat's not either. He ducks into a liquor store for a few minutes, hoping it will let up. He suddenly has to pee something fierce. "Goddamn rain" he mutters, dripping, and the man behind the counter says "Yeah, it's killin' business. Never rains on a weeknight, only weekends," and lets him use the bathroom. Aggie feels obligated to buy something so he gets a half pint of Dewar's. He mulls over whether to open it—the store is air conditioned and he's wet and chilled—but he knows he's had too much already and just sticks the bag in his coat pocket, sighs, then walks back into the rain. Ten minutes later when he gets to the building he's damp from the belly up and soaked from the waist down, he can feel his feet squishing in his shoes. He's a little drunk and a lot pissed: *All the trouble he took, wasted!*

He comes into the mirror-tiled lobby and wipes his face with his hanky which is still wet from wiping his face in the liquor store. "Wet out there," he says with a grin to the guy at the security desk, who nods and says "Guess *so*," then adds: "Mr. Agystyn?"

"Yeah?" says Aggie.

"I thought that was you" Mr. Security says with a smile. "I ain't seen you, must be a couple years. I'm Stuart. Stu. The weekend guy?"

Aggie wrinkles his forehead, then says "Stu. Sure, I remember you. How've you been?"

"Good, I been good." He laughs. "Got a new baby, a boy. First one! Last month. That makes three."

"Congratulations," says Aggie.

"Here" says Stu, "I got some towels." He takes Aggie's dripping coat and offers him a roll of Bounty. "You dry yourself off. What you been doin'?"

Aggie takes the roll and drops it. He starts to bend over, which makes him dizzy, and he leans against the security desk.

"Here" says Stu. "I'll get it. You okay, Mr. Agystyn?" Aggie sits on the desk, suddenly and heavily. "Yeah" he manages. "Just a little dizzy. Goddamn rain," he mutters. "Couldn't get a cab."

Stu gives him the towels again and watches as Aggie tries to dry himself. "So where you headed?" Stu asks him.

"Twenty-eight D" Aggie says. "Twenty-eighth floor."

Stu smiles. "Sure is. Mr. Embry's unit. Lot of people up there." He laughs. "I just heard something t'night about him gettin' married. Thanksgiving weekend, I think. Maybe this's his bachelor party."

Aggie laughs. "Getting married," he says. "How 'bout that!"

Stu announces him and offers to hang his coat in the security closet so it'll dry faster. Aggie nods thanks. The elevator rushes up to twenty-eight; it makes him dizzy and he holds onto the door; when it opens he steps out slowly. The hallway looks just like the one on nine, where their unit was: wallpaper with silver lilies on a pale blue background, blue-gray ceramic flower sconces every few feet with white silk lilies in them, navy carpeting. Aggie is still wet. And disheveled. He arranged his suit in the lobby, dried his shoes, re-combed his thin hair. But he looks like hell. For a moment he thinks about getting back into the elevator and going home, or maybe back to Pancho's Villa, but then the elevator starts its descent and he's stuck there. He can press the button and wait, or he can go forward into the fray.

"Fuck it" he murmurs, and walks to the end of the hall. He hears sounds through the door: voices, music, laughter. He taps with the brass knocker that's a pair of initials: BE. Once, twice, three times. "Hey," he shouts, "open the goddamn," and before he says *door* it opens and Merilyn's there. She's wearing pale blue slacks and a fluffy lavender cashmere sweater. A silver-circled sapphire on a chain, silver, maybe platinum, hangs between her breasts, and an unfamiliar diamond ring is on her left hand.

"Aggie," she says with a big smile. "You came."

"Uh-huh," he mutters. A vagrant drop of water falls from his ear to the carpet.

Merilyn's smile disappears. It's replaced by concern. She sniffs the air discreetly. "Are you—okay?" she asks softly.

Aggie nods. "I'm fine. Just fine."

"Well," she says hesitantly. "Come in. I'll get you a towel. Oh, dear. Your shoes are soaked. Why don't you take them" she indicates "off" and points to a closet just inside the doorway.

"Sure," says Aggie. He tries to take off a shoe but he can't balance himself and gives up. "Hey—guess what. I joined a gym. And I had a job innerview, I mean, in*ter*view, this morning. Big deal job at a big deal company."

"That's wonderful," says Merilyn as a man Aggie recognizes as Bartlett Embry walks into the foyer behind her.

"Aggie," he says. "I'm really glad you came. Come on in, you look like you just got out of the pool," he says and laughs. "Mer, get him a towel, okay? Aggie, you want some dry clothes? I can get you a sweatshirt or something; it'll be loose, but it'll be dry. How 'bout a drink?"

"Sure," Aggie says. He swings and just misses Bartlett's chin.

He doesn't have much on the punch and Bartlett grabs his fist in mid-follow-through. Merilyn gasps and goes to call a cab but Oliver offers to drive him home, and he and Bartlett ease Aggie to the elevator. Stu puts him into his coat while Oliver gets his car, and together they load him into it. Oliver puts the car, a year old Lexus, into gear; they drive off through the rain.

"Jesus, Dad," Oliver says, staring at the road but shaking his head.

He's never gotten along particularly well with his son, never really *liked* him. Oliver was a straight A student through high school and college, got his BA and is a soon-to-be-finished thesis away from an MBA. He's a rising shark at the securities firm where *everyone* likes him. From his earliest years, he's never needed Aggie, never wanted fathering from him. He asked Mer to drive him to Little League, and she always helped him with his homework. Oliver and Moli, a doe-eyed, size two, intense young woman who edits the *Law Review* and sways instead of walks, plan to get married as soon as she passes the bar.

"Mm?" Aggie mumbles.

Oliver looks at him. "Jesus," he mutters and taps, *thuds*, on the steering wheel with the heel of his hand. "*Jesus H. Christ!*" he says through clenched teeth; this time it's an expletive. "You - fucking - failure." He shakes his head. "I can't believe they even in*vi*ted you."

They drive the rest of the way in silence. Oliver helps him into the elevator, holds him steady as it crawls upward, unlocks the door with Aggie's keys and guides him through it. He watches Aggie stumble in and onto the sofa where he sits, glassy-eyed.

"Good night" Oliver says. He drops the keys on the coffee table and leaves. *At least he didn't slam the door*, Aggie thinks.

He peels off his wet coat, takes the bottle of Scotch from the pocket, kicks off his shoes and sits there, thinking *I should've eaten something*, then *I should make some coffee* and *I better take some aspirin*. But he doesn't move, except to pick up the remote. He clicks the TV on, mutes the sound, and watches cartoons, mice and cats and dogs and bulls, all chasing each other relentlessly, until he falls asleep.

Saturday morning he wakes up at 10:00, stiff and with the mother of all hangovers. The TV is still on and more creatures, this time alien-looking ones, are chasing each other across the silent screen. He turns the set off, strips and heats a cup of leftover coffee. He doesn't trust himself in the shower yet.

He remembers last night clearly and doesn't want to think about it. He supposes he'll call Merilyn later, apologize to her and to Bartlett: *I was an ass, I'm sorry, I just had a few drinks on an empty stomach, you know how that is.* Thank God nobody else saw him, except Oliver. He'll call Oliver and apologize to him too, though he really has no interest in ingratiating himself with that smug little bastard.

Aggie gazes out the kitchen window which overlooks the alley. It's dark and raining. *Gatos y perros.* He doesn't know what he's going to do today: A walk is out, unless the rain lets up, and he's *way* too groggy to even think about the gym. He'll do it tomorrow. Anyway, Tom said he should skip a day now and then. Then he remembers: He was going to look up internet dating services. Nobody can see him looking like this, so the 'net is the perfect place to "be." Maybe he can even get a date for tonight, that would help him forget about last night's fiasco. If he does, he won't drink. Anything.

He turns on the computer and heats another cup of coffee

while it loads. He checks his voicemail—nothing—then logs into his e-mail, sees one from Penny from last night and, below it, one from "jpalchuk@academyelectriccorp.biz" that came in at 6:56 p.m. according to the "date/time" column of his inbox. Damn it, he thinks, I should've checked one more time before I went out. Well, it *was* Friday *and* after hours. He can reply now, she probably won't get it till Monday but what the hell, if they're there on Saturday he'll get cleaned up and go in. He swallows some coffee and clicks the message.

"Dear Mr. Agystyn:" he reads. *"I want to thank you again for interviewing with us for Academy Electric's Accounting Supervisor position. I appreciate your interest in the company and the chance to talk with you about it.*

"As you know, we've seen a number of candidates for the position and, while your credentials are, as I said, excellent, Ms. Voynovich and I have discussed them and we feel there are several others whose backgrounds are also strong, and whose specific experience in this industry makes them better suited to our needs.

"With your permission, I'll keep your résumé on file and, should something else in our accounting area become available, I'll get in touch with you about it.

"Again, thank you, and I wish you much success.

"Sincerely,

"Judy Palchuk

"Vice President, Human Resources

"Academy Electric Corporation"

He reads the message twice, the second time very slowly. Then he stares at the screen, as though something is going to change what's written there. He takes a sip of coffee, reads the message one more time, then deletes it. His head still aches but he feels perfectly sober. He finishes the coffee and takes a shower.

He hurries through the downpour to Express Ribs for an early lunch; Enriqué reminds him: They'll deliver as of Monday, he won't need to go out in *this*. When he's done, Aggie rents a DVD from the video store that's next to it, goes home, puts it in the player and sits watching it. When it ends he plays it again, this time with the sound off. The people on the screen move from place to place, senselessly, cars chase cars, things explode in technicolor silence. He debates calling Bartlett and Merilyn to apologize and decides not to. Monday will be soon enough. He checks his voicemail again. Merilyn's called: Is he okay? He deletes the message and checks his e-mail. He realizes he's forgotten to open Penny's, the only unread one in his inbox. He clicks it and reads:

"Dad!

*"The Soc paper is **in** and the results are back from the Chem quiz: 98%, an A!*

"Mom said you might be going to her party, well, Mr. Embry's party, tonight. I hope you have a great time. Really, he's not too bad a guy.

"And I hope the job hunt is going well, too. I know you'll find something really *good. Soon.*

"Talk to you soon.

"Love,

"Penny"

Aggie moves the message to his "Penny" file. He looks outside; it's still raining. The clock on the computer says it's 4:57. Too early for dinner.

He reaches for a cigarette, the pack's empty so he gets a fresh one from the carton, takes it and walks into the living room. The rain is coming down heavier, drumming loudly against the windows. He lights a cigarette, picks up the remote, turns on the TV, looks at the screen. Animated faces look out at him.

THE EASY LOVIN' BLUES

1962

She can hear them rehearsing in the apartment directly above hers, the singer and the trumpeter.

"*I got the easy-lovin' blues, Those easy-lovin' blues*" she sings, while he travels up and down the chords in long, legato lines, the notes a little unevenly blown but played with the same aching heartfeel the words convey. "*I fall in love on Monday, Come the weekend I feel used, 'Cause all the things he said, Whispered in my bed, They just led to the blues. I'm singin' the blues,*" she goes on, her voice deep and dark as the song itself.

In her third-floor apartment Naurean tries to listen to the old phonograph that's playing "Serenade in Blue," the volume high to cover the din upstairs, and she revisits The War, the bands, the days and, especially, the nights of her girlhood. Now she smiles as she watches the young girl in a white silk dress, in the embrace of a tall, dark-haired young man in a dark blue suit; they dance together in wide arcs around the room.

"*My Mama always wanted me t' be a dancer,*" she tells the couple, dreamily. "*When I was a little girl she would take me to Danceland at all hours, and we'd watch the girls swoop 'cross the floor, graceful as swans, the boys whirlin' them so their pretty dresses fluttered. She never danced; not there, anyhow—she couldn't, what with her leg and all—but she did at home, with me. That's how I learned: 'Naurean, you got to learn,' she said, 'a girl's only really alive when she's dancin'.' So I learned. And when I did?—I was aleven—she was so proud. That summer? she picked out a boy for me—Jim was his name—and she stood watchin' with this look of complete rapture 'cross her face as though bein' with Jim made me the most beautiful thing that ever walked upon the earth.*"

The voice in the hall disrupts her reverie.

"Mrs. Rossell?" it bellows. "Hey!"

The young couple fades from sight.

"What?" she whispers, watching them disappear.

"Turn that record down!" the fiery voice commands. "People're tryin' t' sleep … Mrs. Rossell! *Naurean Rossell*?"

"What?" she calls.

"You gone deaf or somethin'?" the voice says, and its owner raps sharply on Naurean's door. "C'n you hear me? I said turn that record down. It's past nine o'clock at night! Decent people're sleepin' this hour."

She stands up and goes to the phonograph, calling "I'm sorry, Mrs. Andrews. Is that better?" but before Mrs. Andrews can answer, she hears another voice at the door—"I'll do it, Gretchen. Leave her alone."—and the turning of the brass doorknob—"Oh, *you're* home," Mrs. Andrews says—and then Amanda opens the door and stands there, facing the dragon.

"Yes, Gretchen," she says, "*I'm* home. Now *you* c'n go home too."

Mrs. Andrews—Gretchen—snorts. "A' right," she mutters—her slippers flip-flop two doors down the uncarpeted hall—"Just, you tell 'er t' *keep* that noise down. Decent people're—"

"—tryin' t' sleep" Amanda says with her, and sighs. "I know, I know. G'd evenin', Gretchen." She steps into the apartment, closes the door behind her and leans against it.

"She is such a…" says Naurean. She turns off the record player and stands, shaking her head, exasperatedly running through the things she *should* have said while Mrs. Andrews was still close enough that she might have heard them.

"I know, I know," Amanda says. She comes in and drops her sweater, bookbag and pocketbook on an end table. "Sorry I'm s' late; I, um—it was so busy, all day, I was six cents off so I had t' stay late t' balance the drawer. I, um, I didn't have time for supper before class so I stopped for some after. I was *so* hungry. Then I decided t'—."

"*Wretch*-en," announces Naurean. "That *ought* t' be her name." She laughs with satisfaction at having de-fired the dragon. "How was work?"

Amanda sighs. "Oh, work is just fine and dandy, Mama. You *know* I just love smilin' and gettin' pinched and givin' other people money eight hours ev'ry day." She sits on the sofa and takes off her shoes. The heels aren't really high, but she's been wearing them since eight in the morning and her feet are killing her. *Someday* she's gonna remember to take a pair of sneakers.

"Well," says Naurean, cheerfully, "It's only for a little while longer."

"Mm," Amanda replies noncommittally.

"It *is* only for a little longer. You'll finish up your course, you'll get yourself a *good* job, executive secr'tary or somethin'. Everything'll change."

Amanda snorts. "I'll get t' sit in 'n office all day 'stead a standin' in the bank. The only thing *that*'ll change is where I'm gettin' pinched."

"Or somethin'. I said 'or somethin'.'" Naurean sits in the stuffed chair across from her daughter and straightens the carefully polished coffee table, which is already in perfect order, restored to its position and shined with Pledge after the students—and their fingerprints—left. "You got all kinds 'f potential; I expect you c'd work your way up t' one of those adminastrative assistant positions. *That's* where you'll meet the really—I mean, those are the really good jobs. Responsible."

"Mm." Amanda leans against the back of the sofa and tucks her feet under her, rubbing one, then the other. "I, I was thinkin' t'day? Maybe I c'd, I don't know, work in a nightclub or somethin'."

"A nightclub?" Naurean says. "Now what put *that* idea in your head?"

Amanda shrugs. "I don't know.—It'd be more excitin' than a bank, anyway."

"Well!"

Amanda reaches into her bag and takes out the brightly colored brochure she stuck in her accounting text, and opens it.

It shows faraway places, exotic structures: the Riviera, the Statue of Liberty, the Eiffel Tower, the pyramids. "Or, maybe one of those travel places," she says, and offers the flyer to Naurean who nods at it a moment, then refolds it and lays it on the table between them. "This girl at the bank?" Amanda goes on, "her sister's at one and she gets t' fly, all over the world practic'ly f'r free. See ev'rything." She picks up the brochure, notices the Eiffel Tower has a smudge, probably from when they were lookin' at it during supper. She puts the flyer in her pocketbook. "Well," she says, "that's just a dream."

Naurean sits beside her on the sofa and gives her a big hug. "You shouldn't be so negative, Mandy. You got to think good things'll happen in order t' make them happen." She smiles.

"Yeah. I'm always *thinkin'* good things're gonna happen, but …" She hugs Naurean back. "You seem t' be in 'n awful good mood."

"Oh, I am," Naurean says, and sits up and claps her hands. "I had five students t'day, two of them new, little girls, and you know what?"—she leans forward and lowers her voice, confidentially—"One 'f them, she was brought in by this young man, her uncle, such a nice young gentleman, and he's a professional dancer, travels *all* over, said he heard about me and told his brother *I* was the one who ought t' be teachin' Lynn Ann—that's her name, the little girl, his niece? And the uncle—he was such a nice young gentleman." She laughs. "He actually asked me t' dance with him. *Insisted.*"

"He did?" Amanda says, not meaning to sound incredulous.

Naurean sniffs. *Amanda*—who is twenty—thinks her mother is old—too old that a "nice young gentleman" would ask her to dance. Much less *insist.* "You don't need to act so surprised."

"Mama, I just …" Amanda says, and shrugs.

Naurean smiles and laughs. Well, yes, Mandy would think that. When she was twenty *she* would have thought that about *her* mama, too. "Anyway," she says, "I said—fin'ly—I said I would." She looks away, remembering: *such* a nice young man. It was like when she was a girl, and *all* the young men wanted to dance with her, and she'd float about the dance floor in her dress, white silk—moiré; nearly transparent under the bright lights—and lace; and her hair: done up with pearls. And a tiara, as a matter of fact. Gold—white gold, to go with the pearls. It had been so lovely. *She* had been so lovely. And she can be again. She's tiny—small people don't show their age the way bigger ones do—she doesn't weigh an ounce more than she did then, her skin still glows, and there aren't any lines on her face, practically. Life wasn't just remembering, not just the past. Such wonderful words: *Would you care to dance with me?* She sighs. "I most definitely would," she says quietly.

"Oh?"

She looks back at Amanda, recalls the conversation. "Oh, not in front of the *stu*dents, of course. But he was practic'ly pleadin'. *And* he paid for Lynn Ann in advance. For *three* weeks. She's gonna come ev'ry Friday." She reaches into her pocket and takes out neatly folded money, a thick packet of mostly dollar bills.

"Well, that's good," says Amanda. "When you goin'?"

Naurean laughs. "Oh, we're not *go*ing. Out, I mean. He's comin' over here. T'morrow night." She hesitates. "I—I thought it would be …easier."

"Mm." Amanda rouses herself and hangs her sweater in the front closet. "Well," she says, "I s'pose I can go t' the movies."

"You don't have t' go anyplace. We're just gonna dance one 'r two dances, then maybe talk a little while." Naurean puts the money into her coin purse and tucks that away.

Amanda takes the barrette out of her hair and shakes it out. She has beautiful hair, it falls over her shoulders, strawberry blond. "Mama, I don't think a man wants t' come over on a Saturday night f'r one 'r two dances and a little talk." She gets her brush from her purse and begins to brush her hair.

"Let me do that?" says Naurean.

"I can do—" she begins, then nods her head and smiles. Mama loves to brush her hair. She hands Naurean the brush and sits with her back to her.

Naurean draws it carefully through the lush brilliance: so much like her own, when she was Mandy's age. Oh, how men admired it! "Now, what would you know about what men want t' do?" she asks coyly.

"Oh, I hear all sorts a things 'bout it, from the girls at the bank." She mutters: "The boys, too."

"And when're you gonna start finding out for yourself?"

Amanda turns and grins. "Prob'ly 'bout the same time you start gettin' gray hairs." Naurean laughs—she just likes to keep her hair lookin' pretty, that's all, and gray just isn't a pretty color—and Amanda turns back. "Anybody else pay you?" she asks.

"Mrs. Doyle gave me six dollars toward Stevie." She resumes brushing.

"Mm. So now she's only *five* weeks behind."

"No," corrects Naurean, "just three. It *was* five, includin' today's, but now it's only three."

"Mama, you need to make her stay up to date. All of them."

"I know, Mandy." She sighs and holds the brush in her lap; "but I can't just turn them out. 'Specially Stevie. He's just about the only little *boy* I have."

"Yes, you can. We got bills too. And I'm not gettin' a raise till the spring."

"Well, I'll talk to her. *All* of them."

"Mm." Amanda gets up, takes the brush and kisses Naurean's head. "Thanks, Mama," she says. "I'm gonna change."

"You goin' somewhere?" Naurean asks hopefully.

"Not unless the bathtub counts," Amanda says en route to the bathroom.

"Y' know, it *is* Friday night."

"I *know*." She stops at the door and turns back in. "We have this conversation *ev'*ry Friday night."

"We wouldn't, if you ever went somewhere."

"Mama!" Amanda says, and turns on the bathtub.

"Yes?" replies Naurean, in perfect innocence.

"Don't you start up on that. 'Sides, you never go anywhere either."

"Well, *I'm*—not a girl any more." Naurean sighs. What's to become of Amanda? She's so bright, so pretty. And so like a ... hermit. *That's* gotta *come from her Daddy's side.* "Anyway, I used to. It's not normal, Mandy, a girl your age *never* goin' anywhere. I worry about you, what's gonna happen if *I*, I mean ... I—"

"I *know* what you mean, Mama," Amanda says. "I'm closin' the door now."

"—mean, my goodness," Naurean continues, "here you are al*rea*dy twenty; how're you gonna *meet* a—anyone? I used t' have lots of friends when I was twenty. Boys *and* girls. And, and, why, when I was your age I went—"

"—dancin' ev'ry night" Amanda says, in perfect unison, then adds: "I know, I know."

The bathroom door closes, all but the crack to let the steam out. Amanda settles into the hot water and closes her eyes. This is where she can dream a little, everything's a little gauzy from the steam and she looks at things the way *she* wants to see them. She can remember, things like supper tonight, and maybe even imagine goin' to one of those places in the brochure. Together. That'd be nice, they'd ride in—.

Naurean calls: "Well I did!" Then she walks to the bathroom, stands by the door and goes on. "It was my duty, those boys, they needed someone to dance with them. The world was comin' apart, I was just a nice little ...flower, *planted*, right there, in the middle of it..."

She hears Amanda's quiet "Oh, Mama" and walks back to the living room, sits on the sofa, and looks at her picture, framed on the mantel. She's nineteen in it, at Danceland in her white silk dress, with such a nice young man in a dark suit—navy, she recalls—at her side. "I look so pretty," she murmurs, "like a flower," and she smiles as she watches the girl in the photograph step forth from it. "One of them told me that," she tells the girl, who smiles at her as the tall, dark young man steps out of the picture as well—now wearing neatly pressed, perfectly creased khakis—and music starts to play. He takes her into his arms and they begin to dance.

"*Jim, his name was*," she remembers aloud. "*'You're a flower,' he said. And he smiled at me like a young gentleman would smile at a flower. At first. Then*—then *he smiled like a young gentleman would smile at a, I don't know, exactly, at a chorus of dancin' girls, I guess, that sly, slick sort of smile that looked so dashin' with his uniform. All the girls at the USO wanted t' dance with him, the minute he came in we all started talkin'.*" She giggles. "*Even me. He was so handsome. When he came up t' me and asked me t' dance? I blushed. Honest to Pete I did. But he danced so well, from the very start I could close my eyes, and it felt like we were some place else, someplace wonderful. I fell in love with him, that very first dance, b'cause*—…" She looks at the dancing couple. There is a white flower pinned on the young man's uniform, over the breast pocket, a white rose in fact, that she's never noticed! "*Because he had a flower on his shirt, this beautiful little white rose, and while we were dancin' he stopped and he took it off and he gave it to me. And then he smiled again, and he said: 'Naurean, you are a wonderful partner.' And I said: 'You mean, a dancin' partner?' And he said: 'I mean, a partner. For dancing, and for always.'*"

She watches; at last, the couple dances away and the music fades. "And three days later we got married," she murmurs, "and two days after that he was sent to the war … And I never saw him again. And then nine months later…" She shakes her head and picks up the photograph. *We looked so handsome together, Jim and me.* "A white rose," she says softly. "Right over his breast."

"He was wearin' a *white rose*?" says Amanda, standing behind her in a white robe.

"Hm? Oh, I didn't know you were—yes," Naurean says, "he did."

Amanda pats her face with a towel. "Hnh. You never told me that. About the flower."

Naurean laughs, an easy laugh. "I didn't?" she says, as a trumpet begins to lilt in long, mournful phrases above them. "Well, silly me. It was *only* the highlight of my twenty-first year."

"Mm," says Amanda, and looks up.

"He was such a gentleman," Naurean says and shakes her head slowly, then notices Mandy staring at the ceiling. "Trumpy better be quiet or Gretchen'll be after him. Though I suppose she can't hear him like we do. She prob'ly can't hear *him* at all. I mean, the way she fawns in the hall whenever he's goin' upstairs. You'd think he was Loo-is Armstrong, somebody like that." She gets her account book from the desk drawer, opens it and begins to note the day's payments. "And *her*—she must think she's some kinda royalty, the way she carries on. '*Lady-blue.*' Hmp. Been here not even a month and she acts like she owns the place." She turns to Amanda who's in the stuffed chair, her eyes closed, and smiling. "This mornin'? She was sittin' right in the *mi*ddle of the steps when I got back from the groc'ry and I asked her, very nicely, to please move so I could get by? And *she* said? She said—"

"Oh, well," Amanda says, "they'll be leavin' in a little while."

"—somethin' *aw*ful, I can't even—Leavin'? They are?"

"Goin' out. They're startin' another job. For a month this time."

"Well!" says Naurean.

The trumpet switches to bop scales, quick staccato runs up and down. Amanda gets up and starts toward her room. "Some little club. The Paradise *Ca*fé it's called."

"When'd you find all this out?"

Amanda stops. "Oh," she says, "I—, um, he was just—um, comin' inta the bank t'day. Just 's I was goin' out. T' lunch."

"You *talked* t' him?"

"Of course I *talked* t' him, Mama." Amanda sighs. "I talk t' him all the time.—He's ni—not so bad."

Naurean returns to her account book, displeased. "Well," she says, "You just be careful."

"I *am* careful, Mama." Amanda opens her door.

"Well," Naurean says again, with a note of forgiveness.

"I'm real careful. I'm a big girl, Mama. I been takin' care 'f myself for a long time now."

"I know." She puts the pen down and looks at her daughter. *The spittin' image*, she thinks. The spittin' image smiles. "I just, I love you so much," Naurean says.

"I love you too, Mama," Amanda answers. They smile at each other a long moment, then she steps into her room.

*

In the apartment above, Trumpy puts his horn on the small desk and opens the top drawer. He reaches in and takes out a small pistol, the .22 The Lady bought in a pawn shop in Pittsburgh. She gave it to him and he takes care of it. *Good* care, like he takes care of her. He holds it by its short barrel and rubs the nickel handle with his sleeve until it gleams.

He's restless now—he'd call for The Lady but she'll come out when she's good and ready; if he calls she'll wait even longer. Usually, playing the trumpet helps, but it doesn't now and he paces to the window: All he can see is the grimy street filled with grimy kids, scraggly trees, scrawny pigeons. Couple cars, a bus blowing smoke out its tailpipe. *Like a big blue fart*, he thinks, and laughs. He starts to point the gun at one of the birds, then thinks better of it and steps back, looks around the living room and sees the picture on the wall, some old painting, a faggy lookin' kid in a wrinkled blue outfit. Came with the place. He plants himself a dozen feet away and, slowly, using both hands, raises the gun level with it. He closes an eye and aims.

From the bedroom, Ladyblue calls. "You about ready?"

He continues to aim. "Uh-huh. 'Bout," he says as she walks into the room holding the syringe casually.

"Hey!" she yells. "Gimme that." She grabs the gun. "You dumb piece of shit. You f'git already? About—." She slaps his face and throws the gun back into the drawer, slams it shut.

"*No,*" says Trumpy, "*no, I remember.* I'm, uh, sorry."

"Yeah?" The Lady says. "You're one sorry motherfucker, all right." She glares at him. "Well? You gonna just stand there?"

"No, I … No." He rolls up his sleeve, takes off his belt and wraps it around his arm while The Lady finishes prepping the syringe and takes the two steps to him.

"Be careful?" Trumpy asks. Needles hurt.

"*I am plenty careful,*" Ladyblue says.

"I—I didn't mean nothin'."

"Then shut the fuck up an' gimme your arm." She reaches for it. He turns toward her, pulling on the belt, keeping it taut. He starts to watch as she brings the needle to his skin, then winces and closes his eyes, turns his head away.

"You better hope nothin' ever happens t' me," she says as the point punctures his skin and delves further, into his vein, "'n' you gotta take care a yourself."

"Yeah," he says through clenched teeth.

Ladyblue laughs. "Your little girlfrien' know you're a junkie?"

"She ain't, she ain't—."

"Goddam right she ain't. *Goddam* right." She presses down on the plunger, slowly, and he feels the heat as the cloudy liquid mixes with his blood.

"It hurts," he says.

She lifts her thumb. "You want me t' stop?"

"No."

"Say 'please don't stop, Ladyblue.'"

"Please don't stop, Ladyblue."

She restarts the pressure. "You act like a goddam six year

old."

"I can't help it."

"Goddam junkie scairt a needles. Jesus."

"I'm sorry."

"You oughta be." She snorts.

His arm is burning up. "Don't go too fast," he pleads.

Ladyblue says "Shit" and presses harder.

"There. Oh, there," says Trumpy. "Oh yeah."

The glass cylinder empties and she yanks out the needle. He yelps, loosens the belt and rubs his arm. "You c'n open your goddam eyes now," she says.

"Okay," he says, and does. The room looks different. He can't say just how, but—no, no it *feels* different. He looks at the trumpet. *It's shining again! It'll be warm, he can make it sound the way he used to, clear, open notes, all the high ones again, like Clifford could hit, big tone, long smooth glissandos and unwavering pitch no matter how long he holds it. Oh, man, he'd be—.*

"How you feel?"

He looks at Ladyblue and giggles. She smiles. "I feel, I feel like dancin'," he says.

"Yeah?"

He giggles again. "Oh yeah. Oh, yeah."

She takes his thin face firmly in one large hand and squeezes it. "You wanna dance for me?"

"Anything you say," he says through his contorted mouth.

"That's right. Anything I say." She releases his face, unbuttons his shirt. He stands there as she moves a hand across his chest, grasps his right nipple between the long nails of her thumb and middle finger and squeezes, not hard, just hard enough he knows she can squeeze *much* harder. She says, very softly, "Go fix this up f'r me," and holds up the syringe.

He winces. Needles *do* scare him. "We gotta go?" he begs. "Gotta go?"

Her nails tighten their grip. "*When I say we gotta go.*" He gasps but nods. "Now go fix this up f'r me, and come back here, and then *you're* gonna …" She touches the needle's tip to her arm.

"Lady…"

She squeezes. His pain is extraordinary. "You're, *gonna*, do, it."

Slowly, he nods. She releases his nipple abruptly—he gasps again: *the pain*—and hands him the syringe. "That's a good boy," she says softly, and smiles.

*

It's early on this mid-September Saturday evening. On the street, there's plenty of light and in it, loud music and louder talk, car horns and barking dogs. A lot of apartment windows are open: It's warm, a little warmer than it should be this time of day and this time of year, but most of the people in this neighborhood don't have air conditioners so there are fans humming in those windows, or leaning against the radiators that won't be needed for a couple months to come. TV sets flicker, radios play and, here and there, a couple, mostly older folks, dances on the rug.

Naurean, dressed in a pale blue (it's *her* color; her Mama always said so) scoop-necked dress that's cut just low enough to be suggestive but high enough not to be revealing (unless she bends forward—something she's well aware of) putters around the apartment nervously, running a dustcloth over things, checking to make sure everything is spic and span. She looks at the clock: 6:56. *Oh, dear he should* she thinks, and finishes the thought aloud "be here any minute and *nothin'* is ready—"

From her room, Amanda calls: "Mama, *why* are you makin' *such* a fuss, I mean, you're acting like the President and Jackie're comin'—."

"—yet, I haven't even finished the dustin'" Naurean continues over her, "and—oh,"—she stops dusting—"would you plug in the coffee maker, I want it t' be fresh and it's not a fuss, I just want things t' look ... nice," she says as Amanda walks into the living wearing a lime poodle skirt and Peter-Pan-collared white blouse, buttoned to the top despite the warmth.

"Things look *fine*, Mama," she says, and continues through the swinging door, into the kitchen.

"Well" says Naurean. "Can you plug in—."

"I'm turnin' on the coffee," she calls.

"Good!" Naurean looks around and decides Amanda is right: Things *do* look fine. "Well," she says. She puts the dust cloth into the bag in the closet, takes a deep breath and is checking herself in the mirror again, adjusting the cultured pearl choker around her throat, when Amanda comes back into the room. "My, you look pretty," Naurean says and moves toward her. "Here, let me fix your hair."

Amanda puts up her hand. "My hair looks fine, Mama."

"It needs a little more..." Undaunted, Naurean pushes it back, re-pins it, behind her ears. "There." She stands back and appraises her daughter. "You c'd use a little more color, honey," she says. "You look pale."

Amanda, who eschews makeup except for work, where Mr. Gillam insists on it, shakes her head. "I am goin' t' the movies? Not dancin'? And I think—."

There's a polite knock on the door. Naurean grabs at the choker. "Oh, he—. Now, you go put on that rouge, Mandy," she says, shooing Amanda toward her room.

"For Pete's sake, Mama."

"Go on, g' on." Amanda, with a snort of amused disgust, goes into her room and closes herself inside. Naurean looks in the mirror once more, straightens herself, says "Well" and goes to the door. She stops at it, collects herself and then, slowly, turns the knob.

The door opens and a young man stands there. He's only a couple inches taller than she is, maybe he's twenty-five, twenty-six, perhaps not even that—she wasn't sure yesterday and she's not sure now. He has light blond hair neatly cut and combed, shiny and just a bit wavy, and his sideburns are trimmed. His eyes are the loveliest shade of blue—she noticed them right away—and his skin is fair, though his beard is heavy: *He probably shaved this morning and his skin is just too tender for him to do it twice in a day.* He wears a blue suit, carefully pressed, though one cuff of the jacket shows signs of wear and has half a button missing, and his tie is a little wider than the fashion these days.

He's not exactly good looking, but he's not *un*attractive and he looks ... friendly. *Yes*, she thinks, *friendly. And he was so kind yesterday.* She smiles at him; he smiles back, holding his hat between his hands. He has a wonderful, generous smile, perfect teeth, and there's a slight hint of the South in the way he speaks, *just* a hint, as though he's lived there but a long time ago.

"Why, Mr. Petterson," she says. "Good evening."

He bows slightly. "Good evenin', Mrs. Rossell." He stands up as straight as he possibly can. "And it's Rex; remember?"

"Rex. Well—*Rex*"—she steps aside to open his path—"please, come in, make yourself comf'table."

"Thank you very much," he says, and steps into the room. She takes his hat, smoothes the ragged feather in its band, and sets it on the shelf in the closet.

"I hope you didn't have any trouble gettin' here," she says. "Saturday night, the buses don't run so often."

"Oh, no. No trouble at all." He laughs and rubs his hands together. "'Sides, I'm used t' waitin' on buses. Goin' from city t' city, they're always late."

. "Well ... that's good," Naurean says. "Not that they're late, just that you're—."

Rex holds up a hand. "I know. I know what y' meant." He walks farther into the big living room and looks around. It's not new to him—he looked around yesterday, too—but it's not familiar, either. A sofa, couple chairs, the usual assorted tables, doo-dads and knick-knacks most everywhere, 'specially on the mantel. Lots of photos too. A record player, the console kind with a radio built in: nice lookin' wood, maybe real oak, beige-with-glittery-gold-thread fabric over the speakers and a shelf with a lot of albums lined up neatly on it. He's looking at the photos on the mantel as Naurean says "C'n I get you somethin' t' drink? There's fresh coffee, and I know we've got—" and Amanda enters, a plash of rouge on each cheek.

"Now, some coffee w'd be nice, thank you," Rex says, looks at Amanda and adds "This your sister?"

For a moment, Naurean is confused. "My sist—?" She stops and laughs, nervously: It's been so long since she's been complimented. By a man. In *that* way, especially. "Oh ... *Mister* Petterson. This is my daughter. Amanda: Mr. Rex Petterson."

"I'm very pleased to meet you, Miss Rossell," Rex says, bows ever so slightly and extends his palm. She's a little bewildered, but she takes it and, before she realizes what he's doing, his dry lips are on the back of her hand.

She pulls it away quickly. "Hello," she says. He smiles.

Naurean doesn't notice. She's a little tizzied, heart fluttering. *My!* she thinks, *it was only a little politeness*, but she needs to re-collect herself; the kitchen is the perfect place. "Well," she says, "why don't you two sit for a minute and I'll get some coffee— cream and sugar, Mr. Petterson?"

He smiles at Amanda. "Uh, no. A little cream."

"Mama," says Amanda, moving toward the kitchen, "I'll get the coffee, why don't you and—."

"No, it's all right, I'll get it. You just entertain Mr. Petterson for a minute." She smiles at him. He looks at her and smiles back, his wonderful smile.

"All right," Amanda says, slowly.

Naurean stands by the kitchen door, still smiling. "Mr. Petterson," she says, "if you'd like some music Amanda will be glad to put it on for you. I won't be a minute." She steps into the kitchen. Amanda stands, watching the door swing.

Rex follows Naurean's path, as though to peek in, but the door stops. He smiles at Amanda and rubs his hands together. "She's, um, she's an interestin' woman. And a charming one."

"Oh, she is," Amanda says. She stands in the middle of the room.

"Ev'rybody says that," he says, with a small laugh. "I expect her charm is half a what makes her so successful."

"Successful?"

Rex sweeps a hand in a wide arc, including the whole room in his assessment. "Runnin' a big dance school like this. All by herself."

"Oh. Mr. Petterson, I don't know what Mama told—."

"With your help, of course," Rex interrupts. "And, course, she's a fine teacher, too. I heard that; and I *observed* it, first hand. Handles children *real* well." He laughs, warm and gently self-deprecating laughter. "I expect I could learn somethin' about that from her." He moves to the stuffed chair and sits.

She remains standing. "Mm. Mama said you travel all over."

Rex leans back and unbuttons his jacket. "I do indeed," he says, crossing his legs.

"It must be interesting, seein' all those dif'rent places."

"Oh, it wa—it *is*," he says, and shifts his body. The chair is a little bigger than he'd like, he feels swallowed by it but—since he just sat down—he doesn't want to get back up right away. He uncrosses his legs and sits forward. "But, *but* I been doin' it all the time," he continues. "All the time. Least, till the past month 'r so. I needed a little time t'... kinda take a break, y' know?"

"Mm."

"It gets kind a wearin', bein' by yourself? All that time. Still, it's a livin'. Course, if I met a nice girl I might like t' settle down. I mean, y' can dance anywhere. I might even like t' have a little dance school myself." He waves toward the kitchen. "And seein' how well Mrs. Rossell does it..."

Amanda looks at him. He shifts again, folds his hands

behind his head and leans back. "Of course. *Would* you like some music, Mr. Petterson?" She goes to the record player.

"Why sure. Anything you like."

She kneels by the shelf and pulls out a handful of albums. "Most 'f what we have is from the thirties and forties," she says as she flips through them.

"Oh, you don't have to 'polagize," he says. "I like that. A lot."

She selects one, gets up, opens the console's lid and turns it on. There's a click, and then the Glenn Miller Orchestra starts "In the Mood."

"Nice," he says. "But I do have to say: It's unusual, *you* likin' *that*. Girls t'day, they don't us'ly care for that. The boys too, the ones *my* age. They all seem t' favor rock an' roll."

Amanda closes the console's lid. "What *is* your age, Mr. Petterson?" she says. "If I may ask." She sits on the far end of the sofa.

"'Bout yours, I guess."

"*I'm* twenty. Mama's forty-one."

Rex chuckles. "Oh," he says, "I expect *she*'d 'f kept that a secret. But I like that: You're straightforward. Directness, that's a *good* quality." He sits forward in the chair again, his hands flat on his knees, and lowers his voice. "I bet you don't go teasin' like some girls do. But now, I'd've taken you for closer t' twenty-five; not that you look old—hardly. Just, you *got* that direct quality about you, and that—look, 'f someone who's more mature an', an' sophist'cated," he says, earnestly. He leans back, but keeps his eyes on hers and adds, ruefully, "Not like those girls I meet on the road. Unh-uh. They're forward, all right, but there's *nothin'* straight about them. I mean, they don't have … grace, there's no style. When I'm on the road? Why, the way those girls act, you'd think they never met someone who really knew what *dancin'* is about. The way they carry on, I mean—well, sometimes it c'n get—well," he says, quietly, intimately, "I could tell you some things."

Amanda nods. "Mm," she murmurs.

Rex sits forward. "This,"—he points—"it's nice music. Nice. 'Specially for dancin'."

Amanda looks toward the kitchen door. "I guess."

Rex tilts his head at her. "I'll bet you're quite a dancer," he says. "I expect you'd be goin' out most ev'ry night."

Amanda shakes her head. "Unh-uh."

"You don't?" She shrugs; he says "I'll bet all the boys'd want t' dance with you."

"I don't know those new dances."

"Then" he says, with a wide smile that extends beyond his voice and wiles its way into his eyes, "I bet they'd love t' teach you. All about it."

"Maybe I just don't care t' learn."

"Now, I think you're just bein' modest," he says casually. He breaks away from her gaze. "That's a good thing in a girl, though. Lot a girls t'day, they're not modest at all. One of the problems with bein' a dancer: Bein' on the road, bein' a *performer*, you meet a lot a girls like that. Not many with good manners. Quiet." He looks at her again. "Homey."

There's a faint sound of a trumpet. Amanda says "Umm" and looks up.

"And pretty, too. Real pretty," says Rex. "About the rosiest cheeks I think I have ever seen." He stands. So does Amanda.

"Y' know, I can't imagine what's keepin' Mama with that coffee," she says quickly and starts for the kitchen, "I'll just go—."

"Amanda?" he says, just a little uncertainly, and she stops. "Long 's you're here, 'n' long 's there's music playin' anyhow, I mean…" He bows, offering his right hand. "Would you, um, care t' dance?"

"I—don't think… And I have to go out. In fact I was just—."

"Now, you got time for one dance," he says genially and reaches for her, starts to pull her into a dance embrace.

She pulls away, *pushes* him away. "Mr. Petterson," she says,

"Mama said you were comin' over t' dance with *her* t'night, and I think maybe you ought t'—."

Rex shakes his head and smiles. "Of *course* I'm gonna dance with *her*. When she gets here. But in the meantime," he extends his hand again, "it's a way f'r us t' get t' know each other a little."

"I…" Amanda looks at his hand, but doesn't touch it.

"Course," says Rex, "if you'd rather, *we* could go somewhere—some other time?" He lets that sink in a moment; she doesn't react, so he reaches the hand around her, then gently draws it to her back, stroking lightly as he does, and pulls her toward him.

She slaps him, hard. Her hand stings but she keeps it poised.

"Now, I was only tryin' to dance with you," he says, and backs away.

"Mama?" Amanda yells, "If I don't leave now I'm gonna miss the beginning. I'll be home about ten. Mama? You hear me?" She hurries to the door and looks at Rex as she opens it, says "Mr. Petterson, I—" but Naurean comes into the living room and says "Mandy? I thought you said the picture doesn't start till—" and Amanda says "Night." She pulls the door closed with a bang.

Naurean stands there, nonplussed. *This! After she's just spent the time trying to calm herself.* "Well," she says, "I can't imagine what got into her."

Rex laughs easily. "Oh, I expect she just remembered her engagement. Girls, they're like that: things just—occur to them."

"Her engagement? Oh, Amanda doesn—" Naurean begins, then: "Yes." She smiles. "I suppose."

He leans by the mantel, sees a photo he overlooked before: a smiling girl in a silky-lookin' dress—looks like it's white but he can't tell for sure, the picture's old, and black and white— standing next to a tall young man who's smiling too. "Amanda's 'n int'restin' girl," he says.

"Oh, she is," Naurean replies, a little nervously. *What could have gotten into her? He'll think I'm the rudest thing!*

"Got a lot 'f—imagination." He looks at her and laughs. "Bet she gets that from you."

"Oh, yes; we're a lot alike. Always have been." She laughs too.

"Um-hmm," says Rex. "Look a lot alike, too." He smiles at her.

She smiles back. "Well, I *did* look like that ..." she says, and touches her hair. "She's my spittin' image, when I was her age." She laughs a note. "I'm sorry t' be takin' so long; the coffee wasn't quite brewed yet. It'll just be another minute." She pushes the kitchen door open. He can see the white stove and refrigerator, the yellow Formica-top table with its four polished metal legs, yellow vinyl covered chairs and the matching yellow, floral print, wallpaper; all spotless.

"Please," she says, "do sit down." She looks at him a moment longer, then goes back into the kitchen; the door swings once and stops.

"Take your time," he calls after her. "I'm enjoyin' the music."

"It's this new electric pot," she calls back. "I can't get used to it. But it's all perc'lated now."

"In the Mood" ends and is replaced by "I've Got a Gal in Kalamazoo." Rex looks closely at the knick-knacks and doo-dads, the photographs, the pictures on the walls. They're nice, the pictures. Old. He's seen pictures like those, in museums once or twice. The photos are mostly of the girl in the silky dress, although she's wearing different clothes and with different people. Some are a little faded. They're mostly all in black and white, 'cept a couple of her where she's older and with a really pretty little girl, maybe twelve or thirteen. Really pretty. He calls: "Yes, it *is* a lovely place you got here."

"Well, thank you," Naurean calls back. "It's kinda old. Not very ... stylish any more, I'm afraid. I'd like t' move." The kitchen door swings open and Naurean enters with two coffee cups on saucers, on a tray; he hurries to hold the door open for her. "Thank you, Rex.—I'd like t' move someplace a little nicer, but Amanda?—she's just a home body and she's used t' this. I guess I am too." She sets the tray on the coffee table and hands him a cup-and-saucer.

"Thank you."

She sighs—a small sigh, not unhappy, just an I-take-my-life-in-stride sort of sigh—takes the other cup to the sofa and sits, gestures, inviting him to join her. He continues to stand at the mantel. "Y' get used t' somewhere, y' just— stay," she says. "And it's modest; some people, they just got t' show off about ev'rything, but I don't think there's a need for that. I mean, you are what you *are*."

Rex nods. "You don't have t' always *wear* a lot 'f lace an' ruffles t' prove you *own* a pretty dress."

"Ex*act*ly! I'm glad *you* understand that."

"Oh," he says, "I do. I do indeed." He taps the photo of the girl in the white silk dress. "This your picture?"

"Uh-huh." Naurean smiles. "At my … cotillion. When I was about Mandy's age."

Rex shakes his head. "Hard t' believe you got a daughter who's—how old is she?"

Naurean hesitates the length of a heartbeat before she says "Eighteen.—Just."

He shakes his head again. "Eighteen!" he says, in wonderment. "You look too young."

"Oh … I don't."

"Yes; you do." he insists, and sits on the other end of the sofa.

"You think so?"

"I do indeed."

"Well …"

The music plays—now it's "Tuxedo Junction"—and they listen in silence. The room feels a little warm to Naurean, but she doesn't want to open the window: too much noise and dirt outside. Besides, it's private in here. An open window would let the world in. And, really, she just doesn't want to move: She's still feeling a little nervous … well, more like shy really. She tries to focus on her coffee but she doesn't really want it. She sips, tiny sips, looks now and then at Rex, quickly, sees he's looking around the room, just holding the saucer like it was delicate china instead of Melmac. She tries to look around too, tries not to look at him.

Finally, Rex turns to her and says "Nice music."

"My fav'rite," she replies. "When I was y—I mean: I used t' go dancin' to it ev'ry night." She laughs, a little musical laugh. "And this song? It was playin' the first time I met my husband. It was *his* fav'rite."

"It doesn't make you sad? To listen?" he asks solicitously.

"Oh, no," Naurean says. "He was a wonderful man, we loved each other very much. Hearin' it? I remember how we were happy." She sets her coffee carefully onto the table. "The, the only sad mem'ry I have of it was, they played it at his wake. A recording. And I kissed him there, for the last time, while it was playin'." She starts to sing, thinks better of it and scats a few bars. Then she laughs. Rex laughs with her. "I *never* could sing," she confesses. "Just dance. Jim—my husband?—Jim 'n' me, we danced t' this all the time. I think he could've been a professional too, if he'd wanted."

Rex puts down his coffee. "I'm sure," he says.

"He was a good man. Very kind." She looks at a photo on the mantel and smiles to it, warmly; the young man in the navy suit smiles back. "He just *doted* on Amanda. And he made sure, Amanda 'n' me, he made sure we'd be provided for. Not that there was ever anything t' worry about, but he didn't want me ever t' *have* t' work. The dance lessons, they're just t' keep me busy"—*Oh, dear, he'll think I don't do a* thing *with myself*—*"and they do*: I mean, I just think it's important for a woman t' have a purpose in her life—b'sides raisin' a daughter, I mean, I don't know what I'd do with*out* her, she's all I got since, since …

Just, I think it's important for ev'ryone, t' have a purpose. Don't you?" she says hopefully.

"I do indeed," he says. "I do indeed."

She nods—*Well. Good.*—and picks up her cup. "That enough cream, Mr. Petterson?"

"Oh, it's fine, it's just still hot." He shifts his shoulders, straightens his tie, pulls at the cuffs of his shirt and clears his throat. "But I, um, Mrs. Rossell, I was wonderin' ..." He rubs his hands together.

"Yes?" she says, mystified that *he* seems so uneasy.

"If you would, um," he stands up and extends his right hand, "care to dance."

She looks at him. He *is* handsome; kind of. She just didn't really look at him closely, before. Short, but lean, *a*gile-lookin' like that Donald O'Connor. But much *better*-lookin'. "You really want t' dance with me?"

Rex's Adam's apple bobs in his throat. "I would be honored," he says softly.

Oh! But ... "Really," she says, "I haven't danced *with* anyone in years. Except my students of course. After Jim, after, he ... And then, I don't know—y' know, you raise a child all by yourself, and givin' all those dance *lessons*, it doesn't leave a lot a time."

Rex grins: a sweet boyish grin. "That's a shame," he says. "Woman like you—I bet all the boys'd want t' dance with you."

"Well ... maybe when I was a girl."

"Oh?" Rex says and steps around the table toward her; his grin broadens. "And you're not a girl any more?" Naurean laughs. "You're a fine dancer—that's what ev'rybody says."

She is giddy. "Oh, they do?"

Rex takes another step toward her, still grinning. "I asked around."

Naurean laughs again.

"And," he stammers. "And..."

"And?" she asks gently.

It's almost a whisper. As though he's terrified to say it he looks away. The grin disappears. "And you're a beautiful woman," he says slowly, somberly.

"I ... Well..." She looks at him. He turns toward her, his face still boyish but now filled with concern, and looks back, then extends his hand. She takes it.

"Maybe we could put on somethin' a little slower?" he says.

"All right." She lets his hand slip from hers, goes to the console and puts on *Music for Lovers Only*.

From outside, there's the wail of trumpet.

"Who's that?" Rex says. "Outside."

"Oh, that's prob'ly just Trumpy," Naurean says, annoyed at the intrusion. "He lives right above us." She whispers. "With a woman. We c'n hear them *all* the time."

"Oh," Rex says knowingly.

"They're both musicians." The needle clicks into a groove and "Alone Together" begins. "How's this?"

"Perfect."

"Well..."

He strides up to her, stands erect and unfurls his arm. "Mrs. Rossell," he says, with perfect formality, "may I have this dance?"

"Mr. Pette'son," she says, allowing herself a hint of drawl, "I would be cha'med."

She felt again as though she'd danced with him every day of her life. *He* made her feel that way. He led perfectly, each move was like they were a single body, rising, falling. So light, so airy; so ... completing. He held her close—barely room for two sheets of paper between them! Now and then she felt his breath on her cheek, now and then his hand gave hers the slightest squeeze. The living room was crowded; it made no difference. He moved them as though they were in a ballroom, an infinity of open space.

She closes her eyes, something she's done only with her most trusted partners, and lets her body flow with his, aware only of the music and of him.

When the first song ends, he holds her, in position, and when the next begins, a waltz, he dips them both gracefully, then leads her turn. She executes it perfectly.

"Yes" he says, when she returns to his embrace, "you are a *fine* dancer, Mrs. Rossell."

She smiles. "Not like I used t' be."

"Why, I can't b'lieve there aren't men askin' you to dance ev'-ry-where you go."

"No," she says. *No.*

He pulls her a little closer. "Well, if you ask me, they're makin' a big mistake then."

She half-sighs, half-giggles. "Oh, Mr. Petterson," she says.

He pulls her closer still. "Rex," he whispers, then adds: "It's Greek for 'King.'"

It's cooling a little now, beginning to get dark, the streetlights are on and most everybody's gone in for supper and to watch Jackie Gleason—or they've gone out, dancing, or to movies or to sit in the park, maybe by The Pond to listen to transistor radios and feed the ducks, or to the new fieldhouse that's just opened, to watch the basketball game. There's a bus now and then, but not much street traffic otherwise, though there are vague sounds he can hear in the distance. The street itself, so alive in the daylight, has settled in for the night. All that's left is the blue, deepening from robin's egg to pale lavender and then gradually to indigo. Lights from the windows here and there, and the streetlights: There's no moon and the stars are barely visible between the thick clouds.

He sits on the narrow steps of the stoop, his eyes closed, for once playing the horn just for himself. He doesn't get t' do that much any more: Playin' in clubs, you had to play what they wanted, mostly pop songs 'r "cool" jazz. Almost never blues. Blues, they're The Lady's favorite; his too. And he 'specially likes ballads, used to be he could lean back and blow a ballad, blue or not, that dripped out of his horn like melted butter: warm, smooth, you just wanted t' be covered in it.

He's halfway through "Willow Weep for Me" when Amanda comes down the steps. He doesn't know it's her, not till she speaks. He'd've been happy just to sit and play, but he likes her. 'Manda's a kid, little confused, maybe, like a lot a kids were, like he'd been, even *after* he was a kid. Until he met The Lady. *She* straightened him out. Maybe she was a little hard on him sometimes, but that was okay. Sometimes, he needed that. He'd never been very good on his own. And there wasn't anyone, anything, else, ever. Just him; and her and his horn. She'd sent him away once. After a day he knew how alone he really was and begged her to let him come back. She'd made him wait a while, then she made him hurt—he still had the marks from the cigarette on the insides of his thighs, and even with the cream and the bandages on he'd throbbed for a week when anything touched one, and The Lady'd touched them all the time—but that was okay. Without her, he knew he would've died. Hurt was okay; better than dying, anyway.

Amanda stands and listens. Trumpy's horn shimmers in the dimming light. His eyes are closed.

The music, it don't come from the horn he'd told her, *it comes from someplace way inside, someplace deep and blue and **you** can't see, nobody can see it. It's just there. All your music's just **there**.*

The night is dry, and she feels a light breeze coming up. She wishes she'd taken a sweater—she might need it later—but now she undoes the top button of her blouse and sits on the step above Trumpy, tucking her skirt under her. She closes her eyes and imagines the music, its story. The place it comes from. She doesn't have that place, and she envies Trumpy his. She pulls the pins from her hair and shakes her head. The strawberry blond falls back over her ears, the way *she* likes it. She looks at him.

"Evenin', Trumpy," she says.

He lowers the trumpet. "Oh. Evenin', 'Manda."

In the living room, Naurean murmurs "Oh, my."

"Mm?" nuzzles Rex.

"You're holdin' me so…"

"Oh…" He starts to ease his grip.

"It's all right. It's just, it's been a long time since anybody … like that, too."

"I see."

"Y' workin' t'night?" Amanda asks.

"Uh-huh," he says. "Start 't nine." He takes a breath and blows the horn again. Deep tones flow out, here and there it's a little ragged, but she's never heard anything like it, not up close, and it sounds beautiful to her.

"Mm" she says, and listens. "C'n I sit with you a minute? Just listen?"

Trumpy nods.

"Nice out," she says, and Trumpy nods again.

She executes another perfect turn and when she comes out of it, he presses her close. She feels her breasts flatten against his chest. He whispers "How long has it been since anyone kissed you?"

Naurean is startled. "I—don't remember," she stammers.

He looks into her eyes and, still dancing, takes his right hand from her back, very gently closes them, and replaces his hand, presses her deeper into him. She trembles. *Oh*, she thinks. Then he kisses her: first her eyes, gently, then her mouth, slowly, deeply. She waits while it happens, then lets it, then joins in the kiss. He pulls away slowly.

"Will you remember that?" he asks softly.

Her eyes open and she looks at his solemn smile. "Oh, yes, Rex," she says, "I *will* remember that. I will."

Trumpy finishes "Willow" with a long, tremeloed E that slowly fades, then he segues into "The Easy-Lovin' Blues." Amanda claps softly. "That's beautiful" she whispers. Eyes closed, he nods a *thanks*.

She listens a while, then says "Didn't have much weather like this, this summer. Been hot … Wish *we* had air conditioning, like the bank. Maybe next year we c'n get one, though, 'r move someplace that's got it 'stead a this old dump. After I finish up with school." She listens. "That's real sad music," she says. "That what they call 'blues'?"

Trumpy plays and nods.

"I like it. Mostly, Mama 'n' me listen to—." Suddenly, she's aware: She is interrupting his reverie, this very private moment. "You mind me always talkin' t' you like this?"

He takes the trumpet from his lips, just a little ways, and smiles. "I like it," he says, and begins to play again.

Amanda laughs a little laugh. "You sure love that trumpet."

He finishes the phrase and places it in his lap. "…' do," he says.

"What're you doin' out here?"

"Oh, just—… The Lady wanted t' be by herself a while."

"Mm" Amanda says. "I still think it's a funny kind a name, Ladyblue."

"She likes it. An' it's … right, I guess. She had a lot a blue times too."

"Mm" Amanda says again.

Trumpy turns and looks at her. She looks pretty, even prettier than she does for work. "You're waitin' on a date, looks like."

"No." She sighs. "Just waitin'."

"Your boyfriend workin'?"

She sits straight up. "Don't have one. I told you that."

He laughs softly. "I forgot," he says.

"Mm. The boys I know?" she says with something between disappointment and disdain, "they're all real—young. All *they* wanna do is—I don't know."

"Uh-huh."

"I'm goin' to the movies, but it doesn't start till eight. Mama's got company."

"Uh-huh," says Trumpy. He looks at her again, then turns back and raises the trumpet.

She listens to his loneliness, realizing it's how *he* talks about it, how he says what's he's got to say.

"Trumpy?" she asks, "You ever wonder? About the world, I mean?"

"Unh-uh" he says between notes.

"I do. All the people I know, except you I guess, they all seem so, so, like they're just doin' what they're *supposed* t' be doin'. Not what they want t' do. And they all seem so ... unhappy. Inside."

He lays the trumpet on his lap again and looks into the dusk.

"Most people," he says, "they *don't* get t' do what they want. Too busy doin' what they got t' do. End up dreamin' 'bout what they want t' do, makin' it up 'stead a doin' it." He laughs, one small, rueful note. "Once? I knew this retarded kid. 'Bout, oh, long time ago—before the war. His Pa—Dave was his name—him 'n' me were friends, and he'd come inta the club with his kid. Kid had a trumpet—little toy, but he loved it too, y' c'd tell. And one day, the kid, he asks his Pa 'C'n I blow on the man's horn?' And me 'n' Dave laughed"—he laughs again now, remembering it—"but I gave it to 'im and he blew on it, an' man, he made a sound come out like I never heard before, just clear an' blue as heav'n. Made me jealous: I wasn't never gonna make a sound 's pure as that ...

"Kid couldn't've been, oh, ten years old. 'All he wants t' do is play' Dave says. All he was ever gonna do, too, bein' a retard.

But that kid, he'd be doin' what he wanted. Not just dreamin'. Most of us, most of us just *got* dreams. And inside? We got a sadness. Way down deep." He sits, working the valves in silence and staring into the falling darkness.

"You do?"

He turns, as though he's surprised she's there. "I s'pose," he says slowly. "I s'pose most ev'rybody does. Always wondered what happened t' him. That kid." He continues to work the valves.

Finally, Amanda says: "You're—really nice."

He replies easily. "So 're you."

"Trumpy?"

"Yeah?" He looks at her.

"I liked havin' supper last night. Thanks."

"Uh-huh," he says, and raises the trumpet.

"And thanks for talkin' t' me," she tells him. He starts to play. She reaches down and touches him, his shoulder, gently. He nods but keeps playing. "Sometimes?" she says, "I don't know … sometimes *I* dream too, 'bout things the rest a the girls I know? and Mama, too, they don't even think about. Sometimes I think I'd be better off if I was a retard, I mean, I'm *always* thinkin'. Dumb stuff. Like, like there was this thing they had, in high school, where one day this lady came in t' talk t' us—career day, they called it—and she talked about all the things people c'd do—be a doctor or a lawyer, or, or fly planes 'r be an engineer. And then she talked about bein' a nurse 'r a kindergarten teacher or a mother, the things *girls* c'd do, and I kept thinkin', what if *I* wanted t' be a lawyer 'r fly a plane, *c'd* I do it? I mean, sometimes I dream about doin' that kind a stuff, and, goin' places like in that flyer, and, and all I'm ever gonna *be* is a secretary for some damn—."

"What're you doin'?" Ladyblue says from the doorway to the vestibule.

Trumpy stops in mid-note and Amanda pulls her hand back. "Oh," he says. "I—Nothin', I was just sittin' 'n' playin' 'n'—."

"'N' whatta*you* want," Ladyblue snarls. She steps down to where Amanda sits.

"I was—."

"Never mind," she says to Trumpy, staring at Amanda the while. "Git upstairs."

Trumpy glances quickly at Amanda, then hurries up the steps and through the door.

The Lady stands there looking after him. Then she turns back to Amanda. "You leave him alone, you hear?" she says.

"We, I wasn't—." She stands up. Ladyblue, on the same stair, is six, seven inches taller, and still looks down to her.

"*You leave him alone*, y' understand? You 'n' that nose-in-the-air mother a yours both better leave, him, be."

Amanda takes a deep breath. "Or else what?"

Slowly, Ladyblue grins. Then she turns away and walks deliberately up the stairs and into the building, leaving Amanda alone.

*

Sunday morning is bright and clear and Naurean wakes early in a wonderful mood. She usually sleeps well, but *this* night she has not only slept, she has dreamed, a garden of earthly delights: dancing, sweet music, gracious arms enclosing her. She's dressed, out the door and back from the bakery with the bag of sweet rolls by 7:30; by 8:00, she's finished one, and her first cup of coffee, and she's in the living room, the radio playing as she dances with an invisible partner. She strokes his face, then closes her eyes and leans to kiss him.

"Mama?" Amanda calls sleepily from her room.

"I—." Naurean opens her eyes. "Oh … Well."

"*Ma*-ma" Amanda continues. "You turn that down a little?" She yawns loudly.

"Time you got up anyhow!" sings Naurean. "It's after eight

o'clock."

"Mama, it's Sunday!"

"Best part of the day's the mornin'! It's when you got the most energy!"

"*It's when* I can sleep late," Amanda says grumpily, but Naurean hears her feet hit the floor.

"You'll get plenty of sleep when you're dead," she laughs, and turns down the radio. "Now, *I've* been up for over an hour. I—"

Amanda stumbles in, yawning and barefoot, her robe tied loosely and a glare in her half-opened eyes. "Oh, *good*," she mumbles, aggrieved, and continues on into the kitchen.

"—went t' the bakery," Naurean continues. "There's fresh coffee and I got some 'f those sticky buns you like, there's one in the oven keepin' nice and—."

"Mm," Amanda grunts.

Naurean sits on the sofa, though she wonders if she'll be *able* to sit much today, she feels *so* energized! "I already poured you some coffee," she bubbles. "A bun's in the oven. How was the picture?"

"Okay."

"Good!"

"You have a good time?" says Amanda as she walks into the living room, coffee cup and a roll balanced precariously in one hand, and sits beside Naurean.

"Oh, yes. I had a *won*derful time," Naurean says. Wait till she *tells* Mandy the whole thing. Too old? She laughs. No, indeed she's not!

"Oh," says Amanda, settling herself in. "I thought maybe, I mean, y' went t' bed awful early." She yawns again. She was asleep by eleven, but most nights, between her classes and homework and studying, she doesn't get to bed till after midnight. And she's up at six-thirty on workdays. Saturdays, too: Most of Naurean's students come on Saturday, so she has to shop, cook, run most of the errands.

"Early?"

"I got home little past ten. Your door was closed." Amanda takes a big swallow of coffee.

"Oh. We … went out."

"You did?"

"To The Paradise Café." Naurean hugs herself. Everything— shined. Shimmered. *Shimmied*. She giggles. "Oh, it's so lovely."

"Yeah, Trumpy says it's pretty expensive." Amanda bites deeply into the sticky bun, getting warm cinnamoned glaze and bits of pecan all over her mouth and fingers. She licks them and is utterly happy.

"We saw them there—him, and that woman, singin'," Naurean adds, wrinkling her nose. "And it's not so bad."

"Oh?" says Amanda, and casually chews the bun.

"The whole evening didn't cost more than thirty-five dollars." Amanda frowns. "How d'—Who paid for it?"

Naurean says, indignantly, "Why he did, of course."

"Well, that's—."

"Least, he's going to," she adds. "Pay me back.—And we danced, oh, we danced." She laughs and claps her hands. "*I* didn't get home till after one."

"I see," Amanda says, and drinks her coffee.

"He is a *won*derful dancer—and so polite. He spent the whole evening making me talk about myself."

"Mama," says Amanda, "how come you paid?"

"Why, I imagine he didn't expect t' be going out." She puts the cup down and heads to the kitchen: She's going to indulge herself with another sticky bun! "We just—decided. On the spur of the moment." She jams the door open.

"Uh-huh."

"He's quite a young man," she says. "Got all these plans, knows exactly what he wants t' do with his life."

"Oh?"

Naurean sticks her head in the doorway. "Uh-huh" she says. "You want another one?" She points at the bun in Amanda's hand.

"Not right now. Thanks."

"He wants t' have a school, too," she says. "A *real* dance *school*. Thinks he's almost ready t' do it, just needs a little more time t' get organized. He thinks there's a real need for it, so children c'n grow up with manners and, and grace. And," she adds confidentially, "he might even want me t' be his partner in it."

Amanda looks at her. "Partn—Mama? All those plans of his, where's he gonna get the money?"

Naurean shrugs and steps back into the kitchen. "I—I suppose he's been savin' it."

"Suppose?" Amanda calls.

"It's not something we ... discussed."

Amanda takes her coffee and goes to the open doorway. "'d you look at him, the way he dressed?" she says.

"I told you," says Naurean as she extracts the heated sweet roll. "He wasn't ex*pec*tin' t' go out." She puts the roll on a small plate and gets a knife and fork, reveling in the smell. "B'sides," she says, "you don't have t' always wear a lot of lace an' ruffles t' prove you own a pretty dress. Professional dancers, they are *well*-paid."

"And how d' you know he's a professional dancer? 'Cause he says he is?"

"Of course." She sits at the kitchen table and cuts a piece of the bun. "And, I c'n tell from *how* he dances." She puts it into her mouth.

"There are a lot of good dancers, Mama," says Amanda. "Mr. Gillam, at the bank? He and his girlfriend've won a bunch a prizes."

Naurean puts down the fork. "Amanda," she says, "why are you inter*fer*in'?"

"Interferin'?"

"Interferin'! I meet someone and, and I have a, a good time with him, and you're actin' like *you* got to look after *me* 'cause he's so terrible I can't take care of myself. Well, I—"

"*Mama*—."

"—think you're just jealous," Naurean continues over her. "Twenty years old and you can't get your*self* a man and you don't want *any*one to have one."

"Mama, that's not true!" She steps into the kitchen, goes toward the table. "And he's just a boy, he isn't more th'n twenty-five himself."

"So what?" Naurean says and cuts another small piece. "How old someone is doesn't matter. Long as he's a gentleman."

"*But he's not a gentleman, Mama*" Amanda says. Naurean looks at her with pursed lips. Amanda sighs and sets her cup on the table. "Mama, he was tryin' t' take advantage— of—."

Naurean stands up abruptly and faces her. "He is *not*. He—"

"Mama, you don't—."

"—loves me. *He said so.*"

"He—he—" Amanda stammers.

"What?" says Naurean. "What're you gonna say? No, Mama, he doesn't? No, Mama, he *couldn't*, you're too old, you're not pretty any more, you're just withered and lonely—"

"No!"

"—and *desperate*" Naurean shouts over her. "*You don't know what it's like*"—she takes a breath and looks down at her plate— "t' be, t' be this old and alone for *so* long. And then a young man, a young gentleman wants to dance with you ... and you feel alive again. Fin'ly."

"Mama, I..." Amanda begins, gently, then, not knowing how to go on, lets her voice trail away.

"Fin'ly. All these years, *all* these years I raised *you*, I tried to look out for *you*, *I* just stopped livin'. You were my life. Men'd ask me somewhere, I'd say: No, I got a daughter, I can't do anything, can't take a chance on gettin'—somethin' happ'ning, and—"

"Mama—."

But Naurean isn't listening. "—so I got older an' older," she says, "all by myself and now look at me, I'm, I'm, like some broken down old maid, no one wants me any more 'cause there's nothin' whole there t' want." She looks up, at Amanda. There's a quiet plea in her voice, in her eyes. "Except Rex, he, he sees what's not broken, how it used t' be before I …"

Amanda reaches her hand to Naurean's face, touches it gently. "Mama," she says, "He tried t' … take advantage. Of me."

"*No!*"

She looks directly into her mother's eyes. "While you were in the kitchen gettin' the coffee, he tried t' get me t' dance with him and—"

"T' dance with you?" Naurean laughs, "Well, there's—."

But Amanda goes on, raising her voice to be heard. "—*then he asked me t' go out with him, and, and he* tried to get familiar."

Naurean slaps her. "No he did not," she says evenly, assuredly. "No he *would* not. You understand me? He did not."

Amanda stands there, her hand still near Naurean's face. Her own face stings. "Oh, Mama," she says sadly, and reaches to embrace her but Naurean steps away. Amanda looks at her a long moment; Naurean stares back. Then Amanda walks out of the kitchen, through the living room and into her room.

"*He did not!* He's a gentleman, Mandy. He is a gentleman!" Naurean shouts after her.

Amanda closes her door.

"A real gentleman," Naurean says softly. "Just like your father.—Why, he even looks like him. And when we dance, it's, it's like all the time's just disappeared. We just … float." She stands in the kitchen, looking at nothing until the music starts and the girl appears, in the arms of the young man, dancing gracefully and smiling. "*Like the moon dancing with the stars over a lake*" she tells the couple, "*and I could see his eyes, all shinin' and bright. But he said it: 'It's such a beautiful night, Naurean, and your eyes? they're so bright. They shine like the moon, I can* see the stars reflectin' in them.'" She smiles; the couple smiles back and draws closer, his hand caresses her intimately and the girl begins to move her hips against his. "*I felt so—silly*" Naurean says. "*I laughed, I didn't know what to say, just, 'Oh, Jim.' And he smiled—the way a young gentleman would smile, lookin' at the moon and the stars on a beautiful night—and he held me, so tight*"—the young man grins as the girl licks his ear, bites it lightly; his hands raise her skirt and disappear under it, Naurean can see them, fondling, squeezing, and hear them both breathing anxiously "*and we just … float there, in the sky, away … Away.*" Their breathing becomes heavier, hungrier, demanding. Naurean fills with fear. "*Go away,*" she commands, but they laugh and their hands move across each other more urgently, in complete disregard of her presence, "*go away!*" she shouts, "*go away go* away go a—No! …

"No," says Naurean, with preternatural calm. She feels a little dizzy and leans against the table, looks, listens, but the couple has disappeared and the music ended. She takes a slow breath, smiles weakly, then sits and, slowly, grimly, lifts a scrap of sticky bun to her mouth.

*

"… *Gonna get rid of the easy, easy-lovin' blues* …" Ladyblue sings, and Trumpy giggles. "Jesus," she says, "you still up?"

"Uh-huh," he answers.

She smiles and continues dressing. "Mmm. That's some good shit."

"Uh-huh."

"Well, git y'urself t'gether." She clasps her bra. "We got rehearsal."

"Uh-huh."

"'Uh-huh,'" Ladyblue mimics. "Will you say somethin' *else*?"

"Uh—Sure," Trumpy answers, and giggles.

"Jesus," she says. "Go sit on the steps. Clear your head. Too goddam hot in here t' think." She pulls her dress over her head and wriggles it down her body.

"Okay," he says, and starts to the door.

"That girl comes out," Ladyblue says, "you leave her alone."

"Girl?"

"You *know* who I mean."

"Oh," he says. "'Manda."

Ladyblue snickers. "*'Oh. 'Manda.'*"

"She, she just likes t' talk."

She pulls the hem down and looks in the mirror. "You like talkin' t' her?"

She says it matter of factly, but he's been with her going on ten years, and he can hear behind her voice. "Well," he says, "kinda." Then he adds quickly "But it don't mean nothin', Lady. She's just a kid, she gets lonely. You used t' git lonely too— remember?"

She whirls on him. "*You shut the fuck up,*" she commands, and he freezes.

"I'm—" he mumbles.

"*And don't give me none a that 'I'm sorry' crap,* you hear me?" she says. He stands, immobile, mute. "You, hear, me?" she repeats.

He nods. "Uh-huh," he answers.

"C'mere, Trumpy."

"Lady—" he begins.

Quietly, she says: "I said, C'mere." He comes. "Now" she says, "You kinda like talkin' to her."

"Just, I don't say nothin'," he mumbles, head down. When she's angry, she doesn't like him to look at her.

"Oh." The Lady nods. "You wanna use it again?" He shakes his head. "*You want ta use it again?*"

He looks up, then down again. "No, no, I—."

She takes his thinning hair in her hand and pulls his face up, so his eyes meet hers. "But you will," she says, "if I tell you to."

He is silent. "*You will if I tell you!*" she shouts into his face, then says, softly. "Won't you?"

"I, I … Lady …" He struggles.

"*Won't you?*"

He tries to look away from her. "I, I didn't *mean* t'," he says. "In Pittsburgh. I didn't mean to."

She releases his hair; he looks down. "You didn't?" she says.

"*Nooo* … I…"

"But, you, did."

He looks up. "It, it was 'n accident, Lady. *You* know it was."

"Oh, 'n accident." He nods. She turns toward the mirror and begins to apply makeup. "*Why'd* we leave Pittsburgh?" she asks, as though she can't quite remember.

Trumpy shifts his weight uncomfortably. "I …" He shakes his head.

"Junkie," she hisses. He nods. "Roll up your sleeve." He does, eyes still cast down. She looks at him. "You want some more?" she asks.

"I …" he begins, then nods.

"You gonna do what I say? No matter what?"

"Uh-huh," he answers.

"*Quit sayin' 'uh-huh'!*"

He stammers. "I—'m sorry."

She drops the lipstick on the bureau. It clatters. "Open your mouth," she says. He does.

She walks into the living room, open the desk drawer and returns casually, holding the gun. She lifts it and puts the barrel into his open mouth.

"The next time…" she says. "The next time?"

Carefully, Trumpy nods.

She circles the .22 around his cheeks, across his tongue, then removes it and hands it to him. "Clean it off," she says. He starts to wipe it on his shirt. "And close your mouth." He does. "And roll down your sleeve" she says and picks up her eyebrow pencil.

"Not till later." He does. When he's finished, she says: "Now git out."

"Lady …" he hazards.

"What?"

"She don't mean nothin'," he pleads. "It ain't like Pittsburgh. 't's not."

Ladyblue looks into the mirror. The pencil has made her eyes darkened slits. Quietly she says: "Get, out … *Now!*"

*

Amanda is gone—she doesn't know where—and Naurean is sitting on the sofa sobbing when the telephone rings. She continues to cry, but worries: Who's calling her this early on a Sunday morning? *Something's happened to Mandy*, she thinks, and sobs again, drying her face with a handkerchief at the same time. "Oh my, I …" she says as the phone rings a second time, a third. "Just a minute," she says to it and breathes a few times quickly, dabs her eyes.

The phone keeps ringing. She takes a last collecting breath, says "Now …" and picks it up. "Yes?" she says into the mouthpiece, then: "Oh, Rex, I … I—just a second …" She collects herself again and continues. "Well, there now." She pushes a smile into her voice, aware it sounds pushed. "No, no," she says, "I'm fine. How are you? … Uh-huh … Uh-huh."

He leaves quickly, without his horn, and goes downstairs. He's frightened: The Lady is mad. He's gotta find a way to make her be not mad, else she'll … He sighs. There's no knowing what she'll do. He still feels the junk, a little. Makes it hard to think, but he's trying. If he tries really hard, he'll think of somethin'.

He comes out of the building, his mind on figuring out what he's gonna do, and almost trips over her, sitting on the steps, elbows on her knees and hands wrapped around her head. "Oh. 'Manda—" he begins, then remembers and says "I better g—."

"Oh, hi," she says unhappily.

He stops. "Somethin' wrong?"

"Oh, just …" She shakes her head and looks up at him. "Mama 'n' me had a … argument, I guess."

"Oh." *He should go. Should* go.

"I'm okay. Just …" Amanda continues.

"Uh-huh," says Trumpy. "But, but I better go, practice, we got this re—."

"C'n you, c'n you talk a while?" she asks him.

He looks into her face. She's been crying. He sighs and wonders: *Can* he help? Well, all she wants is to talk about it. That can't hurt. And The Lady's up gettin' dressed. He'll only talk a couple minutes and then he'll—walk around the block or somethin', till she comes down. A couple minutes'll be okay. "Uh … Well," he says. "A while." He sits beside her.

"Thanks," she says.

He waits for her to say something but she doesn't, so he asks, "You, um, like the picture?"

"It was okay."

"Mm." He waits. Then: "What'd you fight about?"

Amanda shrugs. "Oh, just …"

"Just …?" He works the valves on an invisible trumpet.

"Her … company." She sighs. "Last night."

He nods. "Me and The Lady, we been t'gether a long time but sometimes we fight too." He smiles at her. "It don't mean nothin'."

"I guess," Amanda says.

"We always find a way t', y' know, get along."

"Mm." She looks into his face, beyond the smile. *There's a sadness there*, she thinks. *Way down deep.*

Trumpy sighs. "She sends me away sometimes. *Once*, she did, but she let me come back. After a while."

Naurean taps the arm of the sofa as Rex speaks. "Uh-huh" she says again, "Well, I'm pleased you did." What does he want, she wonders. "No, I've been up for a while," she says, "I was just sittin' here." She wonders: What does *she* want. "Yes, I enjoyed it too" she says, a little reluctantly. If she enjoyed it, why does she feels so, so ...? She listens. He's speaking softly, gaily, the same way he said good night to her, except, except then there'd been a soft shade of sorrow behind his words. Of regret, behind both of their words. "Well, I, I don't know," she says nervously. What if Amanda walks back in? "I mean, t'morrow seems kind of soon. And, and—I've got students comin', I know I'll be tired. I *always* am on a Monday." She sighs. Amanda is wrong about him, she knows that but, after all, Mandy's her *daughter*. Mandy *has* to come first. Maybe after a week 'r two, when she's had a chance to get used to the idea, when she sees how happy Naurean is about him, maybe then Mandy'll think differently. "Well, the whole week is pretty *busy*, I—." Course, though, she *did* have a wonderful time last night, and he was, he *is* such a nice young gentleman. A week or two, all alone again, it seems, it seems like such a long time to wait...

"Mama's been alone a long time," says Amanda. "It's hard for her."

Trumpy nods agreement. "Bein' alone, it's hard for ev'rybody. *I* know."

Amanda shakes her head. "I guess I like bein' by myself. Most 'f the time, anyway."

Trumpy laughs ruefully. "You haven't been alone *enough*. People, they'll do all kinds a things, just not t' be."

"'Sides," says Amanda, "most people, they don't even hear what you're sayin'. I think maybe you're the only one who ever listens t' me. Mama doesn't. I c'd tell her the moon'd turned blue and all she'd hear was it was still shinin', like when she was a girl," she says, trying not to be bitter.

"No," Naurean says, "*nothin*'s wrong, I just haven't done anything like that in a while." In a long while. It'd been so long since she … She laughs lightly, a dismissal. "No, don't worry about that, it wasn't so much and it's not important." She laughs again, a little defensively. "Amanda?" she says, mildly incredulously, "Now, what would she have t' do with it?"

Trumpy picks up a stone chip from the step and plays with it. It's jagged; he presses the point into the heel of his hand and looks at it. There's a small red mark, but no blood. It only hurts a little. "You don't like him, do y'?" he says.

"I—" Amanda says. She *wants* to say: *I do like him. Because Mama does,* I *do*. Instead, she says: "No."

Trumpy nods. "You think she don't love you?"

"She does," she acknowledges. "Just…"

Trumpy rolls the chip between his hands. "Uh-huh?"

"She thinks *he's—in* love; with her."

"Mmh." He presses the point into his palm this time. This time there's a dot of blood. But it still doesn't hurt much. "You think she's gonna keep seein' him?"

"I guess."

"Well." He throws the tiny stone into the street; it hits the hood of a passing car, a shiny new Buick. From the driver's seat an older black woman leans on the horn and looks toward them, but she doesn't stop.

"Oh, no," Naurean assures him, "she liked you just fine, she was just in a hurry." She listens, then smiles. "Well, yes, it did feel … nice." She laughs, a little self-consciously. "I did like it, I did, very much." Yes, she did. She remembers, a piece at a time: the dancing, the embrace, the first kiss. The club, the walk home, the entryway and the door, the words and the promise and … And. "Well, maybe that's so," she admits. "Maybe she *is* a *little* jealous." She laughs again. "I was just teasin' her this mornin', that she was jealous 'cause you're such a handsome young gentleman." There's laughter from his end of the line. She's relieved. "No, no," she says, "she just laughed … Uh-huh. We had a *good* chuckle over it."

Trumpy touches her leg. "Wait a while," he says. "Maybe it'll be okay."

"You think so?" She looks at his hand, just above her knee, wishes he'd keep it there a while.

"Uh-huh," he says.

"Thanks," she replies, and lays her hand over his.

Naurean feels better. Of course Mandy didn't mean what she said; she's just a girl, she didn't have experience in these kinds of things so of course she couldn't understand. It was up to her, Naurean, to be understanding. And she would be. She'd hug Mandy and everything'd be just fine, and she and Rex could go on and they'd, all three of them, be happy.

"Well," she says into the phone, "I … she does have her class t'morrow night … If we came back early …" She hears the excitement in his voice, and that excites her. "All right then. At seven. Tomorrow." She smiles and kisses the mouthpiece quietly. "I'll be waitin'," she whispers. "'Bye." She hangs up the phone, exclaims "Oh!" and whirls into the kitchen, takes a chunk of sticky bun in her hand and giggles as she bites into it and a burst of its sweet, delicious gooeyness floods her senses.

Trumpy laughs. "'t's okay," he says. "Bein' young, it c'n be kinda hard t' know what t' do sometimes." He shakes his head and laughs again. "Bein' forty, forty-five, 't can be hard, too; I mean, sometimes y' got t' do the—."

"Sometimes y' got to do what you're told. Ain't that right, Trumpy?" says Ladyblue from the entryway.

"Uh …" he mumbles.

The Lady walks down the steps. "She soft?" she asks, and reaches for Amanda's hand, still resting on Trumpy's. Amanda jerks it away and Ladyblue grabs her arm. "Oh yeah," she says. "She *is* soft."

"Let me go" Amanda says, struggling.

"Please, Lady…" says Trumpy, his voice strained.

"Oh. *Please.*" She looks at Amanda and, still gripping her arm, nods. "Okay," she says evenly, and lets go.

Amanda pulls her arm to her and rubs it. "He didn't do anything," she says.

Ladyblue nods again, no expression on her face. "We got t' go t' rehearsal," she says simply. "You ready t' go t' rehearsal now, Trumpy?"

His voice and his legs are unsteady. He gets up slowly. "Uh-huh."

"Then go get your trumpet so we c'n go," she tells him in the same calm and pleasant tone.

Except it's not a pleasant tone, he knows, and The Lady isn't calm. The Lady is mad again, mad at him, and she'll make him, make him … "Lady," he says, "I didn't—."

"When we get back," she says with an indifferent smile. "Or t'morrow." She looks at him. "Y' can *say* whatever you want … Y' understand?"

"*I*—" Trumpy says.

She grabs his face. "*What!*" she says. Trumpy shakes his head; she releases it and he starts away. "Ar'n't you gonna say goodbye?" she calls to him.

He stops and turns. "Uh … 'Bye, 'Manda," he says softly and, without glancing at The Lady, continues up the steps.

Amanda watches him go. "'Bye," she says.

Ladyblue turns and follows.

*

She saves the lipstick—Crimson Peach, it's called—till last. Excited as she is she's afraid she'll lick it completely off before he's even seen it. She dresses slowly, carefully, with music streaming in from the living room and enveloping her like the clinging silk of her dress. She picks out an evening bag, a small sequined clutch with a silvery braid for a handle, that complements the cool blue of the dress perfectly. She clips on the earrings—she found the perfect ones in her box, her mama's silver oak leaves—checks the newly applied nail polish—and she's ready! With nearly ten minutes to spare, she notes with satisfaction.

She's reluctant to spoil the effect by *doing* anything, but she feels so good she can't keep still. She laughs, and waves to the young girl in the photograph. The girl waves back. "*I'm* steppin' out t'night," Naurean tells her, "*my* young gentleman asked me!" and the girl smiles. "*First time a* man *ever asked me t' dance,*" Naurean recalls aloud to her, "*I was thirteen; it was the first time I ever went to Danceland by myself, and this young gentleman, Jim, he came up t' me and said he'd seen me there with Mama four 'r five times, and I was always the prettiest girl on the floor.*" The young man steps forth and, this time, the girl watches as he offers his hand to Naurean. She takes it. "*I blushed*" she says, not really caring whether the girl hears her or not, "*honest t' Pete I did—I mean, I'd been wond'rin' what it'd be like, havin' somebody that experienced take me inta his arms like that—but Jim? He just ignored it, like a gentleman would, and he put his arms around me, and then he just leaned me inta him, and I could smell him and he smelled so good*"—he whispers in her ear and she laughs—"'*Oh, this is nice' he said. 'I could do all kinds a dances, all kinds a things, with you.*'"

They dance some more, and his hands and body wander, slowly and sensuously, across and against her, pressing the two of them together. She closes her eyes and smiles, her heart racing.

"*And he held me so tight I thought for a minute I would faint. And when he did that? I knew, I knew what Mama'd been talkin'*"

about, how a girl was only really alive when she was dancin',
b'cause I felt so dif'rent all of a sudden, it was—"

There is a knock.

"*—like I was a real woman … Real …*"

Another knock, a little louder this time.

"Yes?" she says. "Who is it?"

Rex's voice says "Naurean?"

"Oh! Rex."—*She's forgotten the lipstick!*—"Is it seven
already?" she calls and scurries to get it.

"It is indeed."

"Well. I'll be there in *one* second." She applies it quickly,
looks in the mirror, wipes the corners of her mouth and blots
her lips, starts to the door, then remembers: *the package*! She
hurries back to her bedroom calling "One more second," slips
it into her lightly perfumed *décolletage*, and hurries to the door
where she stops, sets herself, and opens it.

"Well," she says and smiles. "Hel*lo*, Miste' Pette'son."

"Well," says Rex, and whistles. She laughs girlishly. "Don't
you look wonderful!" He kisses her cheek quickly. He's wearing
a different outfit, still all blues—dark slacks and a jacket that's
a slightly darker shade, with blazer buttons and some kind of
insignia on the breast pocket. Same wide tie: dark and light gray
stripes. And there's something—a record album, it looks like—
under his arm.

"Oh?" says Naurean. "Thank you for thinking so."

"I wouldn't be the only one who thinks so," he says and steps
into the apartment. He puts his hat and the album on an end
table, rubs his hands together and turns back to her, grinning,
as she says "Well, after teachin' all afternoon a girl likes t' feel
like she's ready to go out." She walks into his arms. He nuzzles
her. She giggles and steps away.

"Here," he says, "I brought you this. To listen to." He hands
her the record. "I guess you don't know a lot of music like it, but
it's one of my favorites. We c'n listen to it later," he says slyly. "It

sounds *real* nice when the lights're out."

She looks at the cover. *American Blues*, it reads. "Thank you," she says, a little surprised but pleased, and lays it on top of the console.

Then she remembers and says: "Oh," reaches into her dress and slowly, a little coyly, withdraws the package. "Here," she says, and offers it on her palm.

"What's this?"

"Well open it, silly."

"All right." She watches with both anticipation and worry. What if he doesn't like it? What if everything he has is silver? But no: A dancer on the road, he *must* have all kinds of things, silver, gold, even black. You had to look good, no matter what you were wearing. "Now, if you don't like it," she says anxiously—her hands are perspiring —"we can take it back and find another."

"Oh, I'm sure I'll—" he says as he lifts the lid off the small box, pulls out the cotton pad and stares. "Well!" he says. "*Well!* That a real diamond?" Naurean nods. "And real gold?"

"Yes," she says.

He lifts it out carefully. It *is* a diamond, small but absolutely, a diamond tie clasp, and on either side of the jewel are an "R" and a "P." Monogrammed, no less! "Well!" he says again. "Bet *this* set you back a pretty penny."

Naurean discreetly dries her hands with her handkerchief. "I saw it in the store," she says, "and I thought, I thought 'That looks just like the sort of thing a young gentleman ought t' have.' And b'sides, you said you didn't have one, so ..." She looks at him hopefully; he smiles. "Put it on?"

Rex does, in front of the hall mirror, and admires himself. "I bet I look like that, what's his name, the one who dances in all those movies? Gene Kelly." He pulls out the tie, holds it up close to the glass and peers at the reflection.

Naurean laughs. "You're better lookin'. Ev'rybody's gonna look at you, ev'rywhere we go t'night." She reaches into the closet for her shawl.

"Umm … I, uh … about—goin' *out* t'night," Rex says.

"Yes?"

"Well, I was thinkin', tonight, instead 'f, I mean, maybe we c'd …" She looks at him, puzzled. "No. You're all dressed up 'n' ev'rything, and y' got me this; just …" He sighs and looks at the floor.

She goes to him and lifts his head. "What, Rex?"

"Well, see," he puts his hand on her face, "the last place I worked—I mean, the last producer—they, uh, see, they went out a business, while we were on the road. And nobody'd been paid for about a month, and they promised us they'd pay us, soon 's they could, but …" She nods. He sighs deeply. "So I'm still waitin'," he says, "and, there aren't a lot a jobs now, dancin'. I think they put us, *me*, on some kind of a blacklist, too, b'cause I've been askin' for my money. Almost every day. That's why I'm stayin' with my sister's family; Lynn Ann's folks? I—"

"Your *sister*? I thought—."

"—mean, for now, but I mean … I mean my brother's. And sister-in-*law's* place." He shakes his head in confusion. "See? I'm just so … disconcerted." He holds her by her elbows, lifting her arms toward him. "B'cause, I mean, I hate other people havin' t', y' know, pay *for* me; 'specially you …" He looks into her eyes. She can see the sad desperation in his.

"Why, Rex, I don't …" she says.

"I feel really bad about it," he continues, "and I'll pay you back. I will."

Without hesitation, Naurean laughs warmly. "Well, I know you will," she says, and kisses him lightly.

"I was goin' t' mention it *Sat*'rday night, but we were havin' such a good time, and I … So, anyway, I thought t'night. … Well, y' know …"

"Now, don't be silly!" Naurean insists. "It's just a few dollars, and of course it's only temporary." She reaches for the evening bag, opens it and takes out four neatly folded tens and a five.

"Here," she says, and hands him two of the tens and the five. "Will this be enough?"

"I—" he says, and nods. She smiles and slips the rest back into her purse. He smiles. "Well," he says and turns to the door, "you all ready?"

She closes the bag and stands there, watching him adjust his cuffs. From down the hall, she can hear loud voices: Mrs. Andrews is going on about something. "Rex?" she says.

"Hm?" He polishes the buttons on his jacket with his sleeve.

"Saturday night, I ... What you said ..."

"About what?" He looks in the mirror, adjusts the tie clasp and whistles softly.

"About ... I just ... If you meant it. All."

He turns to her. "I meant it," he says, looking into her eyes. "All."

"You did."

He steps to her. Her heart pounds. "Didn't it feel like I did?" he says quietly.

"I ..." Her eyes are damp. *She doesn't want to cry*!

He embraces her, then moves into a deep kiss. When they break, Naurean slowly nods.

"We better hurry, if we got t' be back early," he says, and wipes Crimson Peach from his mouth. Then he grins. "Don't want Amanda catchin' us doin' *that*."

"No," says Naurean, both surer and less sure than before. But ... "I mean," she says, "yes. We should."

*

It's past 8:30—she stayed after class to go over a question with the teacher and a few minutes turned into half an hour, and now she's tired and her feet ache. She opens the door, and is surprised to find the living room dark. "Mama?" she calls and flicks on a lamp. "Mama, you here?" When there's no answer she murmurs "Hmh!" Mama didn't say she was goin' anywhere. Well, she prob'ly just went to pick up something at the grocery. Or to sit in the park: It's a nice night and sometimes she needs to just relax after all her teaching. It's still pretty early, she'll probably be home soon. She drops her things on an end table, decides she wants some music and turns on the radio. There's an album called *American Blues* lying on top of the console. Amanda wrinkles her face in puzzlement—that's not Mama's kind of music!—as the radio comes on. She turns the dial till she finds something she likes, turns the volume up, then slumps into the sofa and pulls off her shoes.

The station's playing jazz. She wouldn't have recognized that till a week or two ago. Trumpy's schooled her in it a little, jazz and blues. That was mostly all he talked about during supper on Friday. That and Ladyblue. She wonders if he's home. Prob'ly not, he'd probably be up there playing if he was. Or on the steps. She wonders how he can stay with Ladyblue: That woman! Mama may be wrong about a lot of things, but she's right about *her*. *She's what I bet Mr. Gillam'd call a real bitch*, Amanda thinks. Even Gretchen's not *that* bad!

She yawns, rubs her feet and decides she'll make a can of soup. She's not really hungry but she ought t' eat. But she lounges a little longer, listening to the music. A group of four— she listens carefully; no, five—"players," that's what Trumpy calls them. She recognizes a piano, saxophone, a trumpet; bass, drums. Amanda stretches out and is unbuttoning her blouse when someone knocks, insistently. She sighs and sits up. "All right, Gretchen, I'll turn it down, just—" but it's a man's voice which quietly says "'Manda?"

"Uh ... Trumpy?" she says, surprised. "That you?"

"Uh-huh," he says. "C'n, c'n I come in?"

"Yeah," she answers, mystified but pleased. "Just a second, okay?" She gets up and starts to re-button the blouse, then stops and reconsiders; she re-buttons it part way, leaving a gap through which her bra is plainly visible. She sighs, wishing her breasts were bigger, like Mama's. "Okay," she says. "It's open."

He comes in quietly, closes the door and stands there, working the valves of his trumpet reflexively. "Thanks," he says.

She smiles. "Hi."

"Hi," he answers, not moving. He seems nervous.

To her surprise, she's not. "Somethin' wrong?" she asks.

"Unh-uh," he says, "no, nothin', everythin's fine." He gestures toward the window. "I was lookin' out the window, upstairs? I saw you comin' in."

"Mm," she says.

"You all by yourself?"

"I guess so. I mean, I guess Mama's out."

"Uh-huh," Trumpy says, and takes one cautious step in.

Amanda pulls just a little on her blouse. The gap opens just a little wider. She wishes she'd left another button open. Maybe, maybe she'll undo one when she goes into the kitchen, won't he be surprised when she comes out! She asks, just to make conversation, "How come you're not at the club?"

"Monday night," he says. "'t's closed. Anyway, we, The Lady, she don't wanna do the rest of the gig." He looks away, around the room. "We're, I mean, she's—we're gonna maybe play someplace else."

"Where?"

He shrugs. "Just someplace."

"Oh," she says, trying to mask her disappointment. "You, um, you c'n sit down if you want."

"No," he says quickly, with a jerky smile, "I ... I, um, I just wanted t' talk t' you."

She's glad, and she feels, suddenly, completely relaxed. Maybe. *May be* ... "You *and* your horn?" she says with a little laugh.

Trumpy smiles self-consciously, and shrugs. "I ... just like havin' it."

She sashays a couple of steps toward him. He takes a step back, so he's once again against the door. *In the movies*, she thinks, *she could just walk up to him and put her arms around him, and he'd see her eyes and know and he'd kiss her.* Inwardly, she smiles wryly: *Real life is harder than the movies.* "You gonna play for me?" she asks, trying to sound sultry.

He shuffles his feet. "I …"

"You don't have to. I was just, y' know, teasin'." She smiles.

"Uh-huh." He smiles back.

"It's really nice." She points at the trumpet. "Sounds beautiful. When you play it."

"Thanks."

"Can I—see …" Amanda crosses the short gap between them and, barely, touches the instrument.

He seems to hold his breath. Finally he says "Okay" and lets her take it from him. She caresses the smooth brass, slowly depresses a valve, runs her hand around and inside the bell. "Mm," she says. "Feels …"—she looks at him; his eyes are on her hands moving across the horn—"I don't know." She hands it back. He takes it, lovingly. "Thanks," she says.

"Uh-huh." He cocks his head and listens to the radio a moment, then says "That's nice. Clifford Brown."

"I guess." She sort-of laughs. "I keep listenin', trying to figure out which one's which? But I don't know th'm like you do."

"Mostly all *I* know, is horn men."

"Makes a pretty sound. I like 't a lot."

"Uh-huh."

She waits, but he says nothing else and continues to stand, his hands moving over the trumpet. *He's not really listening to the radio*, she thinks, *but he's definitely thinkin'. About something.* "You want some soda 'r somethin'? 'r somethin' t' eat? I just got out a class. I was gonna make some soup."

"Unh-uh," he says, a little strained.

"Trumpy? You sure you're okay?"

"Oh, yeah. Okay."

She nods and says hopefully: "What'd you want t' talk about?"

"Talk abo—? Oh. Just—'Manda?" he says tautly.

"Mmm?"

"You're, you're a real nice girl." He smiles at her, a real smile this time.

"Thanks." Her eyes *feel* like they're bright.

"Y' know," he goes on, "I like you, a l—."

"Uh, Trumpy," she interrupts, "I—" and reaches toward him.

He backs away. "Oh, no, no—not that way, not that way, y' don't—"

"Oh." She draws her hands back.

"—got t', I mean, I wouldn't do nothin' t'—." He looks down, takes a deep breath and lets it out slowly, then looks back at her. "Just, you're nice t' me and I 'preciate it. Y' know?" he says urgently.

"You're nice t' me, too."

"Uh-huh. But, but, see, The Lady, she ..." he shrugs, sighs, reaches into his pocket, takes out the .22 and fires.

"Trumpy—I ..." Amanda says and looks at him, eyes wide with confusion.

He fires again. Amanda grunts and falls to the floor.

He sees her there, the blood spilling from her chest, and kneels beside her. He wants, he wants her to understand... Her arm is across her body. He touches it. "I'm sorry, 'Manda," he whispers to her. "I'm ... See, The Lady, her, and my horn? They're all I got, and, and, I mean, I don't have much other reason t' live, *'cept* them." Her eyes are open; he closes them. "And, and I don't know how I could give up either one of them. And The Lady, she says she'll send me away, for good, and, an' she'd really do it *this* time, if I didn't d—So I ... so ... I'm sorry." He bends over her body, almost kisses her, but he can't. The Lady, somehow, would know, so he touches her cheek as gently as he can. "I'm sorry," he says, and waits, as if she's going to say something, *she's* sorry, it'll be all right. He shakes his head. It won't be all right. He knows that. He looks at her again, then stands and walks out of the apartment closing the door behind him quietly.

*

She's packing when she hears the gunshot. She looks up from the suitcase full of folded clothes and wonders who else has heard it. Well, it doesn't matter: Nobody's nosy enough to bother about it and fifteen, twenty minutes they'll be gone anyway. She smiles, then she hears the second shot. She gets a dress from a hanger, folds it, and carefully puts it in.

There's no one else in the hall or on the stairs, and he remembers to put the gun back in his pocket as he trudges up them. He's sniffling a little, but he'll stop: The Lady won't like it. He knocks on their door. She says "C'min" and he opens it. She's standing there, by the bed, next to the open suitcase. He walks to it, starts to put in the gun. She stops him and takes it. "I thought I—heard somethin'; downstairs," she says, uncertainly. "Did I hear somethin', Trumpy?"

"I done it, Lady." he mumbles. "I did."

"Done it?" she asks. He nods. "Now, what *am* I gonna see when I look in down there, Trumpy?" She smells the gun, then smiles. "That's a good boy," she says. "Roll up your sleeve."

Though it's still early—not even nine-thirty—the streets are deserted and she's only a little self-conscious as they climb the steps laughing, arm in arm, and he stops to kiss her. "Y' *shouldn't*, out *here*," she says. "Someone might be lookin'" she continues in a teasing sing-song. He grins and pulls her to him. She laughs again and kisses him.

"That's a good girl," Rex says and nuzzles her cheek. "You know what?"

"What?"

"I don't *care* if someone's lookin'." He kisses her. Naurean laughs and breaks away. "Oh, this was a wonderful evening," she says.

"Yes it was," he agrees. "It was indeed. Seems a shame, havin' t' end it. So soon."

"Now, Amanda'll be home and worryin' where I am."

From the stairway, a woman's voice calls "You sure you got ev'rything?"

"Amanda's been runnin' your life long enough," says Rex. "*She's* old enough t' take care of herself."

"Uh-huh. Ev'rything" a man's voice says.

"And it's"—he glances at his watch—"why it's only a quarter after nine! The evenin's young yet!" Rex continues. "And so are we. Come on—there's a place up the block. It's got a jukebox."

"Then *come on*," says the woman.

"A jukebox?" Naurean says in amazement. "They never have any *good* dancin' songs on a *jukebox*. Only for those new ones."

"I'll teach 'em to ya. I bet I c'n teach you a lot a things." He nuzzles Naurean. She laughs. "Come on," he says, "we still got money, don't we."

As she opens the evening bag to check, Ladyblue comes into the vestibule, carrying a suitcase. A step behind her is Trumpy, with several bags and his trumpet case.

She pulls out the two tens. "Sure we do," he says. "Twenty dollars, that's more than enough f'r a joint like that."

"Well—give me a minute," Naurean tells him, putting the bills back into the clutch, "t' say hi to Mandy—I haven't seen her once t'day—and I got to change. I don't want t' be goin' t' a place like that in these." She indicates her evening dress, as Ladyblue steps onto the stoop. "Oh," Naurean says, a little startled when she recognizes who it is. "Evenin'." She steps out of the way as Ladyblue pushes past her.

"Yeah," says Ladyblue.

"Evenin'" Trumpy says.

"You goin' somewhere?" Naurean asks.

"Uh—" Trumpy starts to say, but Ladyblue says "*Come on*!"

and starts down the steps.

"Well!" Naurean says.

"Never mind 'em," says Rex. "You were gonna change?"

"Umm" Naurean murmurs. Then she sees Trumpy. He's stopped on the bottom step and is standing there, looking up at them. "'d you ... want somethin'?" she says to him, more than a little piqued at his rudeness.

He looks at her sadly. "Uh—no. Nothin'," he mumbles. "Just—I'm ..."

"What?"

Trumpy shakes his head and hurries after The Lady who's walking quickly and is well down the block.

"Honest to Pete," exclaims Naurean, "those people, I don't know *what* t' make of them." She starts into the vestibule. "Now, Amanda's up there" she says over her shoulder, "and you be nice t' her."

"Oh, I will," says Rex. "I will indeed. But don't you keep me waitin', now." Naurean laughs. "Y' got one minute, then I'm comin' in after you."

"I should," she calls, "Mama taught me t' always keep a gentleman waitin' or he'd just take me for granted."

Rex nods. "Oh, I bet nobody ever took *you* for granted." Naurean laughs once more. "No," says Rex. "No indeed."

She can hear the radio from the hallway and wonders why Mandy's playing it so loud: Mrs. Andrews will have a conniption! Oh, well, let her! Naurean has had just about enough of uppity snippety women for one day, and *Wretchen* can go to—well, she's too much of a lady to *say* where, even in her thoughts.

She opens the door and steps into the lighted living room, Rex right behind her. She stops, sees, and screams.

She still stands there, clutching the sequined evening bag, even after the police have left. Rex has talked to them, explained how they were out and came home to find her ... like that. No, Rex didn't have any idea who might've done it, he'd only met Amanda once, and then just for a few minutes. In fact, he'd only known Naurean a few days. But he'd take care of her, see that she was all right. The detectives were solicitous; there were other folks in the building they had to talk to. They'd call on Mrs. Rossell tomorrow, when she might be more able to talk. Rex thanked them and the detectives left. Rex closed the door behind them, quietly, then sponged the carpet and laid a cloth over the wet spot.

Now he stands behind her, his arms on her shoulders, speaking softly and nuzzling her. "Come on," he says, softly. "C'mon."

But she is listening to the music and watching the young girl, in her white silk dress, dancing alone. *"Mama always wanted me t' be a dancer"* she says silently. *"'You got to learn,' she said; 'a girl's only really alive when she's dancin'.' So I learned. And when I did, she was so proud. She picked out a boy for me—Rex was his name—and he wore a monogrammed diamond tie clasp, and I—I married him. And at the wedding? I wore a white silk dress and when we danced? Mama watched us, with this look of complete rapture across her face as though bein' with him made me the most beautiful thing ever walked upon the earth. ... And I was."* The young man, short and blond and in a slightly frayed blue suitcoat, takes the young girl's hand and dances with her, oh so gracefully.

Rex leads her to the sofa and seats her, then goes to the console. "What you need's some music," he says. He gets the album he's brought, slips it onto the spindle and moves the needle to the last song on the side. He presses "play"; a lazy trumpet lounges up a scale, and a woman's voice sings. He stands there, listening until the song reaches the bridge.

"At ev'ry first kiss I swooned and I sighed," the singer mourns, *"bewitched, bothered, beguiled."* Rex rubs his hands together and

goes back to the sofa. "Come on," he says softly, "let's dance. It'll make you feel better," and lifts her to her feet. She stares at the girl, the young man, reaches toward them.

"What?" says Rex.

She looks longingly at the girl. *The spittin' image.* She shakes her head. "I ..." she begins.

Rex takes the clutch from her hands, removes the two tens and drops the bag on the sofa. "Now," he says, "I'll take care a this. You don't got t' worry about a thing ... You got me now."

"*This time I was sure that I had a guy, but all I ever had*" sings the record, "*was a child ...*"

"Yes ..." says Naurean to the young girl, who, suddenly alone, continues, unaware, to dance.

"*And the easy-lovin' blues ...*"

"You" she says to Rex as he takes her in his arms and they begin to dance.

"*Those easy-lovin' blues. And though I guess it's just a woman's lot to love and lose, I'll keep on dreamin' of, the one and only love, who's gonna be my easy-lover, too. And when I find him it's good-bye t' blues, bad news and losin' I, am gonna get rid of the easy, easy-lovin' blues.*" The last phrase echoes into the room.

Behind the voice, the trumpet fades. The needle clicks in the groove.

Evan Guilford-Blake

Evan Guilford-Blake writes fiction, plays, poetry and creative non-fiction for adults and children. His stories have appeared in numerous journals and anthologies; they have won 17 competitions and received two Pushcart Prize nominations. *Noir(ish)*, his first novel, is available from Penguin. About 40 of his plays have been produced; thirty are published, and he's won more than 40 playwriting contests.

He and his wife (and inspiration), Roxanna, live in the southeasterm US. More information is at

www.guilford-blake.com/evan

Noir(ish):

http://www.amazon.com/dp/B0095ZP0ZG

See the trailer at http://www.youtube.com/watch?v=k3iBuWV-DJo&feature=youtu.be (The *Noir(ish)* trailer)

The links to other online work include

Stories:

http://www.writecorner.com/winner2009.asp#Blake

(a Pushcart-Prize nominated story; a significantly different version is in *Jam* (Mardibooks), and is part of his collection *Love & Loss & Love*)

http://deepsouthmag.com/2011/05/mama/

http://www.gringolandiasantiago.com/2012/05/05/a-box-of-beautifuls/

http://www.lostcoastreview.com/short-stories/2013/10/16/short-stories-by-martie-mtange-catherine-bailey-sea-siamak-v.html

Plays:

http://www.prickofthespindle.com/drama/7.3/dreamland.html
http://redpainthill.com/issue-2-evan-guilford-blake.php

CPSIA information can be obtained at www.ICGtesting.com
Printed in the USA
LVOW10s1415020915

452540LV00006B/186/P